Out of
the
Picture

Polly Samson was born in London in 1962 and spent much of her childhood in Cornwall and Devon. Her short stories have appeared in the *Observer* and the *Sunday Express* and on BBC Radio Four and BBC Radio Scotland. She has worked in publishing, as a columnist for the *Sunday Times* and has written song lyrics for Pink Floyd. Her story collections *Lying in Bed* and *Perfect Lives* are also published by Virago.

Praise for Polly Samson

'Polly Samson is no minor talent . . . prose that makes you miss your bus stop.' *Guardian*

'Her prose is subtle and unshowy, spare yet juicy. Samson has definitely made her mark.' *The Times*

'Piercing insights . . . the writing engages with its easy charm yet unsettles with its originality and honesty.' *Sunday Times*

'Samson has earned herself a place on people's shelves next to Raffaella Barker, Esther Freud and Barbara Trapido.' *Maggie O'Farrell, Independent on Sunday*

'She pinpoints the telling detail in character or landscape and brings her prose to life with evocative scents and colours.' *Shena McKay, Daily Telegraph*

'Outstanding, and an exciting portent of a great writing future.' *Susan Hill*

'Stylish and truthful. She's got *it*, whatever *it* is.' *Deborah Moggach*

'When I give up she can take over.' *Fay Weldon*

Out of the Picture

Polly Samson

VIRAGO

First published in paperback by Virago Press in 2001
This paperback edition published by Virago Press in 2011
Reprinted 2011

First published by Virago Press in 2000

A CIP catalogue record for this book
is available from the British Library.

ISBN 978-1-84408-806-5

Typeset in Bembo by M Rules
Printed and bound in Great Britain by
Clays Ltd, St Ives plc

Papers used by Virago are from well-managed forests
and other responsible sources.

MIX
Paper from
responsible sources
FSC www.fsc.org   FSC® C104740

Virago Press
An imprint of
Little, Brown Book Group
100 Victoria Embankment
London EC4Y 0DY

An Hachette UK Company
www.hachette.co.uk

www.virago.co.uk

For Charlie

Picture this, says Lizzie. My father left me in the bath.

It's slippery on my mother's knees. The lights are low, perhaps just candles, and the bath is at the end of a long, low room, all panelled in glowing honey-coloured wood. Yes – there are candles, two of them, at the end of the bath; and there's a jug of bluebells too, somewhere close enough to the candles to cast dancing flower shadows onto the ceiling. I know it's at the time of the bluebells, so I guess it's April, or do the bluebells come earlier in Cornwall? We've all three of us been outside in the woods all day. I was crawling in those woods, through the bluebells, which can only have been at that time. I can see them above me, not blue, but pink and mauve, and I can feel the wetness of their stems against my face and the taste of peat and bark in my mouth.

My mother is lying back in the water with her long hair knotted on top of her head and I am above her, looking into her calm eyes, at her glistening face. She is singing, I don't remember what. But she sang old Cole Porter songs to me in those days, in Cornwall, when I was a baby, before she was too unhappy to sing. 'I've Got You Under My Skin' or 'Paper Moon', she's singing something like that.

The door is open and my father, that's my real father, Jack, is standing there at the end of the bathroom, silent as a ghost, watching us through the steam. My mum keeps singing and he drops his arms by his side, as though gravity has got the better of him. This is more than I deserve, he says, and leaves. Forever.

Chapter One

Lizzie is being driven mad by a man in a car that's worth more than her flat. 'Shall we stop off for a walk in the park?' he says, smoothing her dress against her leg, just one hand on the wheel. I'm not a dog, thinks Lizzie, after-dinner walks are not what I need, but she doesn't tell Tony that. Instead she points out that it's a bit late for the park. 'It'll only be full of drunks again.'

'Right,' he says, 'I'll take you straight home then,' and he continues doodling on her thigh while he weaves a swerving, lurching tarantella through the enraged London traffic. They are beyond Marble Arch now, where the gallows used to be, he says. They could hang twenty-four men at a time there, but Lizzie hardly hears him.

'Beautiful evening,' he's oblivious to her mood, turning up the J.J. Cale and deafening himself to her telling him how much she's been looking forward to seeing where he lives.

'Just drop me at my flat,' she says, and she tries not to sound too sulky, too desperate, too like a spaniel, though 'flat' is putting it a bit grandly, she has to admit. Lizzie rents a room at the top of a red brick Victorian house not far from Paddington Station. It's without embellishments, this room: not a fireplace, not a single plaster curlicue on the ceiling. It's a no-trust-fund, no-favours, hard-luck sort of a place, with its kitchen galleyed off along one wall by a chipped Formica-topped counter and the bathless bathroom, not much bigger than a cupboard, that houses a temperamental lavatory and a plastic shower, hooked up in the corner, without a cubicle. Lizzie has found crouching over the lavatory the only practical way of having a shower.

'Your place it is then,' Tony says, his fingers sliding against the thin silk of her dress while his foot stomps between the pedals. Lizzie leans her head against the door and shuts her eyes.

She's thinking about his house, or rather how she imagines it to be. It's the usual scene, with her in his bath, up to her neck in pine-scented bubbles, alone on this occasion, though quite often she pictures him in the bath with her, or sometimes, even better, he's just in the room, talking to her and soaping her back.

He's thinking what a novelty it is to be with a young brunette when blondes have always been his thing. Each time his hand moves towards the inside of her thigh, he can feel her muscles twitch, minutely as when a fly lands on a horse. Her flimsy skirt does little to cover her nerves. Lizzie always wears soft clothes in soft colours. Perhaps it's her way of telling the world that she needs to be loved.

The stale shabbiness of her room, or more precisely what Tony, her new boyfriend, will make of it, is troubling her as he pulls into the right-hand lane, preparing for the Queensway turn-off. And there she is, at it again, thinking of him as her boyfriend. Well, that's quite a joke, and a bit of a worry too; but man friend doesn't sound right and, given their circumstances, boss is inappropriate, and he's not her partner, lover, fiancé or husband. Not yet, anyway, and maybe never.

And he *is* driving her mad, though she suspects she's in love. What's the matter with the man? Lizzie can't see why he doesn't invite her home; after all, that's what people do, isn't it? It seems the obvious next move after three weeks of dinners and walkies in the park. It reminds her of a couple of summers ago, with Sam, when they were both sixteen. He kept refusing to take her to his house too. He said that he didn't want her to meet his mother, despite the fact that he'd been to her house and had loads of meals with her parents and even stayed the night. In the spare room, of course. Well, she'd nagged and nagged and eventually he did take her home. And she stood there, his mother, all electric-shock grey curls and puddle-coloured eyes, stirring a jug of custard. The Devil Child, she said, glaring. Why have you brought the Devil Child into my kitchen? Sam had looked at Lizzie across the room, so embarrassed. They left then and he said, see, I told you it was a bad idea.

The Devil Child, the unwanted, the abandoned. These are all labels to which Lizzie has grown accustomed. Sometimes she looks at the small birthmark on her left hipbone and sees there, in abstract melanin, the horns of Satan himself. A lucky mark, declared her mother, a beauty spot. The Devil Child, said Sam's mother, and Lizzie glossed over the rejection, and took perverse pride in being the sort of girl that boys didn't take home: the siren who makes mothers fear for their sons' tender young hearts.

But as Lizzie knows, Tony doesn't live with his mother. What a bizarre thought. His mother must be at least two hundred years old, a right old granny. But there is something. Long after he drops her off after their evenings of pasta and tiramisu and snatched kisses on a park bench in Kensington Gardens, she lies awake listening to the beehive hum of the traffic and wonders about his secret life: about the domestic arrangements that he's keeping from her. And, to be honest, she has had quite enough mystery in her life already.

'Tony,' she says, gathering her nerve, 'do you live with someone that you don't want me to meet?' His hand is still on her leg; she feels entitled to ask.

Tony looks at her and laughs. What he sees is a small pale face with furrowed brow above round chocolate eyes: like a puppy, so serious. He thinks that she looks adorable biting her lip like that, and about twelve years old.

'Like a girlfriend,' she says, pushing his hand away. 'Stop teasing, you know exactly what I'm asking.'

And he just laughs some more. Nervously? Perhaps, she thinks. 'Sweet thing,' he says, and she is lost to the merry crinkles around his eyes. 'If I wasn't available, I'd tell you.'

Of course, Lizzie knows a little more about Tony than she's letting on. How could she not; everyone talks about him at the office. 'Not bad for a man in his forties,' they all agree. 'Quite a catch,' says Lucy, whose job it is to initiate Lizzie into the workings of Tony's photographic agency, or more precisely the intricacies of the filing system, before she leaves for her new job. She pulls out file drawers with the munificent air and enamelled nails of an old beauty queen handing over her tiara.

'Yeah, but still misses his wife,' says the more homely Paula, who gave Lizzie a potted baby spider plant plucked from its parent at her own desk, and would quite clearly like a young girl to take under her wing. Occasionally, Lizzie catches Paula and Lucy gazing, broodily, towards the closed door of Tony's unoccupied office, a room almost twice the size of the outer office where the four of them have their grey metal desks jammed up, one against the other, nursery classroom style, though instead of an alphabet frieze it's the pouts and poignant pipe-cleaner limbs of some of Tony's own most celebrated fashion pictures that they try to ignore.

'Correction. It's not his wife he misses,' says Lucy. 'It's Sophie. He hardly gets to see her.'

'How sad,' says Lizzie, before Paula silences them, with an overemphatic 'Sshh,' and spike-heeled Katrina appears waving a misfiled print like a weapon. Lizzie's already been warned about Katrina. Touchy, apparently, and rules the office with steely determination.

Katrina flings the picture onto Lizzie's desk then strides to the door of Tony's office. Sometimes she escapes there to work. When she needs to concentrate, she says. Lizzie, too, has enjoyed the odd half-hour swivelling in the nubbly grey tweed chair at Tony's desk; whiling away lunchtime with her sandwich, toying with the row of little suspended silver balls that clack so soothingly into each other. And snooping. She knows that he keeps the middle drawer of his desk locked and that there is a peppermint breath spray pushed to the back of the top one on the right. She has sat there, as he does, facing the silver-framed photograph: an informal David Bailey of Tony with his daughter, a little pink-faced girl in a black leotard. He reminds Lizzie of a lion with his springy hair glinting in the sun and his broad, tanned face, his arms strong, a pair of protective paws, hugging the little girl to his chest. The backdrop is pink roses and Sophie is laughing.

It was on her third day that Lizzie first met the lion in person. Tony breezed in, late for his meeting, but gracious as an ageing matinée idol arriving at a film première. Suddenly everyone was smiling and she cursed herself for having put off the dripping shower for an overdue hairwash the night before and for not wearing something more appealing than her old school skirt to the office. When she went to the loo to brush her hair, Katrina was already in there and Lizzie could smell perfume. That same afternoon he sat on her desk, asking for paperclips (a ruse; Lizzie already knew, how could she not, that he had paperclips and plenty of them in the third drawer down on the left-hand side of his desk).

Was she happy working at the agency? he asked, and were the others being helpful? And she said that yes, they were, but there were one or two aspects that she still found confusing and Tony looked at his watch and said, tell you what, why don't we pop out in half an hour, after we've finished here, have a drink, and I'll see if I can help you.

At the Queensway traffic lights Tony takes his hand from her thigh and gestures at the trees. It's still light over the park, even though they have eaten dinner. Better than a saveloy and chips, Lizzie reckons, that's what she would have had if Tony hadn't taken her to L'Escargot after work. That's what she eats on her way from the tube to her flat, has done most evenings since she left home and moved to the city. 'Ever heard of Capability Brown?' he asks.

'A bit,' says Lizzie, who doesn't have the faintest clue what he's talking about and hopes he's not about to test her. Animal, vegetable or mineral? Soldier, sailor, fisherman, spy? This capability brown could be anything.

'Capability Brown planted all these trees,' he says.

Lizzie's mood lightens, she likes it when Tony tells her interesting things. She's keen to learn. She likes it that he knows more than her. She wriggles deeper into her seat as he tells her about Capability Brown in his felted hat sitting with binoculars while men put poles into the places where the trees would grow: where the saplings of oak, beech and horse chestnut would spread their branches for future generations, long after this Lancelot's own death.

'Good men plant trees,' he announces from his pulpit behind the steering wheel and Lizzie doesn't want to argue. She won't tell him that when she was a baby her real father planted a whole orchard of trees for her, but he didn't stick around to see them grow. Or her either, come to that.

Instead she studies Tony while he speaks. Perhaps it's the wine, but watching him like this makes her almost fizzy inside, like laughing gas or mischief, and she marvels at her own cheerfulness so soon after everything that happened back home. What's it been? Not even a month yet and already she's almost forgotten that her world has been turned upside down – punched and scoured and ripped to ribbons – though she still misses her mother. Tony's eyes look turquoise today, chameleon eyes that shift from bracken to aquamarine, and Lizzie tries to work out if it's the colour of his shirt or the sky, or simply his mood.

There are a number of things that Lizzie likes about him. She likes that he knows more than her, of course, and that his arms are big and strong and he calls her 'sweet thing' and 'sweetheart'. She likes it when he tells her stories from his youth; of Oxford University and Bob Dylan concerts. Mostly he plays the blues in his car these days, but sometimes it's opera and she likes that too. One day, he says, he will take her to Covent Garden, to the Royal Opera House. She likes the fact that he has a round tin of travel sweets in the glove compartment. She twists open the top and chooses a lime green square of boiled sugar, dusty from its bed of white icing. She doesn't have to ask, she can help herself to his sweets. That's another thing she likes about him.

Lizzie sits back in her seat, sucking the edges off the sweet, and closes her eyes while Tony slips his hand beneath her skirt, skilful as a shoplifter: not so high that it tickles, but quite high enough to make his intentions clear. And he's not even drunk, she thinks, though she is. Matters between them are hurtling to their conclusion. She feels like she does when an aeroplane takes off: the what-goes-up-must-come-down stomach rush that accompanies the boiled barley sugars that the air hostesses hand out. She has only flown a few times but she's had more than her fair share of bumpy landings. Flying scares her now.

His hand is still there. She concentrates on what happened earlier. He had finished his veal escalope (milk-fed, according to the menu, he always seemed to order the thing that Lizzie felt the most sorry for), and he reached across to take her hands in his and hinted that one day soon he might take her away for the weekend. The way he looked at her set her stomach off so badly that for the first time in her life she hadn't managed pudding. Then he told her about his cottage. The one in Hampshire that he bought with a nest egg, twenty years ago, before he was even married. He told her about the watercress beds and the stream and how little Sophie had learned to swim there in water so cool and clean that you could count the fish.

'But I suppose you go home to your parents most weekends,' he said, waving the waiter away, dismissing the pudding menus with a flick of his wrist. 'Where is it they live? Did you say Somerset?'

'I don't think I did,' said Lizzie, imagining his cottage and herself gliding through the cool stream. 'But it's Devon, not Somerset.'

'Ah, Devon,' he said, and she nodded.

'So that's where you disappear at the weekends.'

'No,' she said, looking away. 'I don't.'

In fact weekends were a desert for Lizzie. Weekends were

when she longed to disappear, quite literally. Just switch life off for a couple of days, like a little hibernation. She wished she did have a family that she could go back to. A father to cosset her after her grimy week in London, a mother to worry that she was looking thin and feed her roast potatoes. Weekends were when she felt most sad about everything that had happened.

During the week, work – or more precisely the uncertain excitement of whether Tony would come into the office or not – sustained her. But from Friday night to Monday morning she barely left her room. Last Saturday, for instance, the Australian girls on the first floor had a party. It was obviously a party because Lizzie could hear whooping voices and laughter even above the music – the B52s and UB40 – and people kept ringing her bell when they couldn't get an answer below because of the noise. She spent the evening sitting hopefully on the landing at the top of the stairs, where the smell of the garlic bread and chilli con carne was strong enough to make her eyes sting, and she watched the chattering people arrive clutching bottles, but no one saw her there at all.

'Yeah, it was brilliant,' she told Paula back at work. Well, she was always so full of the dinner parties and trips to the theatre that punctuated her weekends.

'Meet anyone nice?'

'Nice? Maybe he was. God, I was drunk though.' And Lizzie had lowered her eyes as though ashamed of her wayward behaviour.

It's only a matter of time, she told herself, things will soon start looking up. All she ever did, in fact, was read. A lot. Well-thumbed, brick-thick novels fished from cardboard boxes outside the second-hand shop. Sometimes she painted. Just watercolours that she hid under her bed, like a teenage boy's pornography, but concealed only from herself, because no one else was ever there to find them. Sometimes she hit the Benylin, swigging half a bottle of sweet red syrup to help her sleep: that woozy dreamless floaty sleep, the best kind. Always paid for in the morning by a pneumatic drill of a headache.

'No,' she said again to Tony, deliberately keeping her voice light, 'I don't disappear at weekends to Devon or anywhere else, come to that.' She squeezed his hands over the table and waited for the invitation.

Tony released her fingers and looked at her almost sternly. Lizzie swigged Chablis from her glass. She needed to swallow.

'Is it the train fare?'

Lizzie snorted and to her horror a gobbet of wine shot from her nose. 'No, I just don't want to see my family any more, that's all.'

Tony regarded her even more severely then, as a headmaster might a truant.

'You must worry them sick, you silly girl. What do you mean, you don't want to see them?' He was leaning back in his chair, putting a distance between them, his eyes sharp, like flints.

Lizzie could feel the threat of tears. She didn't want them to spill down her face. Her mascara wasn't waterproof for one thing. She gulped some more wine and Tony refilled her glass from the bottle.

'Look,' she said, wiping her nose against the back of her hand, 'I can't talk about it, okay?' Tony hadn't moved any closer, his mouth was still a hard line. She took a deep breath, and plunged in, speaking quickly to get it over with: 'My dad did something bad and I don't want to see him. And my mum doesn't know and I don't want to have to tell her. And quite honestly, after what happened, it's better that way.'

Her words were the catalysts she intended, at last he was inflamed. 'Oh, you poor lamb,' he said, and she saw his eyes sparking, his hands reaching for her again across the table. 'You can talk to me about it, you know, it might help.'

And just for one shameful moment Lizzie almost felt glad that her dad had done what he did but now the tears were about to spill and ruin everything so she excused herself and went to the ladies' to blow her nose and wipe the soot from the corners of her eyes. When she returned she told him a bit about her parents, but not about what had happened to make her run away. And she told him that, in any case, her dad wasn't her real father; that her real father was someone who hadn't seen her since she was a baby.

His eyes didn't leave her for a moment while she talked. 'What is it?' she said, but he was intent, as though seeing her for the first time. 'Why do you keep looking at me like that?'

Tony was smiling. He formed a square with his fingers and thumbs and peered at her through it. 'You've got something about you,' he said. 'It's in your eyes, there's something unknowable. Something I'd like to try and capture in a picture.' Lizzie could feel herself blush; again he refilled her glass. 'And skin like honey.'

'Tony, stop it, I haven't!'

'You'd be surprised. Why don't you let me take a few snaps one of these days?'

After that she did quite a bit of talking, and he was rapt. She told him about her three little half-sisters, Anna and Briony and Lou, how they all looked like little photocopies of their father and not a bit like her mother and herself at all. And she told him how noisy they always were and about how she once tried to soundproof her bedroom with bubble wrap and when that hadn't worked she had moved all her things up to the attic and set bags of flour as traps over the door in an effort to keep them out.

After a bit of pressing, Tony allowed her to drop the subject of her parents and she felt like the most interesting girl in the world, a raconteur, a wit. And even if it was nothing more than him wanting to take her picture . . . well, never mind. Tony had done some good work, *Harper's*, that sort of thing. She'd seen some of his pictures in her mother's magazines, knew his name years before she met him, and now here he was, listening and laughing, and his eyes with something in them that she took to be burgeoning affection, or even love. An attentive face was still a novelty to Lizzie. As was the large dark green cup of cappuccino that the waiter brought her (she'd just stopped herself from asking for frothy coffee, thank goodness). Tony had a smaller green cup of espresso that made him shudder slightly with each sip, like medicine. 'Bitter,' he said. He stirred in two sugars, still listening to what she was telling him about a magician she had met in the street on her way to work that morning.

'I swear to you, it's true,' she said. 'He took a lit cigarette from his mouth and crushed it in his fist and then it was gone, not even a puff of smoke. I can't work it out at all, can you?'

Tony shook his head. No, he said, magic wasn't his thing, and then, quite suddenly, he leant over and took her wrist. He pulled her close, guiding her hand beneath the table and pressing it into his lap. 'See the magic you do to me,' he whispered. And of course, Lizzie, who was not yet nineteen, felt flattered.

C h a p t e r   T w o

Lizzie remembers eating sausages with her fingers from a grease-smeared enamel plate, balanced on her lap. She is sitting cross-legged on the prickly grass by the small campfire that her parents lit on summer's evenings in the hay field next to their house. When she thinks about these times she can almost feel her eyes stinging and watering in the smoke and taste the charcoally, ketchuppy food that her mother cooked for her and her three little sisters. She can see her mother singing and stirring various burnt-looking bits of food in a frying pan right over the flames and she can smell the newly cut grass. And there is her dad, just beyond the fire, laughing, with his three little daughters, identical but for their sizes, a trio of Russian dolls waiting to be put back inside the biggest one. The father doll. His hair, their hair, is flaming strawberry beyond the fire as she sits quietly, darkly, watching them and licking her ketchup fingers.

As the three girls shriek for their turn, Peter throws them up in the air. They fly above the horizon and he catches them and swings them around until they are so dizzy that for a while they stagger like little drunks when they walk.

As he sets his smallest daughter onto her feet, he glances over at Lizzie, sees her bite her lip. She turns her face away but he has already read the absence in her eyes.

'Come on Lizzie,' he says, while the little girls clamour at his feet, 'your turn now.'

'No, my turn,' says Lou. 'Not Lizzie,' and she jumps at his legs.

'Lizzie's too big,' says Anna, 'and fat.'

'Lizzie's too fa-at, Lizzie's too fa-at,' sings Briony in her playground voice and the others join in as Peter pushes them away, undoing their suckering hands, his blood daughters' hands, unlatching them finger by finger and holding his arms open to Lizzie.

Lizzie wasn't fat; her friends at school called her stick insect, for goodness sake; but at eleven or twelve she was certainly on the large size for being chucked in the air or swung around by her arms like a helicopter.

'It's okay, Dad,' she says through the smoke. 'I'm too big for all that.' But Peter puts on his rejected-daddy face and insists on swinging her round and around with her dark hair fanning out around her head while the little girls wail and bicker by the fire.

'Peter, do watch your back,' shrieks her mother.

And when he stops swinging her and while the blood is still whizzing behind her eyes he throws Lizzie up into the air, and catches her, despite his bad back.

'Peter, you're such a good father, the best,' says Cordelia, running over and kissing him as her daughter sits giddily at his feet. She knows, they all know, that Lizzie must be loved like the others. Lizzie, her first-born, not Peter's. Blood is thicker than water, hissed Peter's widowed mother when they married, but they banished the thought of another man's blood at the altar. Peter is as fair as dice, and she tells him so.

'Cordelia,' he says, squatting on his haunches as he pulls Lizzie back on her feet and then his wife down onto his lap, 'flattery will get you everywhere.' And Lizzie watches with the others as they kiss and roll on the grass, their backs and legs and hair covered in bits of cut grass and clover. And she is unsure, even then, how she feels about it.

Tony parks his car outside the house where Lizzie lives. He can't believe his luck as he opens the passenger door and she slides out, so pretty and pale in flimsy sky-blue silk, and tips her body against his chest, her face an elfin waiting to be kissed. He holds the dark curls at the back of her neck.

'So, sweet thing,' he says, 'are you going to ask me in this time?' and she says yes but that she hates the flat.

'I don't suppose you've got anything to drink inside?'

'No,' she says, 'not unless you count lemon barley water or milk.'

Tony says that he'll find an off-licence and be back.

'Okay,' says Lizzie, 'it's the top bell and there isn't a lift, so it's seventy-seven stairs up.'

'Stairway to heaven,' says Tony.

'No,' says Lizzie, 'not heaven.'

'I didn't mean the flat,' says Tony.

Lizzie can run up all seventy-seven steps. She is the only person she knows who can do this. Not that she knows many people in London. Not yet, anyway. Just the girls at the office and Simon, an old boyfriend from school who is studying architecture now but is always too busy clubbing with his new gay friends to see her. Then there's Savannah, the best friend she ever had. She lives in London too. At some college or other, Lizzie can't remember which one. Lizzie's best friend from before she was two and now she doesn't even know her address, doesn't care to either. Brought up almost as sisters: united by the fathers who left them as babies. Related by something more painful than the blood exchanged from pinpricks in their fingers. Sharing secrets, homework and shoes. Now Lizzie hopes she'll never see Savannah again as long as she lives.

As babies, Savannah and Lizzie slept in adjacent cots in a room painted the colour of tangerines while their fragile mothers took turns babysitting or spent their time comforting one another in the face of their loss in a world that still scorned single mothers. Sometimes other people would be there too and then there would be music and candles and the smell of sandalwood. Late at night, these friends would look into the nursery where the two girls slept and wonder how it was that men were capable of just walking away like that.

Even after her mum moved out to marry Peter, Lizzie and Savannah continued to think of themselves as more than friends, more than sisters even. Secretly they told each other that they were twins really. Right up until they were eleven or twelve they lived a fantasy life: they were twins all right, but even better than that, they were circus pony twins. Their mothers, Cordelia and Ingrid, had stolen them from Billy Smart's Circus because they each wanted a daughter and the rest of the world was just humouring them, pretending to believe their hard-luck stories of disappearing fathers. Lizzie and Savannah galloped around the garden, tossing their manes, a matching pair of palominos, whinnying and stamping their pretty hooves and planning how they would escape and return to the circus.

But Lizzie tries not to think about Savannah any more. It would be too painful to meet her now, too difficult. Sometimes

Lizzie thinks she spots Savannah on the tube or standing in front of her in the queue at the pictures. She sees a tall girl in the distance, on the opposite platform at Paddington for instance, reach up and twist coils of yellow hair into a pile at the top of her head and hold them there, with elbows bent and head thrown back, her beauty deliberate as a model. And then she sees, she always sees, that the someone isn't Savannah at all, that the face is too ruddy or too old, or too deadened by life to be Savannah. And she feels disappointed first, and then tells herself what a relief it is not to run into her old friend and have to face a scene. No, it's easier this way: much simpler just to cut the ties when the emotional problems are too great. That's what Lizzie thinks now.

Lizzie knows she has just a few moments before Tony will return from the off-licence. She whirls through the flat, tidying her bed, throwing a week's worth of dirty coffee cups into the sink, spraying her perfume onto her wrists, her neck and, although it's extravagant, around the dank-smelling bathroom. She snatches the knickers and tights from where they are hanging to dry over the shower rail and shoves them into the laundry basket. She doesn't think she wants to sleep with Tony – not yet anyway – but that's hardly the point. She quickly squeezes some miracle face cream from a free sachet that fell out of a magazine into her palm and rubs it into her hands, panicking now because she thinks she can hear a car scraping against the kerb outside.

At home Lizzie liked watching her mother putting on hand cream, pulling her long fingers, languorous as a cat. She can see her in the garden as she kisses a peony, and suffers the tender ache of feeling that she is not related to her mother at all. Cordelia is always brimming with emotion, in danger of over-flowing as she exclaims over beauty or love or else tells stories from her life that can sometimes make her cry, as though she is

weeping over a sad part in her own movie. Lizzie is the opposite, slow to smile and rarely tearful, she keeps it all in.
'Inscrutable,' her mother used to say. 'Like mercury. I never
know what she thinks.' They are so different that Lizzie, so
often locked in a world of her own, wonders where she gets it
from.

Savannah used to claim that Lizzie's mum was the most
romantic person she'd ever met. She liked to crouch by Lizzie's
side on the landing and listen to her and Peter in the kitchen.
'Coo, coo, like a pair of love birds,' she would whisper, eagerly.
They were supposed to be in bed but Cordelia's conversations
with her husband were intoxicating to Savannah. Domestic
banter was unknown at her house. Ingrid was either all décol-
letée and satin-shirted over some man or other or else it was just
the two of them in front of the telly. No wonder that whatever
Cordelia was talking about was like balm, even her just telling
Peter, yet again, to watch his weight.

'Aw, you fancy me however fat I am,' he always said, and
Savannah would pop her eyes at Lizzie and blow her cheeks out
like the Michelin man, waiting for Cordelia's habitual response.
'That's not the point, darling, of course *I* fancy you, but if no
one else does, where's the fun in that?'

And then Peter would find them there, clutching the banis-
ters.

'Upstairs,' he would say, 'wicked little nosy parkers.' And he
would tell them that they could read for a bit, if they liked. 'Of
course, *I* fancy you . . .' spluttered Savannah. '. . . but if no one
else does, where's the fun in that,' Lizzie rejoined as they ran up
the stairs with Peter growling like the big bad wolf behind them.

Lizzie and Savannah didn't read, they never did when they
were together. Instead they lay side by side, talking like they
always did and taking it in turns to scratch each other's arms,

gently, rhythmically up and down, circling the elbow and shoulder, up over the front of their arms and then back down the wrist.

They were older then; the circus pony fantasies a pale memory. Often at night they lay like this, stroking arms and talking. Sometimes they discussed their real fathers. Not in any particularly puzzled sort of way, but just sharing random snippets of information they might have gleaned.

'My mum was telling someone the other day that your real dad had terrible B.O. and never washed his hair,' offered Savannah when it was her turn to scratch Lizzie's arm, which had been thrown out of the covers and across her friend's chest.

'Yeah, I've heard my mum go on about that,' said Lizzie. 'A bit harder now, I don't mind if you use all your nails for a bit. I heard her tell someone that however stinky he got, she didn't mind because she loved him enough to think it was okay that he didn't wash because he was obviously much too busy with more important things like his paintings or something. God, I hope I don't get stinky when I grow up.'

'Or so stupid that you don't mind if someone else pongs,' said Savannah, dragging her nails down over Lizzie's arm, making her shiver.

'Has your father ever sent you a present or anything?' asked Lizzie after a while, as Savannah ran her fingernails back up the inside of Lizzie's arm. Savannah told her that sometimes, yes, when she was younger, he had sent her birthday cards, but not always, and that one Christmas he sent a lamp base made from shells from whichever Caribbean Island it was that he was living on then, but that it got broken in the post.

'Ouch, just your fingertips now, to finish off,' said Lizzie, rubbing her arm, which she knew, if she turned on the light, would be covered in criss-crossing red tracks from Savannah's strong nails.

'And your dad?' said Savannah, running her fingers softly as spiders around Lizzie's palm. 'Has he ever sent you anything from wherever he is?'

'No, not even a birthday card,' said Lizzie, resting her head on her friend's shoulder, sleepy at last.

'Well, never mind,' said Savannah, who wished that her mum would marry someone whom she could call Dad. 'At least you have Peter.'

Lizzie is telling Tony about Savannah and how they used to soothe each other to sleep by this scratching and stroking. 'Sounds quite kinky to me,' says Tony. 'Do you want to give her a call and see if she can come round?' He is joking, Lizzie can see that, so she doesn't need to explain that she will never see Savannah again, not as long as she lives. She wishes he wouldn't say things like that though, it makes her feel less certain.

They are both already quite drunk on the champagne that Tony bought at the off-licence. All the same, Lizzie thinks she should apologise for the squalor of her flat, that she should explain that she's just living there until something better comes up.

'None of this horrid furniture is mine,' she points out. 'I had to take what came with the place, there's no way I'd actually choose any of this stuff, especially not that sofa.' Right now she would like to set fire to the monstrosity of brown vinyl that weeps kapok between her bed and the kitchen counter.

'Don't worry. It makes me feel young,' says Tony. 'Like a student again.' But deep down they both know that youth is the last thing she wants from him.

She sits in front of the mirror, at the small dressing table where she has lit a candle. Tony moves behind her and puts his hands to her head, loosens her hair and holds her there, watching her face in the mirror. For a fleeting moment, she thinks that he is going to pick up her hairbrush, brush her hair, tell her she's pretty. But instead he grabs her lipstick, Rimmel All-Day Scarlett O'Hara, and holds her chin in his hand, turning her head to face him. He takes off the top of the tube and throws it on the table. Before she can even think to move, he twists the lipstick and paints it thickly around and around her lips. 'Christ,' he says, looking at her ruined mouth and then he pulls the strap of her dress over her shoulder. Lizzie still can't move or speak though she'd like to hold up her dress. But she's mesmerised by something, the champagne probably, as he wipes his index finger around her mouth until it too is smeared with the lipstick, which he transfers to her nipple, round and around, turning it red.

They lie on the bed together, and even then Lizzie feels like apologising for the cracks in the ceiling. She can see Africa and Asia up there, as well as an elephant and the face of a wicked witch. She can feel that the lipstick has smudged over her face and thinks how awful she must look. Tony's lips are also tinged red from where he has been kissing her, more savagely than anyone has kissed her before. Not that many people have kissed her before. All around her mouth is stinging, almost raw, where his chin and jaw have sandpapered her face. She is confused by the roughness of his fingers, making her cry out, and then, when he is on top of her, by the way he holds her hips, forcing himself into her before she has even worked out if that's what she wants to do. For a long time it seems that his eyes do not meet hers but are fixed on her breasts and his hands on her breasts and all she can think is that it's too late now. At last he tells her, through gritted teeth, that she's beautiful and she shuts her eyes until his three final groans tell her that it's over.

'Christ almighty,' he says as she lies gasping for breath, shocked by the sudden rudeness of it all. 'Where did you learn to do it like that?' And she wonders quite what it is that *she* did do, but nevertheless feels, somewhere inside, quite relieved that he is so impressed.

And now, at last, he is being tender with her, wiping her face with the lipstick-streaked sheet then pulling her head onto his salty-haired chest, stroking her back. She can see the hairs in his nostrils, which are still flaring slightly, and his eyes almost closed, just two dark slots as he looks down at her. Lizzie relaxes into him as his violence dissipates and his voice softens almost to a purr.

'You're quite a girl,' he says. 'You've no idea how much I love it when I'm with you.' And that is enough for her for now, but he goes on. 'You do understand,' he says, 'that it would be a very bad idea indeed if anyone at the office got an inkling about us.'

'I won't say a word,' says Lizzie, wishing that he'd stop speaking and just hold her, which he does for a while and they breathe together, her head rising and falling on his chest. Close up like this she can see a few grey spirals amongst the brown hair that spreads in a ragged vee from his collarbones to the hollow of his solar plexus.

She is almost asleep when he looks at his watch. 'Sweetheart, I must get going now.' He is rolling away from her and sitting up. Lizzie sits up too, shy now, pulling the sheet over her chest.

'Why can't you stay with me?' She is addressing the curve of his back as he crouches naked beside the bed, rummaging through the jumble of their clothes on the floor, separating his things.

'I've got to be up early tomorrow, I've got a meeting,' he explains, untangling his shirt, then raking his fingers through his lion's hair.

She can feel the stray spaniel taking her over: 'Why can't you stay?' and hates how it makes her sound. 'Where are you going?'

'Home,' he says lightly. 'I must get home to have a bath.'

She pauses for a moment, daring herself on, then gathers the sheet around herself and stands up. 'I'll come with you,' she says. 'I'd like to spend the night, no one will know.'

He sees her swathed in the crumpled sheet, like a tarnished Madonna in a halo of damp curls. Her ruined beauty makes him feel sorry for her, and, although it's the last thing he wants to do, he finds himself explaining that he can't take the risk of inviting her home, not now, not ever.

'What if my housekeeper finds you there, what then?' he says, his words ridiculous the moment they leave his lips. He takes refuge in his watch, mumbles to her as he watches the seconds pass. 'You must try and understand how awkward this could be. I'm more than twice your age.'

'Yeah, I know,' she is trying to keep her voice light, inwardly shooing the spaniel away. 'Old enough to be my father. So what about it?'

'It wouldn't matter that much,' he says, 'but, in case you've forgotten, I've got Sophie to consider.'

'I know. So . . .?'

Lizzie can feel him move away from her at the mention of his daughter's name. It's something she's noticed before, on other occasions. She has heard enough already about how sweetly Sophie plays the piano and how good she was as Juliet in her school play, learning all her lines so perfectly. Why, Sophie is practically a child prodigy. She's listened to Tony drone on about the day she was born. 'The most magical moment of my life,' he said. Lizzie sits down on the bed, still entwined in the sheet, feeling the blood drumming in her head, her thoughts beating time.

Tony fumbles for his keys. Lizzie's eyes look huge and glistening, making him feel wretched for what he has done, and what he knows he will do again in the near future.

'I'm sorry, Lizzie,' he says. 'I can't risk upsetting her. She's still raw over the separation.'

'Yes,' says Lizzie, feeling the room swirling around her, regretting the champagne. An image of her mother floats into her mind: Cordelia in a long dress printed yellow with daffodils that flare in the sun as she vaults a fence into the school playground to scare the boys who have made Lizzie cry.

And then she's kissing him goodbye, as passionately as she can muster to reduce her humiliation. So that's it, she thinks as he backs out of the door. These are his conditions.

Conditions for love? Any fool could see that it's unconditional love that Lizzie wants.

When he has gone, she lies watching the vanishing light from the candle that is spluttering to death in the mirror of the dressing table. The deed is done, she thinks. No more anticipation, no more imagining what it would be like to be held by him. No more fantasy. Now I know. And she tries to feel pleased. She hopes she did the right thing, though; it all happened so fast. She'd assumed there would be a few more twists and turns first, perhaps some dancing, or even flowers and chocolates. She hopes all that is yet to come and thinks how much happier she'll feel the next time, when he'll stay and hold her until the morning. She will watch him shave. They will have pain au chocolat.

Most of all, though, she hopes he didn't find her too easy. She can remember those girls at school. Girls who were easy. They always had one button more than anyone else undone on their blouses because their breasts were fully developed, and parents who didn't care. Linda Castleton was the worst. Someone told Lizzie that all the boys once paid her to let them put their fingers inside her and then they all started calling her Captain Birds Eye and went on about fish fingers in the art lesson. Another time, when they came out from sitting their domestic science O level, Linda Castleton had shown Lizzie the place behind the cookery lab where she had been with one of the sixth-formers after youth club. Her used tampon was still there, tinged red despite the rain and the mud from where someone else's boot had trodden it into the ground. It made Lizzie feel sick, but Linda Castleton just laughed.

Lizzie told Savannah about Linda Castleton and they agreed that she was pitiful. While they didn't want to be virgin brides exactly, they hoped they wouldn't have gone all the way with too many people before they married in ivory silk gowns with white gypsophila snowflaked through their long hair. Imagine, they said, being one of those girls on her wedding night, having to confess to sleeping with all those boys. They had their own weddings planned right down to the silver sixpences in their shoes. After much debate, Savannah and Lizzie decided that any more than five sexual partners would bring disgrace to their bridal chambers.

When the candle has burnt itself out, Lizzie lies across her bed next to the window and puts her feet onto the ledge, feeling the scabbing paint and cold chipped plaster with her heels. The sash cord is broken so the window is either closed or wedged fully open to the street. She hates the ceaseless roar of the traffic and the hyena calls of the drunks but finds the cool air on her feet strangely comforting. It's something about the breeze; it connects her with the wider world, away from the close drabness of her room. As she falls asleep she hopes that sex with three people by the age of nearly nineteen is not excessive.

Before it is light, Lizzie fights her way up from a black sleep. She is cold and her face is wet. From the sea water, she thinks, as she struggles to stay afloat, untangling herself from the freezing bedclothes and then realising that her face is wet not from

the sea, but from tears. She has been dreaming of the fishing
harbour again.

As the mist slips from her mind, she forces herself to distil the
images, fruitlessly trying to identify the place that she dreams of.
It is nowhere she's ever been in real life, but whenever she
dreams of the harbour she senses it's as familiar as home. She
can see the tiny wooden boats bobbing up and down, their
chains rattling against the jetty, and feel the rough grittiness of
the concrete beneath her bare feet. There is always a full moon,
although it fails to cast a reflection on the water, which is black
as diesel. In the dream she walks to the end of the jetty, where
there are no boats, and sits down, letting the empty sea lap
against her ankles as she stares up at the starless sky. She can
hear footsteps behind her, but she doesn't turn around. In the
dream she knows who they belong to, and that person will not
harm her. This night, however, the footsteps continued, getting
louder and louder, while she tried in vain to turn her head.
'No,' she screamed to the sky, 'I can't swim.' But then she
could feel hot breath on her neck as someone picked her up and
threw her high into the air and she came whirling down, twisting like a sycamore leaf, until her body cut the freezing black
sea. As she went under, she tried to see who it was standing on
the jetty, but the water was filling her eyes and her screams
were coming back to her as echoes from the bottom of the sea.

Chapter Three

When Lizzie was sixteen she had a holiday job selling ice cream at the seaside. 'It's time you earned a bit of money for yourself,' Cordelia said one morning, thrusting the situations vacant column at her over breakfast. 'You'll be able to save a little and buy some of your own clothes.' Lizzie sulked about it at first, having planned to spend the summer mooching about by the river with her friends and sleeping in late, but when Mr Millard of Milly's Ices told her that he would pay her forty-five pounds a week she began to see things differently. She was sad that she wouldn't be able to join Savannah and a couple of her friends camping in Lyme Regis but then she thought about her Britannia account and how she would have some money to buy a car when the time came, and she got over that too.

On her first morning, Mr Millard showed Lizzie how she should sterilise the chilly metal scoops in a jug of pink liquid and how to hold six cornets in one hand, like a fat bouquet, while she bent over the freezer gouging perfect balls of dairy vanilla from the sticky half-gallon tubs of Millards Ice Cream inside. He taught her to light the gas and fill the aluminium steamer trays with dried onions and tinned frankfurters for the hot dogs and to fill the popcorn-warming cabinet from the ten-pound paper sacks of ready-popped, pre-sugared corn. He told her that when people came up asking for little ice creams for their babies she was to refuse them. 'Any kid can manage a full-size cornet,' he said. 'Don't you let them try that on, bloody cheapskates.'

Lizzie's van didn't go anywhere: it was a trailer stationed as a kiosk for the summer, right on the seafront at Stonmouth Beach where the shrieking of the gulls competed with the mindless jollity of transistor radios and cheap electronic arpeggios from slot machines on the pier. All that Lizzie could see before her were the freshly painted sea rails and, below, the caramel-coloured sand and the frothing coffee sea. 'You're a good girl,' said Mr Millard before he left her in charge, 'and pretty too. Just keep your fingers out of the till and you'll do well.' Lizzie laughed when he left; his sweaty brown complexion and bald head made him look like a frankfurter. She had wanted to squirt him with mustard.

Lizzie pictures herself that first day in Mr Milly's van. She is sitting on the freezer cabinet, kicking her heels, reading *Jaws* by Peter Benchley and staring out at the sea. She could see her family down there on the sand, the little girls, three sprites, dancing in and out of the waves, while she sat in stinking onion steam, hot in her Millards turquoise nylon polyester housecoat, which always made her look about as attractive as one of the dinner ladies at school. They came to the beach to be near her, they said, but seeing her parents paddling in the shallows with Anna skipping between them and Lou and Briony hoisted on their suncreamed shoulders made her feel more distanced from them than she could ever have imagined.

Not that she wanted to be on the beach with them. Not since the last time, anyway, when Cordelia took pictures of them all running hand in hand from the breakers. When they were developed she saw herself barrelling out of the waves like a sea lion with the little girls by her sides, all slender tanned faun limbs. She was appalled by the strangeness of her own body in a blue and white checked bikini and her dad looked too and said, 'My, Lizzie, you're getting quite curvy these days.' And then she hated him but couldn't tell him why and he told her not to be such a sulky little madam.

No fear, she thought as she watched them through the greasy sliding hatch of the window. If she was out there on the beach with them she would have to wear a T-shirt over her swimsuit and they would expect her to act like an adult and watch out that the little ones didn't come to any harm in the waves while they lay on their rainbow towels and read their Agatha Christies.

There were the old people, too, standing in the queue with their shoulders like peeled prawns, and sticky children screaming when the ice cream toppled off their cornets onto the sand. She felt stranded there in the van. Her parents were leaving because it was time for Lou's birthday tea and they wished her luck as a crowd of spotty boys in Kiss Me Quick hats barged in front of them demanding 99s, then complained that she had been mean with the scoop. 'Silly scrubber,' they called her when she told them where they could stick their ice creams if they didn't like it. Things looked up briefly when Sam (in the days before his mother had called her the Devil Child) came sauntering along like Kevin Keegan with his new permed hair, and his cassette player blasting out 'Good Vibrations' by the Beach Boys. Then Mr Millard popped by to see how she was getting on and told her that Sam was not to loiter near the van playing that racket and that she would be out on her ear if he caught her 'entertaining' again.

On her third day, when Lizzie got home, bad-tempered, tired and stinking of onions, her mother told her to smarten herself up a bit because Ingrid and Savannah were coming over for supper with Ingrid's new boyfriend.

'Who is it this time?' asked Lizzie, acutely aware that Savannah hadn't mentioned anything about him, although there hadn't been that much time for gossiping, what with the job and everything. Normally Savannah couldn't wait to describe the full ghastliness of her mother's inamoratos. There had been a widowed fishmonger for a while who gave Lizzie and Savannah the excuse for much hilarity as they referred to Ingrid as 'the fishwife' and dared each other to somehow get fish into every conversation they had with him. 'Just for the halibut,' they said. 'Don't you think you should mullet over for a while,' they advised, gravely avoiding each other's eyes, and 'There's a plaice for everything and everything in its plaice,' when he asked for help with putting the groceries away.

'You don't know how lucky you are to have Peter,' Savannah would say whenever her mother hooked up with a new man. There was one, a chef, much younger than Ingrid, with a foxy goatee beard and copper bracelets, who played 'Smoke on the Water' on his guitar and expected to be thanked and, for a while, after him, was a Belgian confectioner complete with humpty-dumpty paunch and a bra size bigger than either of the girls. Savannah said that her mother always went for men in the food industry because money had been so tight that she often didn't know where the next meal was coming from. Except her real father, of course, he played the drums. 'Yeah, and music is the food of love,' said Lizzie.

The house was in chaos, as usual, when Savannah arrived with her mother and Donald. The little girls were doing finger painting at the kitchen table, although Lou, who was only six, was painting her own legs in stripes of orange and black. Lizzie quite fancied unwinding after her day with the ice cream and

hot dogs in a room far away from her sisters, especially after she
tried to show Anna how to fold the paper to make a butterfly
and Anna screamed at her to leave her paints alone. 'Do let
them be,' said her mother. 'If you want to be helpful you can
peel the spuds.' And then Lizzie wished that she could do finger
painting too, but of course she couldn't tell anyone that.

Lou had just flung herself onto her father's lap, saying that she
was a tiger cub, so he went to the door with his trousers covered
in paint and Lou growling in the hall behind him.

'Ah, these must be your little girls,' said Donald, a short man
with very bright teeth who was dressed rather bizarrely in a
white cheesecloth tunic top over tight white jeans.

'Don't fucking laugh,' muttered Savannah to Lizzie who was
still peeling potatoes at the sink. 'This time she's gone for one of
the seven dwarfs. I can't believe it.'

Anna, Briony and Lou all looked up from their painting and
started to giggle in unison.

'Yes, three little monkeys,' said Peter introducing them one by
one to Donald, who was half squatting to get a better look at
them, as though he were about to lay an egg. 'My, my, there's
no mistaking who their dad is, is there,' he said. 'No fear of the
milkman round here, eh?'

Cordelia failed to disguise her scowl as she banged the meat
tenderiser into the steaks but Ingrid just popped a couple of
raspberries into her mouth and said that Donald cooked the
most delicious Stroganoff she'd ever tasted. But by then he was
swivelling his attention to Lizzie at the sink. 'And this must be
the au pair. Yes?' Cordelia rammed the hammer onto the meat
so hard that it flew out of her hands and hit the cat, sending it
screeching from the room. 'No, this is Lizzie,' said Peter. 'My
oldest daughter. Savannah's friend. Hasn't Ingrid told you about
her?' He hoped that Donald would get the reference and Lizzie

knew exactly what he was trying to convey. 'Blimey, she's so dark, like a little gypsy,' Donald said, fixing Lizzie with a sly grin. 'Not at all like the others.'

Lizzie announced that she and Savannah would grab a sandwich later and they bolted from the room. They went to Lizzie's attic where they put on a Ramones record, painted their faces with Ziggy Stardust lightning bolts in silver eyeshadow and tried to eat Jacob's Cream Crackers without licking their lips. Savannah said that she had given up all hope of her mum meeting anyone decent and they agreed that Donald was the worst so far.

'All they do is smoke dope and sit around listening to Leonard Cohen,' moaned Savannah. 'And then I have to listen to the dwarf groaning through the wall. It's so yucky.'

They both agreed, having witnessed the passing of a soggy butt across the adults' table far too many times, that smoking dope was beyond the pale, and noisy sex even worse. Then Lizzie reminded Savannah about the time when they were little that they had crept downstairs and caught Cordelia red-handed, sticking what looked to them like an oxo cube into the flame of a candle, before crumbling it into her cigarette paper, sprinkling it over the tobacco. She hadn't noticed the two little girls standing gawky as gazelles with big eyes fixed on her.

When Lizzie had asked her what she was doing, Cordelia blushed and said she was just putting something into her cigarette to make it taste nice. Lizzie, who always knew when she was onto something, told her to try chewing gum next time, because that would taste nice too.

'Talking of which, I'm hungry,' Lizzie said after she and Savannah had finished spluttering out clouds of crumbs from the last of the crackers. 'Let's go and pick at what's left of the food, they'll be getting stoned in the sitting room by now.'

'Okay, but to the pub after that,' said Savannah, unplaiting her elastic legs from where she had been sitting in the lotus position on the floor. 'I want to stay out so late that they have to go home without me.'

They circled the table, like a pair of bear cubs over a picnic rug. As they drained a few dregs from a wine bottle, they could hear the grown-ups talking in the next room, just as they knew they would. They finished the last of the potato salad and Cordelia had saved them some steak, which they ate with their fingers, pulling off bits of meat, flashing their fangs at each other, pretending to be savages, although Lizzie thought Savannah looked too much like an angel with her milk and honey skin and hair.

'Unlike you, my little gypsy,' said Savannah, wickedly.

'I'm sorry if I put my foot in it earlier on.' Donald was apologising in the next room and Lizzie and Savannah moved closer to the door to hear him squirm. 'It just didn't occur to me that she was from a previous . . .'

Lizzie stuck her tongue out at the sitting room and under her breath Savannah muttered, 'Wanker.'

'Don't worry about it,' Peter was saying now and Cordelia added, 'Lucky she looks like me and not her biological father. That would be worse, wouldn't it?'

'Ugly fellow, was he?' said Donald, and then roared with solo laughter. Lizzie and Savannah could feel the grown ups' discomfort, tangible as hot ashes, through the closed door.

'No. Not ugly,' said Cordelia. 'Just not father material.'

And then Donald, who was unable to leave the subject alone, asked who, in fact, Lizzie's biological father was. 'Why doesn't she just tell him to piss off and mind his own business,' said Savannah, but Lizzie held her finger to her lips. 'Listen,' she said.

'Lizzie's father is Jack Seymour,' said Peter, and Lizzie was surprised to find that he sounded almost boastful.

'What, *the* Jack Seymour, the painter?' asked Donald. 'The

one who painted *Elena at Rest* in the Tate? I was quite a fan of his in the sixties. I think I even had a poster of something by him, once upon a squat. He's dead now, isn't he?'

'No, not dead,' said Cordelia, warming to the subject despite her better intentions. 'Although I often still scan the obituaries quite hopefully.'

'Ouch, I see, that bad was it?' said Donald.

'No, it's just out of habit really,' said Cordelia, 'and because it would have been so much easier to explain to Lizzie. But he's not dead, no. He just doesn't do anything much to convince the world he's still alive.'

'What, a recluse?' asked Donald.

'I suppose so,' said Cordelia. 'Now, who fancies a game of Scrabble?'

Was that the same week that Savannah had discovered she was pregnant? Lizzie can't remember now. But it was about then that Savannah started spending more time at Lizzie's house than at her own, such was her distaste for the wretched Donald and terror that Ingrid would find out about the termination. Lizzie was the only person who knew about that. She took flowers and Walnut Whips to Savannah at the hospital.

Thinking about Savannah now does nothing to ease Lizzie's discomfort after the freezing water of the harbour in her dream and she doesn't get to sleep again. She tries to push Savannah from her mind and think instead about Tony and about the future, their future, and whether he will ever get over this thing about his daughter. All he's got to do is introduce us, she thinks, as she lies there, in the dark. Who knows, we'd probably get on quite well once she's got used to the idea. We could go shopping together. She squints at her watch in the cold dawn light that is streaking the once white woodchip walls, mottled grey, like cheese mould.

She wishes she could sleep and calculates how much time is left before she has to get up for work. Three and a half hours. Three hours and ten minutes. Two, and then, when almost the entire night has passed her by, she gets up to make coffee.

At home, her mother trickled the beans from her fingers into a little wooden box, with a handle on top and a drawer underneath for the ground coffee. Sometimes Peter roasted green coffee beans and the whole house would smell wonderful for days. Sometimes he would add cardamom pods to the coffee, floating them on top like scarabs. Like in India, he said. Lizzie has inherited her parents' coffee fetish. Despite the fact that she has found the price of food at the Spar on the corner so surprising, she has indulged in vacuum-packed bricks of dark Kenya blend. She thinks it makes the flat smell homely when she boils fresh coffee in a saucepan. Instant coffee does nothing for her and she swallows several cups of the real stuff for breakfast, enough for a kickstart, to make her sluggish blood fizz, just as she did at home every morning before school.

On the dressing table lies a hardened pool of white wax that she digs at with a knife, taking some scrapings of brittle yellowing veneer with it, which makes her think of the deposit that she had to give the landlord as insurance against damages. The deposit came from her Britannia account. It was money saved from selling ice creams in the school holidays. It had been money for a car. Beside the wax is her lipstick; its oily squashed stump of Scarlett O'Hara makes her shudder. She can see herself in the mirror: her eyes look bruised from lack of sleep.

Three-quarters of an hour later, her temper is worse. She can find nothing to wear and now she is late. She has already tried on everything she possesses but even her newish pale-green angora mix sweater makes her look like a fluffy teenager with button breasts and not a woman at all. The only thing she's sure of is that she wants him to go weak at the knees when he sees her. She buttons a tight glacé-cherry-coloured coat-dress that she bought for someone's eighteenth birthday party over her only bra: a lacy black one with scalloped edges and two removable pads, a present from Savannah on her last birthday. It'll have to do. She wishes she had been wearing the bra the night before. She wonders whether Tony will appear to take her out again after work, but she's never been this late before and has to leave her bed looking as seductive as a jumble sale.

As she queues for her ticket at the tube, she can hear someone busking, a male voice and acoustic guitar rising up from the tunnels above the clanking of the escalator and the more distant thunder echoes of trains. And then she sees him, the boy with the guitar. He is standing at the bottom of the escalator, in front of a poster of three puff pastry horns on a plate, oozing cream. 'Naughty, but Nice' says the poster.

'You don't have to put on the red light . . .' he sings. Lizzie recognises him as the same boy who did the conjuring trick in the street, when he made a cigarette disappear into thin air. She thinks he sounds almost like the real Sting, who was every girl's idea of a dream teacher at school, but his looks are darker, less obvious. He has an almost triangular face with a large mobile mouth and shoulder-length dark-brown hair. Not a fantasy teacher at all, but good-looking in an Artful Dodger sort of a way.

'Roxanne . . . ' People rush by, some throwing change into the black top hat at his feet, the sort that white rabbits might jump out of and not a busker's hat at all. He finishes the song as a couple of boys, dressed like him in denim jackets and jeans, stop and talk to him. She can see him laugh, as she stands there, descending towards him, and she watches as he leans his guitar against the wall behind him as one of the others takes up the hat and holds it out to the passers-by. And then he is juggling.

Spinning three silver clubs, which blur like Zeppelins from his hands. His eyebrows have caterpillared together into a single wavy black line and his lips are turned up just at the corners in a circus-clown grin. A blast of warm gritty dust from a departing train hits her face, bringing with it the bad breath smell of the platform. As she rushes past, the boy drops one of the silver clubs. 'Oops,' he says, flicking it back up with a twist of his heel and winking at her, 'another rush of gravity.'

Katrina has asked Lizzie to step into her office, which is, of course, not her office but Tony's. But Tony isn't in today, nor has he been any day since he left Lizzie in her bed. Katrina looks efficient behind his desk, cool as slate in her boxy grey jacket, surveying Lizzie through glassy green eyes beneath her fringe. She blows clouds of cigarette smoke around her as she speaks.

'Well, I'm still waiting for an answer.' She crushes her cigarette in Tony's fish-shaped glass ashtray as Lizzie sits before her, blanking her out, refusing to consider the way she's been dressing all week as totally inappropriate for office life. Lizzie stares at the cigarette butt and can't help feeling that Katrina would rather have stubbed it out on her face.

'I think Mr Ashcroft would prefer you dressed in a more business-like way too,' Katrina continues, although no one calls Tony 'Mr Ashcroft' in the office, not even the man who comes to fix the photocopier. For a moment Lizzie can't think who Mr Ashcroft is.

'Besides which,' she adds, pretending to make notes in the personnel file, 'the weather is starting to turn cold. You must be freezing to death wandering around in such a short skirt.'

Lizzie is in a phone box on the corner of the road between Paddington Station and her flat. In her hand is a scrap of paper from the office on which she has scrawled Tony's home number, copied out from Katrina's black leather address book at lunchtime, just after their contretemps. The autumn wind has spewed rusty brown leaves into the phone box and someone has kicked all of the glass out of the lowest panes. Fragments grind beneath her feet, and she can feel them pitting the soles of her shoes. Katrina is right about the skirt, though, her bare legs are pricking like freshly plucked drumsticks in the draught. Why don't they replace the kick-level glass with something less breakable? But the cold is better than the thick stench of urine, not that the traffic fumes carried in through the lethally edged panes do much to mask it. The walls of the phone box are stuck with a Day-Glo and white collage of business cards advertising the specialities of local hookers. My neighbours, thinks Lizzie. There are pen and ink drawings on some of the cards of water-melon breasts and impossibly high heels and cartoon Honeybunch Kaminsky-type women with their bums in the air, like dogs bowing. Words appear in starbursts, 'new' and 'young' and 'wicked'. Then there are the abbreviations like 'Specialises in Hum and Dom' and 'Special TVs', which Lizzie likes to think of as something sweet and homely: humdrum domesticity in front of *The Generation Game* perhaps.

Lizzie hasn't quite worked out what she wants to say to Tony as she dials his number. 'Hi, you haven't been in the office and I was just calling to check you're okay,' would sound insincere; 'I've been missing you,' too soppy, and 'I've been thinking about the other night,' she wouldn't be able to do without laughing because she thinks it makes her sound like a sex maniac. It would be better if she had something to report from the office, something concrete and business-like, but that's Katrina's job. She decides to go with just whatever comes into her head when the phone is answered by a woman's voice. 'Shit,' she thinks and then remembers that he has a housekeeper. But it isn't a housekeeper's sort of a voice that asks who's calling and tells her to hang on a minute. His bloody girlfriend after all, and she hears the voice calling out that someone-called-Lizzie's on the phone. And then there are footsteps and his voice getting closer. 'Who?' and the girlfriend says, 'I dunno, Daddy, I think she said her name was Lizzie.'

Lizzie has forgiven Tony for the other night when he acted like a stranger on the telephone and also for practically ignoring her all day in the office. She tells him that she understands. They pour whisky into mugs of hot milk from the half bottle he brought.

'Yes, Lizzie, what is it?' he had said earlier, almost impatiently when she stood in front of his desk.

'I was just wondering if you were free for lunch,' she said but before he could answer Katrina's steely voice preceded her body through the door.

'I hope I'm not interrupting anything *important*,' and she came clipping across the room in her pencil skirt and stilettos, like a pair of scissors. 'It's okay, Kat, do sit down,' said Tony. 'Lizzie was just asking if she could have the second Friday of October off. It's her birthday. She wants to visit her parents and they live quite a way away, in Devon, isn't it Lizzie?'

Lizzie had felt like punching him across his desk as he sat there, grinning at Katrina over her head, as if they were discussing the holiday entitlements of the office junior, which, indeed they were.

Lizzie worked through her lunch hour and left early, without asking Katrina's permission and failing to deal with a stack of requests for pictures of Lady Diana Spencer, even though she had been told they were needed urgently by Fleet Street. 'They can bloody wait,' she said, flicking through the pictures of a plump blonde, about her age, getting out of a car in cardigan and pearls and the various other shots of the same blonde with chubby-legged children in her arms. 'They can't be that urgent.'

The young magician with the top hat and long denim legs
was at the tube with his guitar when she got off, but she
marched past, ignoring his wistful, circus smile and muttering to
herself. The heavy slices of sky above the houses matched the
colour of the road as she scuffed through the composting leaves
in the gutter, barely noticing the stench of dog shit that perme-
ated their mush. She could smell the rain, though, before she
felt the first drop, which exploded on her forehead like a wish.

Tony has explained himself now. She knows how busy he was
with Sophie at home, and that when Sophie's on half-term he
never goes into the office. She knows that Sophie might be upset
by strange women calling him at home. She knows too that he
plans to take her away for a long weekend, for her birthday, the
second weekend of October. That was what he was arranging earlier with Katrina while she stood there fuming and looking so
beautiful, like an enraged Carmen, he said. He is sitting on the edge
of her bed, relieved that she finally allowed him in, that she stopped
telling him to just go away through the intercom. He felt such a
twit down there in the street pleading with the closed door, getting
soaked to the skin. What if someone had seen him there? In
Paddington! They would have thought he was visiting a prostitute!

Tony is asleep in her bed now, anchored there on his back
with the arm that she has been lying on held out beside him like
a rail. The rain has stopped, leaving behind it the smell of
second-hand books and coal dust. Lizzie sits up and watches
him dream. The years have dropped away as if there are hidden
guy ropes in the pillow, but it's just gravity that has smoothed his
face to its more youthful shape – he has cheekbones! – and he
looks to her like a spoiled boy, a Caravaggio. She prefers him
awake, when his yellow-flecked eyes are open, and she can gaze
into the years, like into an encyclopaedia.

Chapter Four

Cordelia used to say that unless you knew something about ants, you didn't stand a chance with Lizzie. Not that the books on ants that she and Peter gave her were ever read much and, silly girl, she overfed the colony in the ant farm they bought her last year, for her eighth birthday. They died from an overdose of mango, said Cordelia, sorrowfully, as they emptied the sand and the brittle little bodies onto the compost heap. Lizzie had grown quite fond of those ants, but in all honesty, she prefers her knowledge first-hand and from nature itself. 'She's such a solitary child, always with her eye on the ground, watching what will happen next,' says Cordelia. 'I swear she talks more to the ants than she does to us. Ants and Muttley. Dear old dog.'

Muttley drools beside Lizzie as she crouches on the ground, ignoring the little girls' noisy splashing in the paddling pool. Both she and the dog are watching the cracks in the paving stones where she has sprinkled some sugar. Lizzie likes to set up little obstacle races for the ants, trailing demerara over bricks and dolls legs, and sometimes, when he is asleep, over Muttley's feathery tail. She imagines Muttley's tail as a warm, dark forest and her own fingers as the hands of God. She watches the ants swim their way out of lemonade lakes, and fight to be free of spiders' webs. Once, when she injured one – just enough – she observed the teams of ambulance ants swarming around, finally carrying the maimed one off on a straw stretcher. She knows how clever they are. How strong. How intent on keeping their course. She knows how they taste. They taste of lemon sherbet.

Cordelia is taking photographs with her new instamatic camera of Anna and Briony in their bright-blue paddling pool on the bright-green lawn. Lizzie thinks her mother looks ridiculous, with her swelling pregnant belly and permanently pink cheeks. Like a Weeble, the wibbly wobbly doll you can never knock down. You can't get close enough for a cuddle now, all that fatness is always in the way. And Anna and Briony, too, they race to get to her lap first when she heaves herself into her chair and says, now, let's see what's on the telly.

'Come on Lizzie,' sings Cordelia across the garden to where Lizzie crouches with the dog, 'come over here and let me take a picture of you with your sisters.'

Lizzie doesn't want her photo taken. She always ends up looking like an over-sized, dark-haired rag doll, a lanky Looby Loo between a matching pair of cute strawberry-blonde Andy Pandies. Photographs simply show up the discrepancies, leaving her stranded in a land of otherness, and she would rather imagine the differences didn't exist.

Lizzie stands by the paddling pool, scowling at the sun. She hates the feeling of Anna's wet hands, like jellyfish, on her legs, and the sight of Briony's soaked nappy makes her sick to her stomach.

'Oh, Lizzie, *do* try to look happy,' says Cordelia with her finger wavering over the shutter. 'It's such a lovely light at the moment.' In fact Cordelia wishes that she had kept her mouth shut, her eldest daughter looks like a spare part next to the toddlers' paddling pool. It would be different if she was actually taking part in the Happy Family Moment, splashing the little ones, say, or letting them splash her.

'You never put any of me in the album, anyway,' mutters Lizzie, who wants to get back to the ants. 'They're all of Anna and Briony. You only ever stick my stupid school ones in.'

Lizzie has hit a sensitive nerve. Cordelia feels the twinge quite physically, as though a piece of elastic has been flicked at her heart. It is perfectly true that her leather-bound albums have become centred on the two younger girls. But isn't that just the way, she tells herself, everyone always takes loads of their babies' first days, first smiles, first steps. Anna and then Briony, crawling like tigers through long grass. Anna at the breast. Briony eating sand on the beach. Besides, it's hard to get a good shot of Lizzie since she acquired those big teeth, and she's always so solemn. And when she does smile, Cordelia thinks, well, then she looks like Jack and she can't bear to stick them in.

Cordelia puts her hands on her belly, feels the new baby heave from left to right, pushing inside her like a fist kneading dough, then giving three sharp prods under her ribs.

'Come inside with me a minute,' she says to Lizzie, moving her hands around to the small of her back, trying to straighten herself. 'I want to show you something.'

Lizzie knows what Cordelia wants to show her. It's the red vinyl photograph album that she keeps in her studio, on a shelf above her porcelain jars of brushes and solvents. The leather family books are with the Britannicas in the sitting room but the red one is in there, in the dusty room where Cordelia is supposed to paint but never finds the time.

She's done it before, this stuff with the red vinyl album. Lizzie defocuses her eyes, like she always does.

'This is the day you were born,' says Cordelia, hauling Lizzie onto her lap, pressing her against the solid round drum of her stomach. Lizzie concentrates on identifying the fading smells of lemon hand cream and grass clippings and, fainter still, linseed oil and turpentine. 'And this is you having your breakfast, and this is you too – look at the face you are pulling! You look like Les Dawson! And this,' she says, turning the page again, 'this is you in the bath.'

Lizzie can see more than she wants through the mist, but she doesn't wish to hurt her mother's feelings. She would like to be back with the ants, where she was comfortable, not here in the harsh north light of the studio. Through the blurring she can see her biological father, in hazy dots of blue, honey and black, holding a baby in a white shawl. And there he is again sitting in the bath, a strained smile on his face, a tiny Eskimo on his chest, his feet veined like Gorgonzola cheese. Her eyes ache from the effort of squinting them at the page, it feels painful, as though rubber bands are breaking in their sockets.

The final page has a picture of the three of them together. A miraculous sunset behind them turns the bare dug earth to clumps of gold, from which rows of twiggy saplings stand up, looking to Lizzie like starved limbs. It's a bigger picture than any of the others, blown up to fill the whole page. Cordelia is in a purple smock with tiny mirrors on the bodice that flash in the sunlight and her dark hair hangs either side of her face like the opening to a tent. She is holding the baby Lizzie, but the baby's arms are stretched out to Jack. Jack is standing, long-legged in jeans, with one big boot resting on a shovel. His hair is a famil-iar dark cloud and he is looking away from the camera and straight into the baby's – her – eyes, smiling or laughing.

'And this one,' says Cordelia, sighing, 'this is of the orchard that your biological father planted for you.' 'Biological father' – how Lizzie hates that term. It makes her think of washing powder and test tubes. 'There were one hundred trees,' continues Cordelia, failing to notice Lizzie wince. 'Apple, pear, damson and plum. I should think they have fruit by now.'

'I just don't want her to think the subject is closed,' Cordelia explains later to Peter, while Lizzie reads in bed. 'I want her to know that any time she feels she wants to talk about Jack, that will be okay. It's healthier that way, don't you think?' and although she juts her chin, her words lack conviction.

Peter comes to tuck Lizzie up, taking Laura Ingalls Wilder from her hands, finding her bookmark, placing it in the page. He kneels by the bed and smooths her hair, but she turns away. She feels drained. 'You're not my real father,' she thinks and he senses an absence, as though all love has disappeared from her desiccated heart, like water down a plughole.

And then Cordelia comes in to wish her God bless. She's stoned, or drunk, or just very tired. 'Don't ever shave your legs,' she says. 'That's the best advice I can give you.' But as Lizzie is only nine years old, it really is the last thing on her mind.

Lizzie is sick of the sight of herself. She catches her reflection in the enormous new mirror every time she moves, to plump up the tapestry cushions, for example, or when she's making her bed. Especially when she is making her bed. She has been busy with improvements to her flat – what with Tony being around so much – just a few knick-knacks here and there and some Athena posters on the walls. Even the monstrous brown sofa looks better now it is clothed in a peach-coloured Chinese silk throw that she found at Camden Market. Her new pay rise is enough to cover extravagances like that from time to time. The mirror, all five foot square of it, was her birthday present from Tony. It was probably quite expensive, too, with its plaster frame of gilded vine leaves and cherubs and the vast expanse of glass that pursues her around the room, even when he is not.

It took three men to carry the mirror up the stairs and even then they were sweating and glaring at her, as though she'd specially had them erected to make their lives difficult. She doesn't know if Tony noticed the fat, wheezing one nudge the boy in the ripped Buzzcocks T-shirt when he told them to lean it against the wall opposite the bed. She did though.

The man who comes from Westminster Council hates the stairs too. Once every two weeks he staggers up to spray around the skirting boards with pesticide. Lizzie shovels up the dead and dying cockroaches between two pieces of cardboard for days after his visits and every morning, without fail, she is greeted by one struggling for life in the lavatory, waving its legs, like a prophesy.

'It's a solution made from chrysanthemums,' says the man from the council. 'It won't hurt you.' But he wears a mask and grey protective overalls and Lizzie read somewhere that if ever there was a nuclear attack, cockroaches would be the only survivors.

She has two varieties of cockroach, or so he tells her. Now she knows that the fat black ones are the Germans and the faster, more streamlined kidney beans are the Orientals. The first one she saw was a German. She thought it was a beetle and, remembering the Melanie song about the friendly little beetle in a matchbox, she trapped it under an upturned glass. It reminded her of when she was little, watching the ants, but it did nothing but glare at her from inside the glass. She had been planning to call it Ringo.

Now that she's been told that she has an infestation, her skin shrinks if she even says the word cockroach. The man from the council has grown accustomed to her referring to them as 'cucarachas' and 'CRs'. He seems to enjoy her discomfort and tells her about another flat, not far away, where a single mother was driven to attempted suicide because she found cockroaches crawling all over her baby in his cot. No matter how many times we treated that flat, he tells her, they just kept on coming back. Just like here. Soon after the woman with the baby was gone, the old lady in the next flat died.

'They only found her because of the smell and the buzzing of the flies,' he says gleefully. 'When they did, she'd been dead a fortnight, and all over the floor were little ramekins of rotting Kitekat. The crazy old bag had only been feeding the blighters for years. Had books on them, and everything.'

Lizzie's eyes are trained, and she is ready for combat with her rolled-up newspaper when she gets up in the middle of the night. The cockroaches are invariably too quick for her, and she swears she can hear hysterical, high-pitched giggling as they scurry away and disappear under the carpet. She hasn't told Tony about them and hopes he doesn't notice. Once, while he slept, she found a hard brown egg case in the corner under her bed. It was tapered at both ends and coiled around with a spiral like varnished leather string. She held it in the palm of her hand, considering whether to show it to the man from the council. In the end, she couldn't wait that long and flushed it down the lavatory. Ha, she thought, cockroach abortion. Cockroach genocide. And she thought about the woman with the baby and ate two plain chocolate Bounty bars to celebrate.

Lizzie is telling the man from the council about the egg case. 'It'll get washed up somewhere,' he says, pulling on thick grey rubber gloves before he mixes the harmless chrysanthemum solution. 'It'll still hatch a thousand cockroaches you know.'

Today he says he's going to set some traps under the cooker and in the bathroom, to gauge how serious her problem is.

'These are the traps,' he explains constructing little cardboard pyramids from folded yellow cardboard, his eyes greedy as he looks at her from above the gauze of his mask. 'Inside, there's a sticky strip and a pheromone tablet that attracts the male cock- roaches.'

'Just the males?'

'Yeah, that's right. It smells like a sexy lady cockroach, see,' he says, setting the traps behind the lavatory. 'And what use is a sexy lady without a man, eh?'

When he's gone, and before Tony arrives, Lizzie pushes the cockroach traps further behind the basin pedestal. She knows it's irrational but she thinks that having cockroaches is akin to having herpes.

She doesn't like the way the pesticide smells, either: it brings out a dampness reminiscent of previous tenants' feet from the carpet. She pours oils onto an incense burner and boils coffee until the saucepan is scorched brown at the bottom. She learned about essential oils from Ingrid, who once did a course at the local tech. She chooses ylang-ylang and neroli because Ingrid told her and Savannah that they were the most seductive scents. A bit like the pheromone tablet, she thinks, and she laughs at herself as she scurries around the flat, polishing red apples to a lacquer shine and arranging them just so in the fruit bowl on the kitchen counter. She puts *The Rachel Papers* next to her bed and stuffs *Cosmo* under a pile of old *National Geographic*s that she found in a charity shop. This is like witchcraft, she thinks, as she changes her underwear from plain cotton to lace and retunes the radio from Capital to Radio 3 because she likes Tony to think that's her taste as well as his.

Ah, but it's worth it, she reassures herself, all this effort: Tony has been behaving almost like a proper boyfriend since their weekend away went so horribly wrong. He has stayed the night with her almost every time this month, and on Bonfire Night he took her to a fireworks display on Primrose Hill. He held her in front of him, with his damp woolly coat wrapped around her, like a big protective bear, as the rockets scorched the night sky and made her bury her head into his jumper with their too-loud bangs. He wrote 'I love you' in a fizzing silver blur with a sparkler, and introduced her to a photographer he met there without once excusing her as someone who works for him.

Before that, though, her birthday weekend. What there was of it was a disaster. Her present was to follow he said, and she had felt childishly disappointed for a while and then excited when he told her that it would be delivered to her flat that week. Had he intimated that he would take her to Paris or Rome? Lizzie can't remember now. What she does recall is that his cottage was not how she'd imagined it. It was in a street with other houses, for one thing, and everywhere she looked was a woman's touch. There were silver bowls of dried pink rosebuds, porcelain figurines of little girls with puppies and hoops and frilly flowered covers on the chairs.

'My wife did it all up,' he explained, switching on the log-effect fire. 'She likes Victoriana.' When he asked her what she would like to drink (it was her birthday, she'd been hoping for champagne already in ice), she said, without thinking, that she would like Bacardi and Coke and she was sure he sneered at her when he said that they would have to go to the pub for that.

Upstairs there were just two bedrooms and the bathroom was a brightly lit, poky extension over the garage, with a view to the street. 'Why don't you have a bath while I sort out some food,' he said, and Lizzie felt that she should have been pleased.

He showed her his room, where a huge Victorian bedstead

dominated, its high wrought-iron head and tail boards forbidding as a cage. The walls were papered with thirsty-looking roses and there was a reclining nude, painted in smudgy oils, with nipples like raspberries and frightened-looking eyes in an improbable shade of cornflower blue. 'That's the wife, I'm afraid,' said Tony, stepping back to study the picture as though he had just come across it for the first time, in a gallery perhaps. 'I'll take it down if you think it'll put you off.'

Lizzie couldn't imagine what it was like to sleep in a room with such a badly executed picture. And of his ex-wife too! But Tony explained that because the divorce wasn't finalised, she still had some rights to the cottage and he didn't want a fuss.

'And it might upset Sophie to find it gone, it is her mother after all.'

After that she looked into the other bedroom while he scrambled some eggs downstairs. It was Sophie's room, with a heavenly little carved wooden sleigh bed and a whole constellation of luminous stars stuck over the ceiling. She felt like Goldilocks as she stood at the door and wanted to lie down, right there, and fall asleep. 'Ah,' she thought, with the soft wool of the striped rug beneath her toes, 'and this one's just right.'

By the time they went upstairs, after they had washed up and Tony had caught the end of the rugby on the box, Lizzie felt about as glamorous as a suburban housewife.

'This isn't your birthday present, but I bought it for you anyway,' he said nervously as she started to undress while he watched her, motionless as an owl, from the bedroom chair. He thrust towards her a polythene bag with 'Body Belles' written on the side in pink curlicued script. Even before she opened it, Lizzie guessed with a heavy heart that it would be underwear. She wondered if it would contain something embarrassing like crotchless pants, but she needn't have worried: inside was a long white cotton nightgown with ruffles around the collar. It was the sort of nightie she had worn when she was six. After that Tony wanted to fuck her while she leant out of the window, but for reasons that she didn't want to explain to him she couldn't go through with it and she pulled the nightdress back down over her legs.

'Why not? What's the matter?' he said when she stood by the window with her black, refusing eyes, driving him nuts in the white gown.

'I don't want to talk about it,' she said and then he said that she was cold as a clam.

'If you never want to talk about anything, how am I supposed to know what you're thinking?' he said. And that reminded her of her mother. What with that and the bad memories brought on by the open window, she almost cried.

Later he turned away from her in the iron bed and she stared at the window through the bars at her feet and thought how she would like to escape to the little room with the stars on the ceiling.

Tony had promised Lizzie that they would walk through the fields to a little pub that did the best smoked-salmon sandwiches in the world. 'But it's pissing down,' he said when she reminded him of this after he let her win at Monopoly (she was the dog, she always was because he looked like a miniature silver Muttley and Tony said he didn't care what he was, so she gave him the iron).

'We won't dissolve, you know,' she said, feeling that if he didn't move off the sofa soon she would set fire to the sports pages in his hands. 'Come on, it's ages since I've walked in the country.'

She had to borrow a coat, though, and Tony said that she could use the riding mac that was hanging behind the kitchen door, because that was the only waterproof other than his Barbour jacket and he would be wearing that.

It had been raining all night and they tramped through sodden grass, along the footpath, with the spongy ground wringing out a footprintful of brown mud with each step. The river that Tony had described as so clear was the colour of Bovril and had burst its banks, making shallow pools in the middle of fields for opportunistic ducks and depositing the balding corpses of tennis balls and plastic bottles along the way. Mournful-looking cows stood huddled in the corners of fields, and the view over the valley that Tony had told her about was obliterated by the grey rain that was driving towards them in angry needles that made their faces sting.

'It's no good,' said Tony eventually, when they had trudged through a field where the pigs had pulverised the ground to a mud bath that sucked at their boots. 'I think we should head back, there's not a patch of blue in the sky.'

Lizzie had been pretending that they were explorers, wading together through the swamps (which, naturally enough, contained crocodiles). She had been imagining their arrival at the pub: there would be an open fire and they would steam there together, with her hair hanging in wet corkscrews and Tony rubbing it dry with a towel that he begged from the publican. They would eat the sandwiches, which really would be the best smoked salmon in the world, and drink brandies or rums to warm themselves up from the inside. It would become one of their shared memories: Do you remember that day in October when we walked through the torrential rain and got so drunk at the pub that we couldn't walk back and had to stay the night in that little haunted room with the creaky bed and the beams?

'Come on,' he said.

'Okay,' said Lizzie reluctantly as the water dripped from her hair and trickled inside the collar of the mac. 'I suppose you're right.'

And it was when they got back that she met Sophie. What a surprise that was! Dear little Sophie, who looked much younger than her thirteen years with eyes puffy from crying, had got a lift down to pay a surprise visit to her father and to tell him that their Siamese cat had been run over.

Sophie was weeping about the cat and Tony was holding her to him, patting her on the back and telling her that he would buy her a new kitten. He said that they would go to the big pet shop on Camden Parkway and she could choose a new one right away. He promised. Lizzie didn't know what to do with herself as she stood in the cottage kitchen, dripping onto the doormat and wondering if Tony was expecting her to just turn tail and get the train home. He could always tell Sophie that I'm an apparition brought on by her grief, she thought. But then Sophie peeped out from her father's arms and gasped. 'Who's she?' she said, pulling away from him. 'And why is she wearing my coat?'

On the way back to London, Lizzie sat in the back of the car. Sophie and Tony talked about their Christmas arrangements. He had been thinking of Meribel but Sophie said that she was bored with skiing and couldn't they go somewhere hot instead. Lizzie watched them as though through a screen of glass in a taxi. As they left the dual carriageway, Sophie took the round tin of travel sweets from the glove compartment and popped one into her mouth. She offered her father one, but not Lizzie. A bit rude that, thought Lizzie, considering that I'm just his devoted secretary. It was kind of me to come all this way with those urgent letters. I deserve a sweet.

That had been the worst, that time leaving the cottage in the pouring rain with Tony holding his coat over Sophie's fair head to protect her from the wet, but also to shield her from Lizzie, who was bringing up the rear. It was nowhere near as bad as what had happened with her dad, of that Lizzie's sure, but it was fairly close to rock bottom. Things have improved since then though. Tony was proud of the way she conducted herself in front of Sophie, he said, and he was sorry that her birthday had been ruined. He had been trying to make it up to her, really he had. He sent her white tuber roses that smelled of heaven and said that he would take her to Paris.

Before the flowers arrived, however, and for a long time after Tony and Sophie dropped her off on their way to Camden Parkway, she felt wrung out. Like her mother's floorcloth, twisted until it was limp but still slightly seeping with salty liquids. She made it up the stairs, her breath held high in her chest like a balloon, and across from the door, where a single Oriental cockroach lay dying on its back, waving its legs in the air, reproachfully. Her head hit the pillow and her exhalation brought the emptiness inside crashing through her like a wave of homesickness. She could taste her loneliness in the back of her throat, warm and salty as chicken soup. She was missing something so badly that she had to hug her knees to her chest and concentrate on breathing in, rocking herself back and forth, and breathing out. She didn't know what to cry out when the tears started, but her misery was demanding a name. It could have been Tony, but it wasn't. 'Muttley,' she sobbed, trying to convince herself. 'Muttley, where are you?' And after a while she blew her nose on the sheet, got up, made coffee, and told herself how pathetic she was to be crying about a dog when there were people starving in the world.

She drank her coffee while it was still hot enough to scald her throat and imagined Tony with his daughter in the pet shop. She would be able to have anything she wanted, that Sophie, she could point her finger at a rare cockatoo and it would be hers. But in the end she would get a kitten. A guilt kitten. Taken from its mother and mewling in a cardboard box with holes punched in the top.

It hadn't been quite that straightforward when she and Peter got Muttley. Lizzie remembers the late summer day he took her to the dogs' home. Just the two of them. Nothing very surprising about that, she thinks now with the bitterness of hindsight: stray dogs, stray children, they were all the same to him. She had never been anywhere alone with him before, and he was still Peter then, not Dad. Cordelia said that she could call him Daddy if she wished, but each time Lizzie dared herself to try, the word stuck in her throat. Sometimes she said it, standing on tiptoes, into the bathroom mirror and then it felt like a naughty word, like one of the things that she could only say if her mother wasn't listening. Like bloody or bugger.

He was driving his silver car with the roof down. She was sitting next to him, holding her hair in her hands because the ribbon had blown free and it was whipping into her eyes, making them water, and he had refused to stop the car to let her go back and find it. Only a couple of months before, she had watched him take her mother to be his lawful wedded wife. She had been a bit put out about that, though, when the registrar said lawful.

'She's not awful,' she squeaked and Peter's mother had put her finger to her lips then held her hand in her own, which Lizzie hadn't liked because it felt like a lizard.

Peter parked his car just beyond the peeling blue gates of the dogs' home, under a cherry tree that was hung with clusters of yellow and red cherries. 'Look at this,' he said, 'they're ripe.' And he hoisted Lizzie onto his shoulders and when she came down she had two pairs of cherries linked by wishbone stalks and he showed her how to hang them over her ears like earrings.

Inside, Peter sat her on his lap in the office while the sallow-faced dog woman filled in a form, asking questions like had they a garden? and was it well fenced? all the time coughing into her greying handkerchief. Lizzie was scanning the photographs on the wall of depressed-looking greyhounds and playful terriers leaping for balls and large brown dogs that looked like Scooby-Doo. She was wondering whether or not she liked sitting on Peter's lap. The woman asked what sort of dog they were looking for.

'Well, something trustworthy, obviously,' said Peter. 'It will have to be good with very young children so it might be better if we got a breed that is known to be perfectly safe with babies.'

Lizzie felt hot with fury to be referred to as a baby but the woman ticked the box and said that she would show them what they had. So then Lizzie was so excited that she forgot to point out that she was nearly six and not a baby at all.

The coughing woman took them to a door in the wall that had a notice pinned up on it that Peter wanted her to try to read for herself. The kennels will not be liable for any injury sustained. He read it for her.

The noise started as soon as Peter opened the door and Lizzie felt the vibrations of barking dogs resonating up her spine. An Alsatian threw itself against its cage, rattling the bars, its origami lips pleated back from hard candy gums and glittering wolf's teeth. Two big black dogs in another cage flew at them snarling then turned on each other after they walked past. So many big dogs hurling themselves against the thin bars that separated them from tearing her apart made Lizzie feel like a criminal, with the smell of dog shit permeating her skin, so that she might never be clean again. She was glad that Peter was there, grateful that he had picked her up and was carrying her, reassuring her that the dogs didn't mean to harm her.

Some of the older dogs just lay with their faces on their paws, cocking one eye hopefully as they went by, or else disconsolately sniffed at their folded blanket beds in the corner of their cages. There was a caramel-coloured bitch who looked like a moth-eaten teddy bear. She stood up with her paws between the bars until a small tan terrier came up yapping, nipping her on one of her hindlegs then chasing her whimpering and apologetic to the back of the cage. There was a sleepy Labrador the colour of lemon meringue topping whom Peter called Honey, and a small brown dog with curling grey whiskers around his snout and a tail that spiralled over his back, as though he wanted the whole world to inspect his bottom. Then, beyond more terrorist Alsatians, who made up the majority, was Muttley, although he wasn't Muttley then, he was Dog No. 55, young mongrel, needs training, and that Lizzie had read for herself.

After Lizzie had sat in a choked, misty silence all the way home, Peter told Cordelia about the meringue-coloured Labrador, saying that he thought it would be the best option as Labradors were known to be good with small children. Lizzie said that the little black and white mongrel with the bushy ginger eyebrows wouldn't hurt a fly and Peter said that 'needs training' was code for badly behaved, even dangerous.

'You would love my dog the best, Mummy,' said Lizzie burrowing into Cordelia's warm, almond-scented chest, daring Peter with an excluding stare. Nothing was resolved by bedtime so Lizzie did a picture of the black and white dog in crayon and slid it under the kitchen door while Peter and Cordelia ate their supper.

After school the following day, when Cordelia had grown weary of all mention of black and white dogs and was distracting Lizzie by dressing her up as a bride in old net curtains with a daisy-chain headdress, they heard a car pull up and then footsteps on the gravel.

'Come on, let's see if that's Daddy,' said Cordelia, pulling Lizzie behind her. As Peter opened the gate, the black and white mongrel bowled in, scooting to Lizzie and hurling himself against her with such force that he knocked her over and she banged her head on the garden table leg. Then he raced around the lawn, so fast that he rolled over and over, and he cocked his leg against the rose bushes while Lizzie screamed with pleasure.

The dog was licking her face, his tongue like wet velvet, when Peter said, 'He's all yours, you know honey,' and then Cordelia knelt down next to her and the dog who was beating a tattoo with his feathery tail on the grass. 'And that's not all,' she said, gently, too gently. 'By next Easter you'll have a new baby brother or sister too, but the dog will always be just yours.'

Then Lizzie didn't know what was happening to her and she buried her head deeper into the wiry white ruff, where the skin was warm and pink. She was laughing and crying then, all at the same time. Like a rainbow.

Chapter Five

Why does this keep happening to me? They all go. They all go so suddenly. Lizzie now but it was my mother who started the rot, running off to Melbourne like that and getting herself killed. And then there was Jack. For him I set fire to my town clothes, my King's Road fashions and dolly bird fripperies. We made a big bonfire at his cottage and threw it all on and warmed our hands on the flames of all that was trivial about me. I moved there, to Cornwall, and didn't send a single change of address, wanting to spare him the callowness of my friends. I was his muse, you see. That's what he said. He needed me there to paint, not only when he was painting me but when he was painting anything, a tree, whatever.

'If you are ever angry with me, I shall die,' he said and made me promise that I would never lose my temper. Well, that was easy enough and we toasted my promise with hot sweet tea and Gauloises while he painted me with a smile on my face.

That night I dreamt I was pregnant. I ran along dark wood-panelled corridors towards a glowing light from a door that was ajar some way ahead of me. In that room Jack was painting the wall with a flotilla of boats that were on fire, that was where the light was coming from. The rest of the room was in darkness and I lay on a cream damask day bed, in the dark, with my hands resting on my stomach, feeling excited about what I had to tell him. But before I could get his attention, he stopped painting the wall and the flames diminished. He crouched on the floor, doodling his brushes in a sticky pool of red paint on the boards at his feet, and told me that he had something to confess. He was looking up from the floor and straight at me, his eyes like anthracite, as I lay rigid and frozen on the bed.

'I should have told you at the beginning,' he said. 'I have a rare disease, there is no cure. It's fatal.'

I could taste metal at the back of my throat as he went on.

'If I ever have a baby, I will die. I have this illness, you see, it's unfortunate. If I procreate I die.' Then he stood up and started to daub the wall with more red and orange flames and I was clinging to his knees. 'I'm having our baby,' I cried, and then he was kissing the nape of my neck, gently, just as he did every morning when I woke up with his hands clasped at my heart.

'Don't ever shout at me,' he said. And, for a while, it was easy to keep my promise. I wasn't angry, I was in love. We travelled England by train, it made no difference which town we were in, Canterbury, Glasgow, Exeter and York – anywhere with a cathedral, because Jack was obsessed with them that year.

A woman gets the face she deserves at forty. On the morning of her fortieth birthday Cordelia cannot imagine what she has done to deserve hers. It's not the jet lag that is crumpling her skin, she's been back too long for that. The longest days of her existence, and still not a word from Lizzie. She felt so strong as she stepped from the plane, so optimistic, but all that feels like a life-time ago, now.

The Himalayas: it was supposed to be a cure. A cure for the years of stagnation, rooted to that sofa, pinned there by the babies sucking her dry, pulling at her stay-at-home-breasts; all those years spent putting herself on hold. Those three weeks trekking with Ingrid made her feel like a person again. An intrepid woman with blisters and ideas, one who would eat cur-ried goat and meditate in temples. Instead of just someone's mother. She's been someone's mother for half her life. Jesus, I was just twenty, she thinks, not so much older than Lizzie is now, when she was born. And now, on the morning of her fortieth birthday, Lizzie is still missing. She has disappeared, without an explanation.

'Just like my mother did,' says Cordelia out loud. 'Just like Jack.'

Each disappearance more painful than the last, and some-where, she can't help suspecting, the fault must lie with herself. That's three times she's been deserted. When her mother went, she had her whole life ahead of her, but it didn't seem worth having. Then Jack walked out, and it was only Lizzie's life that made her hang on to her own. Now losing Lizzie puts her right up against the edge. If Lizzie doesn't come back, she'll jump.

'Gone, what do you mean, gone?' she said to Peter when he stood at the front door, his face drawn, shaded grey with stubble. His hands were damp on her bare arms. The taxi driver was still waiting to be paid for the ride from the station and she thrust pound notes into his hands from her purse, as though she were stuffing a turkey.

'Gone. Three days. I can't find her.'

'Jesus, Peter, what's happened?'

'I don't know. We had a row. She said she was going to London.'

Somehow Cordelia was through the door and he was steering her, guiding her like a wobbly supermarket trolley, towards her chair. It was the early afternoon but the house was in darkness, silent as a church. Cordelia could smell dust and the rotting stems of some agonised irises, gone brittle and brown in a vase on the table.

'Where in London? Have you called the police?'

Peter sat on the arm of the chair, pushing his thumbs into her shoulders, making her more tense, which was not his intention.

'She'll calm down,' he said. 'Give her time.'

'What happened?'

Peter groaned, hung his head, and Cordelia looked sharply at him, trying to read his eyes, but they were shut, his eyelids creased, in a face twisted with pain.

'Peter,' she said, feeling the first finger of doubt poke at her, strumming the nerves at the bottom of her spine, making her sit very upright. His eyes were still screwed shut and his fingers pulled at his face, the nails digging into his corrugated forehead, clawing at the skin as though he were trying to diminish himself.

'Peter?'

'We had a row, she screamed at me. She told me I wasn't her dad and then stormed off. I don't know what to do,' he said, looking at her between his knuckles. 'I've got to go and pick the girls up from school, they've been in a terrible state ever since. I should've phoned you, but how could I have reached you? Oh, shit, Cordelia, I've really messed up.'

And then she was comforting him as he collapsed on top of her, sobbing, his words coming out as staccato bursts, not making any sense. 'Hurt . . . Fucking hurt . . . years of it . . . always second best . . . until I could burst . . . you'll leave me . . .

Cordelia . . . I try to do my best . . . Not easy . . . Why has this happened . . . Fucking hurtful . . . never good enough . . . Lizzie . . . Cordelia . . . I don't know what happened . . .'

So many nightmare images passed before Cordelia's eyes as she sat there with her husband banging his forehead against her shoulder, while they both struggled for breath. Lizzie at King's Cross Station with track marks up her arms, Lizzie lying dead with flies feasting on her bleeding, broken body, Lizzie in the back of a car with handcuffs and a blindfold, Lizzie being taken away by a man in a car with nothing in front of her but the long black road, spinning her away from home. Away from safety. Flames. Water. Blades. Needles. Hammers. Ligatures. Men.

'Peter?'

'Huh,' it was as though she was jolting him back to consciousness from a daydream.

'What, no forwarding address?' she said, and Peter shook his head. 'You don't know where she is?'

'I'm sorry,' he said.

'What about St Martin's, she's supposed to be starting in September,' and then she thought how irrelevant college was now. 'I mean, where the hell is she? Oh Jesus, Peter.'

'I'm sorry,' he said again. But then it really was time to collect the three girls. Cordelia stayed behind, feverishly calling everyone she knew in London, while Peter heaved his defeated body into the Rover and drove the five short miles to the girls' school.

She went right through the phone book but no one had spoken to Lizzie, not even Savannah, though she said that Simon Deeson had met her one morning in Paddington Station and that she'd seemed fine. 'What's going on with her?' pleaded Cordelia, and Savannah said that she and Lizzie had fallen out too but she didn't know why. 'She's got a job, though,' said

Savannah. 'Simon says that she's got a flat and a job working for someone famous, a photographer I think he said, in the West End.'

'Find her,' said Cordelia. 'Promise me you'll find out where she is,' and Savannah said that she would do her best though there was something strange about her voice that made Cordelia doubt that she would try hard enough.

It is the morning of her fortieth birthday and Cordelia doesn't know what she has done to deserve any of this. Peter gives her a carved jade Buddha and the three girls come into the bathroom and sing 'Happy Birthday', their long legs sticking out from the bottom of Peter's big T-shirts, requisitioned these days for sleeping in. Like Lizzie did before them. They sit on the edge of the bath, these three beautiful pink girls, and watch nervously as Cordelia opens her presents. Some body lotion from Anna, crystallised violets from Briony, a Japanese fan from Lou. Peter brings her the post and the four of them are silent as she flicks through the envelopes, scrutinising the handwriting on each one. They watch as the tears spill down her cheeks. 'Not even a card,' she says. 'Nothing from Lizzie at all.'

'You must pull yourself together,' says Peter when the three girls have left her there, weeping at the basin. 'Cordelia, I mean it, it's not fair on them that you're crying like this all the time.'

Cordelia looks up from the basin, sees herself in the mirror, her unbrushed hair like shredded wool around her face, which is blotched and swollen as pork skin from crying, peeling still from the Himalayas. He has been telling her to stop being hysterical all week, he who didn't stop her daughter from leaving. Why didn't he stop her? He has made no sense. What is she supposed to think? Suspicion stabs at her and she fights it. She pushes the evil, glinting thoughts to the back of her mind, dodging from damage as though fighting for her life. Constantly on her toes, ducking and diving, longing only for the intrusive voice in her head to stop threatening her like this.

'Come on,' he says, 'get it together or you'll look fifty, not forty.' Peter is trying to chivvy her along, to cheer her up, but she lodges the black brick of his insult in a pit, deep inside, where it will remain until she needs it to fuel a greater anger in times to come.

Chapter Six

Tony doesn't drive with his fingers doodling on Lizzie's leg these days. There's no need to now, and he can concentrate on burning rubber at the traffic lights, thrilling to the sight of other people's cars in the rear-view mirror, almost stationary in the smoke. When he gets her back to her flat she will open up for him like a – well, like a what, he thinks, like a jewelled box? Like a sea anemone? A Venus flytrap? A silk handkerchief? He looks at her beside him for inspiration. She is gnawing on her middle finger where the writing bump is and for a moment he almost dislikes her. But then some boys, bottled like pickles in a Ford Fiesta, try to overtake him on the inside and he jams his right foot down hard to the floor. Lizzie lurches back in her seat and her hand flies from her mouth. When he gets her there, he knows she will sit on the end of the bed, just like he's told her to, and he will kneel behind her to remove her clothes, watching his hands in the gilded mirror as he slowly opens the buttons on her shirt.

Lizzie wishes that Tony wouldn't drive so erratically, the angry blares of the other cars' horns make her jump and the boys they have just swerved past jeered, the driver sticking his middle finger up at her as though he was forcing an entry and he had hate in his eyes. She slides further down the elephant-grey leather seat and looks out at the late November drizzle, caught like swirls of mica in the headlights. It's like night all the time now. There is just a moment's reprise in her dark days, when the sickly sun is being strangled by the clouds as she trudges to Paddington each morning, but then she goes down into the tunnel and emerges just footsteps from the office. There's no window by her desk because Katrina bagged the only one years before she started. It's always dark again by the time she leaves. These days she feels like an anaemic beanshoot, sprouting thinly towards the light. The slick black streets are punctuated by the muzzy orange glow from streetlamps that she still associates with throat sweets, pumpkins and Tizer.

They reach her street and Tony starts to change down as they approach her building.

'I'll grab a takeaway from the Thai,' he says, but then Lizzie throws herself down in her seat.

'Oh fuck, no,' she says. 'Drive on.'

'What?' he is starting to turn in, with the click–click–click of the indicators, persistent as a metronome.

'I said drive on, just drive on.' Her hand is tugging at his sleeve, and she is pale as talc. He slips the car up a gear and sails past the woman who is standing waiting on the steps, hunched up in a long tweed coat under a blue umbrella.

'Oh God, I think she saw me,' she says.

'Who?'

'My mum,' says Lizzie. 'What does she think she's doing?'

'Obviously she's come to see you,' says Tony, rounding the corner then pulling up in front of the pub. He doesn't know what to do because Lizzie is fluttering all over like a distressed chicken. He's gone off the idea of Thai food and a night in her flat is out of the question. 'You'll have to go back,' he says. 'You can't leave her just standing there, she must be drenched to the skin.'

'But it's pouring,' says Lizzie. 'I haven't got my coat.' But then she thinks of how wet her mother must be and how awkward Tony's presence. No need to complicate matters. She has known that her mum would find her eventually. Has only been surprised that it's taken her this long. She can't imagine what her dad told her when she returned from her trip to find she'd moved out. She hasn't wanted to hurt her mother's feelings, but what can she say? She would have got in touch, left a forwarding address even, but she hasn't been able to come up with a good enough excuse for her leaving. She doesn't want to break her mum's heart with the truth.

'Go on,' Tony leans across her to open her door, 'be a brave girl. Call me later,' he says before he drives off in a hiss of tyres, leaving her standing outside the brightly lit pub with the rain splotching her blouse.

She doesn't know how long she stands there, long enough for her to be able to see her arms through the cold clinging of wet silk that has turned from shell pink to damson. She hears the door of the pub open behind her, releasing a warm steam of beer fumes and smoke and the football-crowd sounds of the drinkers.

'All right, darling,' mocks a man's voice close enough for her to smell the cheese and onion crisps on his breath. He is shaped like a cottage loaf with an uncooked face. 'Fancy sucking my knob, eh?'

And she starts to run down the street, hearing his laughter hacking behind her but getting more distant as her feet find the puddles and the water that smells of drains splashes up her legs.

She can see Cordelia ahead of her now, two hands on the umbrella that Lizzie knows has the stars on the inside, like a miniature version of the planetarium. At the same moment Cordelia sees her and she drops the umbrella onto the steps and Lizzie falls against her, burying her head into the rough wool of her coat, which smells of wet moss and dog, just as it always has when it rains. And she stays there breathing in the safe smells of her mother and if she had any words they would just choke in her throat.

She feels Cordelia pulling her arms and then she is holding her in front of her, staring into her eyes, scanning her face as though looking for signs or damage. She tries to bury herself again but Cordelia holds her back like a delinquent puppy. 'We need to talk,' she says, and even through the rain that is running down their faces Lizzie can see that she is crying.

'What's going on?' Cordelia says, and then, 'Come on, open the door.'

Lizzie fishes for the keys in her bag, playing for time, feeling something like popcorn jumping in her heart, and still at a loss. As she fumbles among the sweet wrappers and loose change, she tries to bully her defeated brain into coming up with something, anything, to explain her sudden flight.

She can hear Cordelia wheezing slightly as she follows her up the seventy-seven stairs and Lizzie waits ahead, without looking back, while she rests panting on the landing before the final flight.

She clicks on the light and turns around to see her mother's wet leather boot slide over a cockroach and hears the customary crack as it squashes onto the lino of the hall. She hauls herself from the kitchen area to the bed and back again while Cordelia shrugs off her wet coat and hangs it over the back of a chair. Lizzie pours coffee then cold water from the dripping tap into the saucepan and sets it to boil. She watches her mother sit down on the monstrous sofa, splattering the Chinese silk throw with starbursts that she shakes from her waterlogged hair. Lizzie joins her, still in her soaked shirt and skirt, and they sit there mute for a while as though in front of the telly.

'Do you want to start at the beginning?' Cordelia finally asks and Lizzie stares at her own hands, scraping out the black crescents from under her nails, and shakes her head.

'I've been worried sick about you, what happened?' she says.

'Nothing,' says Lizzie, concentrating on the dirt that is trapped under her thumb.

'Well, something did,' says Cordelia. 'So don't just say nothing like that, I'm your bloody mother.'

'I just want to be on my own.' Lizzie can sense the danger, dark and threatening as thin ice.

And then she can see that Cordelia is about to cry again, and she feels her guts turn to gravy, so she puts her arms around her and says, 'I do love you, Mum, I just can't explain.'

And Cordelia hugs her back, which is all she wants but she persists, picking at her, trying to unravel her like knitting.

'What's going on?'

'Why did you leave?'

'What have we done wrong?'

'Who was that man?'

'Why did he just drive past like that?'

'Jesus, Lizzie, I think you should explain.'

So Lizzie presses her face close into her mother's shoulder, enough to turn her lies to mumbles. 'He's a friend from work,' she says. 'I didn't see you there and I had to buy milk so I got my friend to drop me at the shop.'

'You got soaked to the skin to buy milk?'

Cordelia stands up. She is shaking so hard that her wedding

rings jingle against each other. The minuteness of the sound is drowned out by the clangering of the saucepan where boiling coffee is exploding onto the gas, putting it out with a popping hiss. Lizzie jumps up and Cordelia follows her to the stove. As Lizzie pours the burnt coffee into two mugs, Cordelia opens the fridge. 'Look,' she says, without triumph, 'you have two cartons of milk in here already.'

Lizzie knows this, of course she does: she has whole milk for herself, but Tony prefers semi-skimmed.

Cordelia slams her mug down on the kitchen counter and flies at her daughter, shaking her as though she were a badly behaved toddler.

'Why won't you see us, what have we done? Why did you run away from Peter like that?'

'I dunno, I dunno, I don't know!' Lizzie screams back, shrugging her shoulders from her mother's hands.

Cordelia takes her by the shoulders again, but this time she doesn't shake her. Her face is close enough for Lizzie to see the red veins webbing her eyes from the corners where the tears have started to swell again.

'What has your father done to you?' she says, her voice shaking and as high-pitched as helium.

So, thinks Lizzie, she suspects something then. She feels powerful. A few well-chosen lies – he touched me up, or something – could blow their marriage apart. Come to think of it, lies wouldn't be necessary. The truth would do.

'He's not my fucking father,' she screams and pulls herself away again. Cordelia falls against the kitchen counter. Although she is silent, Lizzie knows she is sobbing: it's the way her arms are bent, Cordelia always manages to look as though she's praying when she cries.

'He's not my father.' Lizzie feels the power of the words and the adrenaline pumping her up until she might whizz around the room like a deflating balloon, out of all control, spitting syllables from her mouth. 'I don't know why you're making such a fuss. I'm nineteen for Christ's sake, it's time to fly the nest. I just can't be fucked with the family, if you want to know the truth. And I can't stand him, he makes me feel sick.'

'He's not your father?' Cordelia looks up from her hands. 'He's been good to you,' she says, and Lizzie sinks to the bed, noticing how relieved she looks to still be able to say it.

Mother and daughter are quiet then. For a long time it seems to Lizzie that they are merely feuding characters in a cartoon video and some kid has pressed the pause button. A stillness comes over the flat, and the rain has stopped outside. Eventually Cordelia gets up from the kitchen counter and comes over to the bed. She sits down behind Lizzie, who is leaning against the window, resting her face on the cool, wet pane, has been for so long that there are indentations in her forehead. Cordelia strokes her daughter's hair back from the hairline, circling her damp eyes and temples with her fingertips, then takes her head and rests it in her lap. Lizzie closes her eyes, willing her not to start up again.

'Do you remember that time in the very posh restaurant when Peter asked if he could be your daddy one day?' she says, her fingers cool on Lizzie's hot eyelids. 'It was the first time we'd been back to Cornwall since all that business with your biological father and I was very nervous.'

The bluebells, thinks Lizzie. The bath, the bluebells, two candles, steam. Your face, glistening, singing. 'Paper Moon'. He, not Peter, is standing at the door.

'Do you remember,' prompts Cordelia again, 'when Peter took us to the Lobster Pot in Mousehole?'

'Yes, I remember,' says Lizzie, and then in a weary monotone,

'The waiters were all dressed up in black tie and Dad told me they were penguins. And you found a pearl in one of your oysters and you gave it to him and I was so cross I had to go and sulk in the loo, which had real flowers in it.'

'And then you got your revenge, didn't you, embarrassing us like that!'

Lizzie remembers what she did, and knows that her mother doesn't really think it had anything to do with revenge, that she's just trying to force a conversation about Peter, attempting to reel her in using nostalgia as bait.

'It was no big deal,' she says. 'I just found those nice little bags all strung up behind the door. I didn't know what they were for.'

'Yes, you did, didn't you,' says Cordelia, smiling, 'but then you ran back waving them above your head, right down the red-carpeted aisle between all those tables of people in their best clothes, shouting, "Look, look, this *really* is a good restaurant 'cos look they provide special bags to take food home in." God, I could have died on the spot and the old colonel on the next table almost did.'

'Yeah, and then you said to Peter that you hoped he knew what he was letting himself in for, as though I was stupid or something,' says Lizzie, the hurt as real to her now as it was then.

'Oh, I didn't say any such thing.'

'Yes you did, and then later on Peter went on about how a pearl starts out as a piece of irritating grit that the mother oyster had to protect by covering it in something or other that makes the pearl and you laughed and looked at me, meaningfully. Yes you did. You can't deny it. I can remember it.'

Cordelia tries not to be rattled by Lizzie's version. She had brought the subject up because she was trying to illustrate how special it was that Peter had not only asked for her hand in marriage but had asked for Lizzie's hand too. He had got down on bended knee in that restaurant and asked her if she would consider being his daughter. He'd even given her a little silver ring. Just how many men would do that?

'Well, you said some very unpleasant things at that time too,' says Cordelia, looking down at Lizzie's face in her lap, still able to see the baby within the girl, as she would forever more.

'Peter put up with a lot from you. Remember, you were the one who wouldn't let him kiss you goodnight for years.'

'Yes, yes,' says Lizzie, knowing what is coming next because it has become the stuff of family folklore, 'and you asked me why I wouldn't let him, and I said it was because his skin was all wrong. And you said, "What do you mean wrong?" And I said, "It's the smell" and you said "What smell?" and I said, "The poo smell." Well, I've told you before, I only said that because it was the naughtiest thing I could think of and I wanted you all to myself.'

Cordelia starts to laugh again. 'Oh listen to us, Lizzie,' she says. 'Going on about all this. Don't you think it's time you came home?'

Lizzie can feel herself being tugged back. She sits up and pulls herself free of her mother's supplicating touch. 'I'm not coming home, Mum,' she says, lurching from the bed. 'I've told you, I don't want to be part of the family any more. You've got your real daughters, you and Dad, why can't you just leave me be?'

Cordelia is crying again. She has buttoned up her coat and is standing by the door with her umbrella. She passes her hand over her forehead, which is worn into smooth ridges like drift-wood. She looks bewildered, as though she has been washed up there by a freak storm. Lizzie knows that she should stop her from leaving but she's exhausted and the blankness is enveloping her again. She just wants all the noise to stop. She can't throw off the dense clouds of nothingness that she has wrapped around herself. Any move towards her mother now will guarantee that she will have to go home and she doesn't want to face Peter, or ever see him again.

Perhaps I'm insane, she thinks, like my real father. She remembers hearing her mother talking one night when she should have been asleep; that's how she ever found out anything about her real father. Always through an open window or a crack in the door. It was a hot night, and the scent of the jasmine was coming through her window on a warm breeze. Briony, the second of her little sisters, had been born quite recently, so she must have been about eight. Lizzie doesn't know why she remembers the evening so vividly: the smell of the jasmine, the voices on the terrace, the silky edge of her old baby blanket between her fingers . . .

She could hear the clinking of wine glasses and her mother's voice, the confessional voice that she saved for talking to Ingrid. 'I never thought to ask, you know,' Cordelia said. 'But then I never asked him those normal questions, you know the ones, the nosy questions like: When did you lose your virginity? How many people have you slept with? That sort of thing. Quite honestly, I didn't have the faintest clue about him.'

'I remember,' said Ingrid. 'I mean, you didn't even know if he was a leg or a tit man.' And Lizzie could hear them giggling like girls below her bedroom window.

'Yeah, well, I look back and can't believe how blank I was when I was young. Once Jack told me that he was in a mental hospital but it never occurred to me to ask why. In the bed next to him, he said, was a man who believed that he had animals growing inside his stomach. Every couple of weeks these animals would get so huge that the man had to have them surgically removed or he would go beserk. Jack said that they would actually take him and anaesthetise him, to convince him they had operated. And do you know what I said to Jack when he told me this story?'

'No, go on.'

'I asked him what sort of animals they were. I never once said, "And, Jack dear, what exactly were *you* doing in that mental hospital?"'

'And what were the animals?' asked Ingrid, spluttering into her wine. 'Meercats,' said her mother and then they both laughed and Lizzie didn't get to sleep for ages after that.

'You know what?' Cordelia jolts her back to the present. She's still in her coat, standing at the door, blowing her nose on a shredded ball of Kleenex. 'I swore that I'd never say this to you but you're just like your father, like Jack, I mean.'

Cordelia is in physical pain, that much is obvious from the crumpling of her face, but still Lizzie does not move towards her. She can't. She is speechless, amazed that her mother has just said the name Jack to her. Normally she referred to him as 'your biological father', which made Lizzie feel like a laboratory experiment. Perhaps they should talk about it now, but it's already too late. Cordelia has pulled open the door and still shouting is stumbling like a blind woman down the stairs.

'You don't say anything. You're all shut down. No one ever knows what you feel or think. You just cut people off all the time. Like poor Savannah. She's been ringing me in tears. And your dad. What has Peter done to deserve this? Jesus, Lizzie, what have I done? Yes, you're like Jack, I can see it now. You'll just close the door behind me. I always thought this would happen.'

When she has gone, Lizzie feels as empty and useless as a deflated balloon. Strangely, she doesn't feel like calling Tony like she said she would. The vacuum is too big for him to fill. And she knows, she's always known, that it is not the dog that she misses so much that it hurts. It's her father. The one she has never known. The bastard. The heel. Her real father. Jack. Jack Seymour. Her biological father. No matter what she calls him.

Chapter Seven

Lizzie is at the Tate Gallery. She is standing at the information desk plucking at furred bobbles from around the buttonholes of her coat, rolling them between her fingers. 'No answer from the department yet,' says the girl in the black jacket, covering the receiver with her hand, 'but you're a bit early.' Lizzie is always early for appointments, especially for things she dreads, like the dentist or the headmaster's office. The day of her appointment to view her father's painting has been marked in pencil in her diary since she got the registrar's reply. In pencil because she has considered rubbing it out, and forgetting all about Jack Seymour.

She got her nerves up three weeks ago, the day after Cordelia's visit in fact. Then she visited the Tate, less anxious than now, thinking like a fool that his painting would just be hanging there, waiting for her. They had always told her about her biological father and the Tate, expected her to feel proud or something. She assumed it would be there, for anyone to see. Even her, after all this time. Cordelia once suggested they go to London to see

it, but Lizzie wangled her way out of that one. She told her that
she didn't like figurative art.

'Hi Jim. Your two o'clock's here at the desk. Elizabeth
Weller to view the Jack Seymour.'

That juxtaposition of names: Weller and Seymour. Thank
goodness her name changed when Peter adopted her, it would
be too humiliating if she were still Seymour. She can't remember a time that she signed herself Lizzie Seymour, but then she
hadn't been writing for long before Cordelia suggested the
new name. 'Lizzie Weller, it sounds like a famous actress,' she
said, planting a kiss on Lizzie's forehead as Peter filled in the
forms.

The girl replaces the receiver, tells Lizzie that someone will be
right up to take her down to the stores. Lizzie puts the rolled
ball of fluff into her pocket, tucks her hair behind her ears. Her
mouth is dry as felt. It's not as though I'm seeing *him*, she tells
herself, it's only a picture. She wishes she'd just found it there in
the Gallery when she first came, all this having to write for a
viewing appointment is such a palaver. The letter took her a
waste-paper basketful of drafts, and that effort places too much
emphasis on the picture. Words on paper – 'requests permission
to view' – turn a glimpse into something more important, like
espionage. It's as though finding her father through his painting
is meaningful and that makes her feel needy and pathetic. It's just
curiosity, she tells herself, that's all it is, and she untucks the hair
from behind her ears because she can feel them sticking out and
fears they might be red.

Jim appears at her side, a neat stick insect of a man, dressed in
a V-neck jumper over a white shirt and polka-dot tie. She has
been expecting someone older, in overalls or a peaked hat. He
shakes her hand and steers her through the greenish light and the
swimming-pool atmosphere of the vestibule to a door in front of

the café. He has a piece of paper in his hand with the location of the painting written on it in felt-tip pen.

They go down the stairs and he rattles a series of knobs on a heavy iron door and pushes it open with his shoulder. It makes a sound like a relieved sigh as he shuts it behind her. He leads her along a brightly lit corridor, through another set of heavy doors, flood doors, he explains, because we're underground. He takes a bunch of keys from his pocket and unlocks yet another door, painted yellow this time, and marked D&E. There is a vast grey room in front of her. No natural light but electric, bright from fluorescent tubes suspended above their heads. Another technician is there, pulling out the metal racks, meshed like giant cages, and unhooking polythene-wrapped pictures. 'Hi Jim,' he says, without clocking Lizzie, and disappears with a picture through some dark-blue curtains in front of a bank of grey wooden plan chests. Lizzie's feet feel saturated with gravity against the concrete floor. It's a bit like the reptile house at the zoo, so much to see to the left and the right, not all of it pleasant.

'It's huge down here,' she says by way of making conversation.

'Amazing, isn't it,' says Jim, gesturing at the racks. 'Picassos, Turners, Canalettos, they're all here. Come this way, the painting you want is over here.'

They walk to one of the metal racks, which is already pulled out from the wall with the picture hooked to it, waiting for her. A grey plastic chair is placed in front of it. Lizzie averts her eyes from the picture as Jim gestures to the chair. 'You've got half an hour,' he says. 'I'll just help Gary over there, so give me a shout when you want to leave.'

The painting is before her, just eighteen inches square, a dark brown interior. *Elena at Rest*. Jack Seymour's most famous picture. 1961, the year of Lizzie's birth. A woman looks up from a cream-coloured day bed, Titian-haired and naked. Milky flesh like blown glass, so smooth. Too smooth, because Lizzie can't detect a single brush stroke. It's as though it has been airbrushed, or like a badly focused photograph. The woman is curled into an almost foetal position, all long limbs and greyhound curves, but her head is raised. Her face is pastel pure as a sugared almond, but Elena's eyes bore out of the canvas, scorching as ice. There is an oval mirror on the wall, above the bed where Elena lies, so cold and perfect. In the mirror is a man's face, clouds of dark hair, worried brown eyes, the end of a paintbrush between his teeth. It is the same as the face of the man in Cordelia's red vinyl photograph album.

'Hey, fuck-features,' says Lizzie in her mind. At least she hopes it's in her mind because Jim is standing close behind her. She stares at the painting and it dissolves in front of her eyes, leaving just the man's face in the mirror. But now she is viewing it through steam. There are bluebells and candles and she can smell the milky soap. Imperial Leather. And the man's expression is just the same, the eyes brown and worried.

'So, why this painting?' says Jim as she stands from the chair, swallowing hard to stem the swell of disappointment.

'It's by my dad,' she says, holding the back of the chair as though the store room is in motion and she needs to steady herself.

'Hey, that's funny,' he says.

'Funny, why?' asks Lizzie, regretting the word dad.

'Because I know the woman,' he says. 'Elena. Mind you, everyone's painted her. Hockney, Kitaj, loads of art students. She spends her life at rest.' And he starts to laugh.

Lizzie decides that she might as well take the rest of the day off. Such a bad headache, she'd already told Katrina on the telephone that morning. She can shave her legs and wash her hair, sort out some clothes to wear. Tony has promised to pop round later with some chicken soup. 'From Reuben's restaurant,' he said. 'Jewish penicillin. The best.'

In the pocket of her coat she has Elena's address. Jim said that he was sure she wouldn't mind if she wrote to her. 'Just tell her you met me,' he said. 'She's a lovely lady.' He was so helpful, that Jim, he told her how impressed he was that she was writing a book about her father's life and work, and asked if she had seen the three other portraits in Edinburgh and the one in Sheffield.

She should check them out, he said.

Lizzie likes being out in the afternoon light and the fine drizzle feels cool as seaspray on her face. She walks up Vauxhall Bridge Road, feeling the piece of paper in her pocket, smiling at people who do not smile back. That's what she always noticed about London when she was little. The way people avert their eyes, wary that anyone passing them might be a loony or a pickpocket or in need of a favour. Peter always said that it was a tribal thing: that any one person can only afford to know three hundred others, so in big towns they have to look away to avoid contact. Lizzie also knows that when Jack Seymour was a young man he tried an experiment that involved standing in Marylebone High Street with wodges of pound notes, attempting to give them away. She heard Cordelia tell Peter about it, one night when she was supposed to be in bed. No one took Jack's money, Cordelia said, and Peter laughed and said, 'Well, hon, who could blame them?'

Lizzie stops at a flower stall outside Victoria Station. The flower seller is a fat man in a green apron who is reading the *Evening Standard*. An ivory-faced woman in a black vinyl raincoat buys a bunch of thirty white roses. 'It's my boyfriend's birthday,' she says. 'I'm giving him thirty of everything.' 'Lucky bugger,' says the flower seller as she clips away in her high-heeled patent boots with the tightly packed bundle held before her like a bridal bouquet.

Lizzie looks at waxy lilies in a bucket, creamy open trumpets with tonsils of saffron, and at bunches of unappealing hot-house carnations in bubblegum pinks and nylon football-shirt red. There is cloudy white gypsophila, which brings a lump to her throat as it reminds her of Savannah and the day they stole some from Cordelia's birthday bouquet and threaded it through their hair, swivelling before their bridal images in her bedroom mirror. Lizzie would like to take the lilies, but they are too expensive. She buys five stems of gerberas, three yellow and two orange, and a bunch of white marguerites. The fat man takes her money and adds three white roses and a sprig of gypsophila. 'For you darling, no charge for the baby's breath or the roses,' and wraps the bunch in a slick of green paper.

Lizzie doesn't know three hundred people, nothing like, so she continues smiling at people on the tube. It's quite good fun, travelling at this time of day. She has a seat and no one crushes her or expects her to travel with her nose against their armpit. She holds the flowers before her, disappointed that they smell only musty, like old bank notes. She amuses herself by imagining breaking up the bunch and offering the odd stem to her fellow passengers, but then the woman on the opposite seat glares at her and, for the first time, a fellow commuter actually speaks.

'D'you think you could stop looking at me like that,' says the woman, about thirty, her eyes watery behind pebbly glasses.

'Sorry,' says Lizzie and the woman turns to her companion, a red-wattled man in a City suit. 'Grinning away like that when John Lennon's been shot.'

'Sorry,' mumbles Lizzie again and they resume ignoring her as the train rattles through the dark towards Paddington Station.

'Lovely flowers,' says the boy with all the tricks as she walks from the station. 'Hey, and a lovely smile today too,' he adds, the cigarette dancing between his lips as he speaks. He is there again, hanging around, no guitar but the three silver juggling clubs are sticking out of a squashy blue and red bag on the pavement. Lizzie wonders if he spends all his time hanging around the station. Perhaps he makes a good living at it, she thinks, but doubts it when she looks into the black hat at his feet, a few silver coins glinting there amongst the coppers.

'Can I ask you something?' she says, pulling the flowers inside her coat to protect them from the gusts of gritty wind that are blowing up the street towards the station.

'Ask away,' says the boy, in a voice that sounds too rich and big for his skinny frame. 'Anything you like.'

'How do you do that trick with the cigarette?'

'Which one?' says the boy, pulling on the cigarette between his teeth, making the end glow red, his hands stuffed in the pockets of his brown wool jacket.

'Aw, you know,' she says.

'What, this one?' He takes a tuppenny piece from the hat, holding it, outstretched, between finger and thumb, then, as she watches, passes the lit cigarette straight through its centre.

'Yeah, that one too,' says Lizzie, staring at the coin as he chucks it back, with a clonk, into the hat. 'But I meant the one where you made the cigarette disappear.'

'What, into thin air?'

'Yes,' she says. 'Like you did down the bottom of the escalators that time.'

'Into thin air,' says the boy again, impishly turning up the corners of his lips. 'Did I really now?'

'Yes,' says Lizzie. 'You did.'

The boy scratches his head, appears to be thinking long and

hard. He takes the cigarette from his mouth, looks at it, takes another puff. 'Let's see,' he says. He waves the cigarette in the air between them, then stubs it out into his fist, rubs both hands together and holds them out to her. His hands are clean with long thin fingers that he waves in front of her face.

'It's gone,' she says.

'Ah, yes. Just as well,' he says, 'filthy habit.'

'But how?' She is still staring at his hands.

'Magic,' he says.

Lizzie has to remind herself that she is supposed to have a headache when Tony arrives bringing a polystyrene cup of chicken soup. The soup is thin and salty with hot white noodles at the bottom. She sits at the kitchen counter blowing on the spoon while Tony leafs through a pile of letters and cards that she has left stacked beside the cooker.

'Bit nosy, aren't you?' she says.

'Yup,' says Tony. 'Where did all this stuff come from anyway?'

'My mum left it.'

'Some of it's months out of date,' he says. 'Look at this, you naughty girl, your library book's five months overdue. Newton Abbot Library will have you thrown in prison, you know.'

'Yeah, well, I expect my mum's taken it back by now,' she says, throwing her head back to drain the last of the slippery noodles from the cup.

Tony continues reading her post, stacking her birthday cards in one pile, reading them out to her as though she were a blind person.

'St Martin's, eh? Didn't know you were artistic,' he says, flipping her letter of acceptance over in his hands.

'I'm not, they'll take anyone these days,' says Lizzie, sliding off the kitchen stool and attempting to wrestle the rest of the post from his big hands.

'Come on, stop reading my letters, it's a crime you know.'

'Yup, and so's stealing library books. If you didn't have a headache I'd have to smack your bum for that,' he says, snatching the envelopes back.

'A birthday card from Savannah, isn't that your lesbie friend?'

'Tony, stop it.'

'Ah, sweet, look at that, she says she still loves you.'

'Tony, I mean it, put my things down.'

'And who's this Sam?' he asks, a proper gold-edged invitation in his hand. He flips the card on top of her head, says, 'Eh?' and Lizzie succeeds in twisting the pile of letters from his grip, ripping one of the cards, because he hangs on to them, laughing in her face, then releases them so suddenly that she falls backwards.

'So, what about this Sam's party,' he says, still laughing at her as she stands before him, shoving her letters into the belt of her dress.

'Well, are you going, it's soon you know.'

'It's not until next month.'

'Are you going?'

'I just might,' she snaps. 'Sam's my ex-boyfriend and loads of my friends will be there.'

Until that moment she had little intention of going to Sam's party but now looking at Tony mocking her and twisting the signet ring round and round on his finger like that, she thinks that she will go, just to spite him. He does enough to make her jealous, flirting with Katrina all the time in the office. Kat, she thinks, bloody Kat, that's what he calls her. And she thinks of all his little disappearing tricks when he doesn't get to the office for days on end and she's not allowed to even call him at home to check if he's okay. And all the nights that he gets up from her bed and goes home. Because he wants a bath, for God's sake. Well, she could do with a bath herself but he never thinks of that. And he thinks that the pay rise he's given her is enough for her to move somewhere decent that doesn't have a paltry dripping shower, but how would he know about rent, him in his bloody ivory tower in Campden Hill Square, with Harold Pinter saying good morning to him in the street and his wine cellar full of claret from Sotheby's.

'Yeah,' she says, moving away from him and sitting on the bed. 'I am going to Sam's party. It's going to be a lot of fun.' She can see herself in the mirror as she speaks. She is wearing a long, diaphanous pink dress that Tony bought her. Like a bloody fairy, she thinks and despises the sight of her own nipples poking the fabric.

'Well, don't expect me to go all the way to Devon with you,' says Tony, and Lizzie, warming to the row, tells him that obviously she doesn't expect him to, because he's not invited.

'In fact,' he says, and she notices a ticking in his cheek, just above the thrust of his jaw, 'don't expect me to go anywhere with you any more.' His lips are surprisingly thin and pale as veal but still Lizzie wants to throw herself at his feet, to wrap her arms around his knees to stop him leaving. She has pains like pins and needles behind her eyes and she knows that she's about to start shaking. But Tony is already at the door, holding it open.

'This can't go on,' he says, looking back at her over his shoulder.

'Why not, what have I done?' She starts to stand up from the bed but forbids herself from moving towards him. 'Treat them mean, keep them keen' – Ingrid's favourite saying is running unbidden through her head like a mantra.

Tony is glaring at her from the door. 'Go to your fucking party,' he says. 'Have a good time.'

'Tony, what's the matter? What have I done?'

'I'm sick to death of the way you've been gossiping about us to the others.' His eyes are spiteful, as vivid green as leaves before an electric storm. 'You've made me feel a complete fool, you know.'

'I haven't, Tony . . .'

'You've been shouting your silly little mouth off, don't deny it.' His temper has flared so fast that Lizzie doesn't know what to say as he stands smouldering in judgement at her door, though she knows her silence irritates him.

'Katrina warned me about you right from the start,' he says nastily. Still Lizzie is trying to catch up with him as he goes on. 'I'm not prepared to put up with it, don't say I didn't warn you to keep your little trap shut.'

Tony glares at her one more time before he slams the door behind him, leaving Lizzie stunned by the bed. The mantra slows down in her head, words distorting like a record that is playing at half speed. She pulls the crumpled papers from her waist, ripping cards and letters to shreds and scattering them at her bare feet. She throws herself onto the quilt and for the second time in three weeks listens to the agonising clunk of the door downstairs and the sound of someone leaving her alone, the echoes of shouting still ringing in her ears.

Chapter Eight

When Anna was born, I was summoned into my parents' bedroom. She arrived in the middle of the night, and I hadn't heard a thing. When I went to bed the night before I had my mum all to myself, and then, hey presto, in the morning, there she was, this ugly, livid pink, screaming thing and my mother looking down on her with milky tenderness.

'Would you like to hold her?' she whispered as I stood by the bed, awkward as a stork, first on one foot, then the other. Hold that thing? I felt I should, and sat down on the bed with my hands in front of me as though waiting for a blessing. They put the bawling baby into my arms, its mottled liver-sausage limbs flailing from the four corners of a white vest. I could tell they didn't really want me to hold her. Mum had her arms below mine, as though I might drop her or something. I didn't know what I was supposed to do with this thing once I was holding it.

'What's the matter, don't you like her?'

'It's not that,' I said, while my mum lifted Anna back under the covers and I tried not to breathe the sweet, condensed air that was

all around. It was my class assembly that morning and I was supposed to be reading my ant poem in front of the whole school.

'What shall we do?' My mother was nuzzling her face against
the top of Anna's head.

'Leave it to me,' said Peter and he left his newborn daughter
and my mother and drove me to school. I did my poem like
nothing much had happened to change my life and he took
some photographs for my mum who, for the first time ever,
couldn't be there herself.

Lizzie tells Paula something about her resentment when the first
of her sisters was born, but not about Peter's gallantry over the
school assembly. Paula snaps her fingers and holds out her hand.
'Put it there,' she says. 'When my little brother was born, I . . .'

Katrina slices into their conversation. 'Now, you two,' she
says as she looms over their desks, checking through their red
plastic out-trays for signs of work. 'When you've quite finished
gossiping, there's things to be done.'

'So, anyway, I didn't like him one little bit and they made me
go to stay at my grandma's after they found the Sellotape over his
mouth,' continues Paula, half-heartedly sticking two fingers up at
Katrina's departing charcoal wool back. Paula rifles through the
papers on her desk, picking between them, trying to find something interesting to do. 'How's it going with your man?' she
says, yawning. 'You made up yet?'

'No, haven't seen him since,' says Lizzie.

'Give him time, he'll soon be back with his tail between his
legs,' says Paula, putting her feet up on the desk and reading
through a request from the *Express*.

'I don't know,' says Lizzie, chewing her middle finger. 'It's
been over a week.'

'These older men,' says Paula, sagely, 'they're all the same. I bet he's itching to get back with you. I bet he's just been busy with his boys, how many did you say he has?'

'Five,' says Lizzie. 'Five little boys under eleven years old.'

'Well, no wonder he gets ratty,' says Paula.

Lizzie has a secret card index in her bag on which she writes all the lies that she tells Paula. Forty-five, it says, divorced dentist, red MGB, lives in Camberwell. Cottage near Godalming. Name Andrew. She regrets the five sons because now she'll have to give them names and schools and pets and annoying habits. It's so complicated, this lying business, but at least it means that she has someone to talk to about Tony, even if she can never reveal that the divorced dentist is really their boss. The trouble she takes to keep their secret makes Tony's accusations all the more unjust.

'I hate Katrina,' she says.

'Ssh, she's coming back,' says Paula. 'Here, give me a hand with this, will you? It's the "Where Are They Now?" feature. I'm supposed to have had all the pictures collated by yesterday afternoon. Katrina will give me a rocket if she finds out it hasn't gone yet.'

Lizzie accepts half the typed list of names from Paula, two sheets of paper, and takes it to the windowless concrete chill of the filing room. 'Sixties Giants', it says at the top of the first sheet, 'Where Are They Now?' She starts collecting the pictures, ticking off the names and slamming the metal file drawers shut with her knee as she goes. Donald Cammell, Ossie Clark, Penelope Tree. She finds three pictures of Syd Barrett but on closer inspection finds that two of them have been mislabelled. Or one of them has. She puts the pictures to one side. She'll have to ask Katrina to verify which is the real Syd Barrett, the one with the bird's-nest hair and swirly shirt or the sex god with the fleshy lips and a guitar. She finds the picture of Peter Green, but only after

Paula has told her to look under Fleetwood Mac. She is doing well, though, the first page is almost entirely done. She takes the second page, reads down the list, Jean Shrimpton, Simon Dee, James Fox, and then it jumps out at her, Jack Seymour. Well, yes, she thinks, of course he'd be part of it. *Where is he now?*

Lizzie finds the picture, not under Artists or Painters but from a cross-reference to Anarchists. Jack Seymour stands at the head of a crowd, squinting at the camera, two high dabs of eyebrows, a putty nose, black cavern of a mouth, obviously shouting something. His hair is as thick and curly as her own, and he has a girl on either side. Two slight blondes with long pony fringes obscuring their eyes, above dark Mao collars. Neither girl is her mother. Lizzie flips the picture over. There is a caption on the back, Grosvenor Square, 1968, it says, and below that a typed biog note stuck on with yellowing Sellotape: 'SEYMOUR, Jack, artist, London School; *b.* Penzance, 7th November 1912; *s.* of James and Elizabeth Seymour; *educ:* Westminster; Slade Sch.; Ruskin Sch. of Art, Oxford; RCA'.

She sits on the floor with the picture in her hands. 'Well, Dad,' she says to his contorted face, 'there you are.' She considers the information taped to the back, the typed words swim before her eyes, merging into lines of fuzzy black caterpillars. 'Old and posh,' she says. If she ever was told, she has long forgotten that he was well into his forties when she was born. Good God, she thinks, it was his birthday last month. He's pushing seventy. An old man.

Lizzie always assumed that he was the same generation as Cordelia and Peter, but what has she ever really known about Jack? Not much. What she could tell would fit on the back of the photograph. Just the things from eavesdropping on her parents. Wild stories of wild times. Rude words that she looked up later in the dictionary.

She stares at her father's face, and the picture fragments before her eyes. She is a child again; doing a jigsaw, sitting on her heels, with her eyes at the same level as the top of the coffee table. No one knows that she is there. It is hours past her bedtime. The little girls are in bed. They all go at the same time. Cordelia rounds them up and reads them stories on a feather-cushioned sofa while they snuggle around her like sleepy puppies. Sometimes she asks Lizzie to join them but Lizzie usually finds an excuse. She feels too disparate among them, standing out from their homogeneous mass, like an albino or a freak. With each birth she longed to see someone she could relate to: another Eskimo baby, dark, like the one in Cordelia's red photograph album. But Peter's strawberry blond hair, blue eyes and pink skin won through each time. Cordelia always laughs about it, says that she has weak genes. Lizzie stares at Anna, Briony and Lou and sees three little pigs. 'Fairytale Vikings,' corrects Cordelia.

The jigsaw sky and the edges are all done, her three sisters helped themselves a bit earlier. Lizzie can see where Lou has jammed in bits using brute force and she removes them, swearing under her breath, rejigs and corrects. She hopes that the younger girls haven't lost pieces and wishes they wouldn't touch her things. They move around like a cloud, those three, whispering and picking wild flowers.

Lizzie is tired, so tired that the completed bits of the jigsaw keep sliding out of focus before her, but she won't go to bed until they discover her there, and that could be hours yet. It will be midnight or past before Peter goes around the house to lock up. He'll have had a few drinks by then.

'Lizzie, really,' he'll say, 'whatever do you think you're doing still up at this time?' And she'll pretend to be surprised when he tells her that it's tomorrow already.

Peter will help her upstairs then, complain that she's getting too big to be carried, let her sleep in her vest and pants without brushing her teeth. When he tucks her in he'll kneel at her bedside and hold her to him. Late at night like this, with no one else there, she lets him squeeze her in his arms, and kiss her neck and her forehead. There are no little girls to insinuate themselves between them. And then her mother will come in. 'Oh Lizzie, you naughty girl,' she'll say and she'll feel guilty that she forgot all about her, that she failed to put her to bed at the proper time and that Lizzie's eyes will be bruised by accusing shadows in the morning.

But that will be later. Right now they have forgotten that she exists as they dip wafer-thin slices of lamb with their chopsticks into the boiling Mongolian hot-pot set in the middle of the kitchen table. Lizzie helped earlier, rolling napkins into swans, while her mother sliced the still frozen lamb to make pale purple slivers so thin that they could see right through them to the green fish pattern on the plates.

Children have been exiled from their thoughts as they drink hot saki from the tiny silvered porcelain cups that Peter brought back from Tokyo, the warmth and sweetness flavouring their slices of personal history. Lizzie can hear them. They are all talking at once, about Woody Guthrie, magic mushrooms and Glastonbury; titillating each other with stories from the past; from the sixties. Lizzie likes to listen out for words, intriguing words to look up in the dictionary. Once, she tried to look up 'alesbian' because she heard her mother say that she had a lesbian dream and Lizzie thought it was one word beginning with 'a'. They are clattering pans and whooping, their voices thrilled as kids on a treasure hunt.

Lizzie gets up from the floor because her knees are hurting. She moves to the carved rosewood chair, the one that no one ever wants to sit on. It isn't very comfortable but it is right next to the kitchen door.

They are drunk, in there, or stoned, or both, and sooner or later her mother will start talking about Jack. Lizzie can feel it in her bones. Most of the things she knows about Jack she has heard through open windows or late at night, like this, tuning in to her parents' conversations. The pieces fit together to form a peculiar, perplexing picture: of a man who has spent time in a mental hospital; who exhibited his paintings in public lavatories; got arrested for smoking dope in Marylebone police station while asking for directions to the zoo; who appeared in an underground movie, naked but for a gallon of fishing maggots; who threw himself into the Thames, with bricks in his pockets, when a girlfriend left him. A man who hasn't bothered to see his own daughter since she was a baby.

Lizzie adjusts her position on the hard rosewood chair, dangles her legs over the arm, yawning and stretching and wishing that Savannah was there to listen in with her. Predictably, the grown-ups are talking about sex.

'Absolutely not,' says her mother. They've been discussing Buddhist monks. Peter was wondering if they had wet dreams. Lizzie doesn't know what a wet dream is, though she knows that Buddha is a pot-bellied ornament. 'I've probably told you how Jack had been celibate for years before he met me.' Lizzie has heard about this before; she has looked up 'selibut' and eventually 'celibate' in the dictionary.

'I bet he wasn't really,' says Peter.

'Yes, he was, eight years,' says Cordelia, a little stridently.

'Nah,' says Ingrid, 'I never believed that.'

'He just said it to get you into bed,' and Lizzie hears Peter and Ingrid and Ingrid's boyfriend splutter like drains as Cordelia continues with her story.

'Really, he was. In fact, I just thought he was gay when I first started sitting for him. Any time sex reared its ugly head in a conversation, he used to contort his face in a chalk-scraping-on-a-blackboard sort of a way. I think it was because he'd read somewhere that the enlightened ones believed creativity was lost through ejaculation.'

'Yeah, sure,' says Ingrid, 'then what about that thing with Joan Smolski? That wasn't that long before you.'

'I've told you about *that*?' Cordelia sounds surprised but Lizzie can't imagine why. She always tells everyone about everything. And she repeats herself.

'What about Joan?' says Peter.

'You know her, Peter? You do?'

'Not exactly,' says Peter, 'but isn't she Theodore Smolski's daughter. I nearly bought one of his paintings once. *Jazz Musicians*, I think.'

'Well, to cut a long story short, Joan was a friend of Jack's, before me though, because she hated me. Anyway, Jack told me she came to Cornwall when her mother died because he said that the cottage and the woods had restorative properties. He was just trying to be kind.'

'Pah, *kind*, him,' spits Peter.

'Wait,' says Cordelia, 'Ingrid knows this story. So Joan arrived and they walked in the woods together and he gave her a hug to try and cheer her up because she was crying. Before he could stop her, she was rubbing her knee against him and well, you know . . . The thing was, that while he was telling me this, I really thought he *was* gay, his face was a picture of revulsion and he was shuddering at the memory. Mind you, I hadn't seen Joan then. She's enough to make anyone shudder. Face like a walnut. So Jack pushed her off and told her he was celibate.'

'So what?' says Peter. Lizzie is almost asleep with boredom on the chair behind the door. She has to practise putting her toes up to her mouth and all Cordelia's yoga positions to keep herself awake. And she's cold.

'I'm getting to it. So I asked Jack why Joan Smolski thought she could do that. You know, why she believed that sex was on the cards. Really, I just wanted to know if he *was* gay. "Did you ever sleep with her?" I said. And he said that yes, he had, just the once, years before. Then he smirked. "Well," he said, "actually it was twice but the second time was because her father wanted to paint us."'

'What, on the job?' says Peter.

'That's what he told me.'

'How revolting, and his own daughter too.'

Lizzie stretches like a cat, gets up and flicks a few stray pieces of jigsaw off the table, aiming for an empty ashtray on the floor. She is too young to find anything remotely of interest in her mother's story, she can't quite work it out for one thing, but she squirrels away the information, labelling it in her mind under 'Jack'.

There's an old man in the piazza playing the spoons and stomping his feet. He reminds Lizzie of a pumpkin, in his faded yellow Jack Daniel's T-shirt, and there are fatty pleats at the back of his neck under a tweed flat cap. He's not part of the act, that's a younger man with an amplifier and an electric guitar, singing about revolution, but Lizzie can't tear her eyes from the spoon-player as he flicks his wrists so fast that the spoons and his hands become a blur.

'Not bad, that,' says Tony. 'Almost as good as The Beatles.' Lizzie steers her attention back to the singer, his deliberate Keith Richard stance, the guitar hanging lower than the crotch of his jeans, his eyes screwing heavenwards as he tries to wrestle every last bit of meaning from the song. Tony's arm is around her shoulders, pulling her close, his blue cashmere scarf cosy around her neck. She pulls the scarf up over her face and breathes in the smell of him; petrol and toast and grapefruit. She intends to keep this scarf when he leaves for St Lucia for Christmas. She would like to sleep with it when he's gone. A girl in a black leather jacket is dancing, another old man is sitting on the steps behind, nodding in time to the music, others shuffle from foot to foot.

'I love Covent Garden,' she sighs. 'It's the most romantic place on earth.' She is so happy to be there, part of the crowd, with the wet cobbles beneath her feet, the smell of pizza bread, and best of all Tony nuzzling his face in her hair, the lights from the covered market so golden between graceful stone pillars.

'It's a tourist trap,' says Tony. 'You should've seen it when it was still a fruit and veg and flower market, now *that* was romantic.'

She can hear more music coming from inside, piped 'Jingle Bells' and there are three giant reindeer strung over the entrance with twists of Christmas lights and tinselled tails. Tony squeezes her shoulders, the old man with the spoons bows to the crowd and walks off, lame now. 'Come on,' Tony says, 'let's go and find that Christmas present.'

He said he didn't have a clue what to get her but she can't face the embarrassment of choosing her own gift. She would like him to surprise her with a little gold chain with a heart or a string of seed pearls – or even a pretty ring – but she can't tell him that. He has brought her to Covent Garden because there's a shop here he likes. It sells all manner of novelties: illuminated plastic goose-shaped lamps, inflatable lips chairs, giant cups and saucers painted with Liquorice Allsorts, china soap-holders shaped like baths complete with bubbles and bathing beauties.

'Just buy me a pineapple,' she says as they stand in the street at the other end of the piazza, watching an old-fashioned merry-go-round, glowing golden from hundreds of lightbulbs strung around the top. 'A pineapple?'

'Yeah, that's right,' she says. 'I'd like you to choose me one, the most beautiful pineapple money can buy.'

'Okay, if that's all you want,' he says and takes her hand and kisses it three times, gently, from her knuckles to the small, round bone that he says is like a cherry pip embedded in her wrist. It's heaven being with him now, Lizzie thinks. The distorted notes of the organ on the merry-go-round swirl around them; she soaks up all his new affection like a battle-weary soldier bathing on the sun-spangled shores of peacetime. It's as though they have survived a war together, found something stronger on the other side of the wall, at least that's how Tony put it.

He said he thought her little card index about the divorced dentist was the funniest thing, and that Katrina had always been a bit of a trouble-maker. And he said that making up was so much fun that they should fall out more often. Lizzie wasn't so sure about the last bit.

There are old-fashioned horses on the merry-go-round that rise and fall on painted poles. They are gleaming gold with big teeth in dark pink mouths, and wild, scared eyes, just like in Mary Poppins.

'Come on,' says Lizzie, taking Tony by the hand. 'Let's have a ride.'

They are laughing together as they sit side by side on adjoining horses, the small crowd around them swirling slowly as the carousel spins, the sound of the fairground organ mingling with voices and laughter. Tony leans over to Lizzie, who is on the inside horse, and kisses her on the lips as she looks at the people standing on the cobbles as they pass by. Lizzie's horse rises as Tony's falls, and he reaches for her mouth each time they pass. There's a group of schoolgirls, waiting their turn, in navy gaberdine and stripy yellow and blue scarves, there's a woman in a bright orange dress, three boys chewing gum and a man with a shopping bag. The carousel spins around, the horses rise and fall. One of the gaberdine girls is pointing now, her mouth a perfect 'O'. Lizzie looks back as her horse swoops up above Tony's, she is dreading that she saw what she thought she saw. Yes, she did. It's Sophie. Tony hasn't seen her yet and the carousel is slowing. Lizzie pulls away from him, puts both hands on the red and white stripy pole. The carousel is stopping. 'Shit,' says Tony.

The brightness leaves her blood. 'I know,' she says as her heart sinks like a stone in a pond sending out ripples of shock waves. And yet. And yet, there's a part of her that feels almost pleased that Sophie has seen her there but that soon passes when she looks at Tony's stricken face.

Tony jumps from the carousel, leaving Lizzie still sitting on the garish painted horse. She sees him lurch after Sophie, calling her name, while the close-knit schoolgirls exclaim to each other behind their hands, fluttering them like Oriental fans, their eyes thrilled circles, enjoying the drama unfolding before them. Lizzie sees Tony catch Sophie halfway down the street. She steps from the horse, the schoolgirls are staring from her to Tony and Sophie, pointing and shrugging their shoulders. She holds Tony's scarf to her face and breathes in as she watches him flag down a taxi and usher his daughter inside before him. He doesn't look back to where she stands, thinking of bluebells, with the carousel and the fairground organ starting up again behind her.

Chapter Nine

Someone once told Lizzie that the way a girl loses her virginity will influence the way she makes love forever more. Paula says that's rubbish because she lost hers in her boyfriend Ian's Ford Escort but that hasn't given her a predilection for lovers' laybys. 'Quite the opposite,' she says, licking her finger to scrub at the biro ink, a reminder from the office still on her hand. 'I always like things just so: soft music, candlelight, clean sheets, champagne if possible.'

She and Lizzie are sharing a bottle of Riesling and a few confidences while Paula's boyfriend is at judo. 'He's a black belt,' Paula says with hennish pride. 'He's got a great bod, you'll see.'

Lizzie likes it at Paula's flat. It feels like a proper home with its grey-piped buttermilk sofas and the kitchen wall stuck with holiday snapshots of Paula and Ian, going back to the time that he had long hair and she wore hoopy earrings and mini-skirts. There's Paula riding a donkey in Greece; Ian splashing sangria into his mouth from a little basket held aloft; Paula up to her neck in bubbles in a ski-chalet bathroom; Paula and Ian holding hands across a trattoria table with a red hibiscus in Paula's hair that perfectly matches the camera-flash red of Ian's eyes.

'So how old were you?' asks Paula and Lizzie regrets starting the conversation, only it was Paula who started it really by telling her that Ian is the only man she's ever slept with. Nevertheless she worries that she's turning into Cordelia, always talking about sex and relationships as though nothing else in the world matters a jot.

'Eighteen,' she lies. 'Not so long ago, when you think about it.'

'And was it a good experience?'

'I suppose it must have been because we spent the entire summer sneaking off to do it some more,' says Lizzie, getting nearer the truth this time.

'So has that influenced you, you know what you were saying about the first time and all that?' Paula is checking her watch, bright-eyed because Ian will be home within the hour and she wants Lizzie to admire him. Lizzie fully understands why she has been invited: in the morning she must tell the others how handsome Paula's Ian is. But right now Paula wants intimate details and Lizzie shirks behind a cushion that she has pulled onto her lap.

'Me? Oh, I don't know. I just meant that if it's a bad experience, you know, rape, whatever, that it can make it a problem forever afterwards, but if it's fun, well then I suppose it'll always be good.'

Lizzie doesn't want to tell Paula about her first time. Tony asked her about that once too, but she didn't tell him either. How could she? Four or five years have done little to distance the facts that she was just fifteen and Savannah was in the room the entire time. She accepts another glass of wine from Paula and shivers at the thought of the even rhythm of Savannah's breathing just feet from her mattress on the floor, the only sound since the music stopped and the party calmed down in the sitting room. (Lizzie dealt with that when Ingrid's neighbours started threatening to call the police. Sam stood by her side, which gave her the confidence to pull the plug from the wall when three heavily eye-linered girls and a boy in a leather jacket, who barely even knew Savannah, put the music back on after Lizzie switched it off. 'Who do you think you are anyway?' asked one of the girls, and another said, 'Yeah, Miss Pancake Chest, who do you think you're pushing around eh?'

Sam almost lost his temper then, rounded them up, herded them to the front door, big shouldered and bolshy: 'Come on, you lot, out.')

Not even half an hour later she was lying on a mattress in Savannah's room with Sam at her side, although Ingrid had forbidden any boys from staying the night. But Ingrid wasn't there and other couples were all over the house, in the spare room, in the sitting room, even in Ingrid's out-of-bounds bedroom, and there Lizzie lay, less tipsy than most, in Savannah's little room across the hall. Sam was sharing Lizzie's mattress because there was nowhere else for him to sleep, or so he said. They had to whisper because Savannah, whose sixteenth birthday it was, freaked out at midnight and Sam had helped Lizzie to carry her to bed. 'Not even a fucking card from the bastard,' she cried as Sam removed her shoes, and Lizzie unhooked the spider's-web earrings from her ears. Sam sat silently patting Savannah's clenched hand as she and Lizzie had a brief, slurred discussion about how rotten their real fathers were, before she fell asleep with her golden hair poured over her pillow like honey.

'She's beautiful, isn't she?' Sam said and Lizzie agreed, although she didn't really want him to notice.

'What's all that stuff about your real father?' She could feel the warmth of his breath on her neck as they lay beneath the blankets, shyly holding hands, trying not to giggle when Savannah started to snuffle in her sleep.

'Oh, nothing,' Lizzie tried to leave it there but Sam said that he didn't know she was adopted and in the end she had to tell him that Peter wasn't her real father and that, no, her real father wasn't dead. 'It just gets a bit inconvenient, that's all,' she said, brushing him off with a well-rehearsed line. 'You know when you have to fill out medical forms at school and you don't know which boxes to tick in the bits about heart disease, diabetes and leprosy or whatever in your immediate family.'

'When I have children,' said Sam, gripping her hand tighter, 'nothing, but nothing will stop me from being there for them. Blimey, you and Savannah . . .'

'Yeah, well, it happens,' said Lizzie and he squeezed her hand in such a comforting way that she didn't argue when he started to peel her jumper over her head.

They lay in the dark silently kissing each other, with Sam's hands warm against her skin and Lizzie feeling so wanted that she wished it would never end. For moments afterwards it was as though some missing part of her had been found and she nestled into Sam as he slept, his big bear breaths comforting as a rocking chair, lulling her towards her dreams.

'How was it Lizzie?' Savannah broke in, shattering the night like a stone through a window. Lizzie's eyes snapped open, and she could see her friend, lit by the streak of blue coming through the curtains, propped up on one elbow, not asleep after all, whispering from her bed. 'Did it hurt?'

In the morning Savannah cooked them sausages, egg and beans, perfect as in a café, and brought the plates in on a tray with a rose in an Orangina bottle and two mugs of tea. 'Ta da,' she said, laying the tray across their knees. Lizzie didn't dare move in case there was blood on the sheets. Savannah sat on the mattress with them, her eyes shining, as though they were all three celebrating something together.

'So, you should bring your man round another time,' says Paula when the wine is finished and she and Ian stand, close as Siamese twins, on their doorstep, an arm either side of their double body waving her out into the street-lit night. Lizzie turns back, sees them hovering there, fused together in the doorway, with the halo from the hall light around them. 'Yeah, okay,' she says, almost giggling at the thought. 'I just might do that.' And she thanks Paula for the wine, says, 'Nice to meet you, Ian.'

She pulls Tony's blue scarf over her face, his smell is fading, even though she blows hot breaths into the cashmere and she can feel it warm and damp around her mouth. She thinks about Paula and Ian, settling down with their takeaways in front of the telly and is hit by a wave of salty nostalgia as she hurries down their street, to the bus. She hasn't spoken to Tony since Covent Garden, doesn't know where she stands. She'll see him tomorrow, though, after work. He sent her a note on his pale-blue headed paper asking her to meet him at his house at half past six. At his house! Lizzie skips the last few yards towards the bus stop, planning what she will wear. She's been waiting for the invitation for a long time, so long that she thinks she might ask him to carry her over the threshold. Well, not really, but it is a landmark occasion. Perhaps he wants to introduce me to Sophie, she thinks, properly this time.

'This is Lizzie,' he might say, 'my girlfriend.' And the fantasy Sophie would smile and say that's what she guessed all along, that she was just waiting to be introduced. And Tony would say, 'I'm sure you two will get along really well. How about if Lizzie comes for Christmas to St Lucia too?' And Sophie would say what a good idea that was and ask Lizzie if she would help her to choose a swimsuit before they left.

The jumper she has been knitting for Tony is under her bed,

wrapped in tissue paper. It is dark blue mohair with pale blue hoops. When she gets back, still a little sozzled from Paula's wine, Lizzie pulls it out, unpicks the seam at the neck, which looks a bit raggedy, and threads her darning needle with the dark blue wool, spitting fibres from her tongue, and restitches it, sitting on the floor with her back resting against the mirror. The jumper feels rough in her hands, and not for the first time she worries that he might find it a bit itchy. Or perhaps mohair isn't his thing, but it knits up so much faster than anything else, and the mistakes don't show. He always wears such smooth fabrics, though, sheeny merino wool and powder puff cashmeres that she loves to throw on in the morning when she makes the coffee, the soft folds of Tonyness almost reaching her knees.

He is such a big man that she felt daunted as she started the ribbing for each piece and sat up in bed, muttering knit one, purl one, knit one, purl one, willing it to grow, for nights on end until it was getting light outside. She calculates that this jumper has taken her over sixty hours to knit. So Tony had better like it, itchy or not.

Lizzie rewraps it in the crackly paper, gets up and stretches, rubbing her shoulders where they are stiff from leaning over her work. She thinks she'll take it to his house tomorrow, tell him not to open it until Christmas Day, although she doubts he'll be needing it in St Lucia. Well not to worry, perhaps it gets cool there in the evenings. She replaces the package under her bed, just in case Tony decides to pay her a late-night visit – he does that more and more these days, usually when he's been drinking at his club, so she's always prepared in bed: slightly ashamed, with her hair brushed and perfume behind her ears. Next to the package is her watercolour box – a proper wooden one, with porcelain mixing dishes that Cordelia gave her once, and her brass-zippered portfolio, and a thick brown pad of cartridge paper. Lizzie hauls out the paper and painting box, decides that she will make a Christmas card for Tony. It's already past midnight but she's become accustomed to staying up late with the jumper.

She sits at the kitchen counter with the bitter varnished end of a paintbrush between her teeth, the others in a honey jar of water. She has stretched a piece of paper and taped it down on the bread board. She starts to doodle a wavering line of Prussian blue across the dampened paper: this is how she always paints, she picks a colour and a shape and waits to see what will happen. The line of blue becomes a river, with a rough grassy bank sprouting dock leaves, mottled green and maroon with bobbly seed-heads and silvered rosettes of thistles. There are people on the river bank, some lying back on their elbows, others sitting upright watching a group of children splash each other at the water's edge.

She is painting by the light of the flickering fluorescent tube that hangs from the greasy kitchen ceiling but in her mind she is there, at the river, with her family, on a muggy summer's day that keeps threatening to be bright but never quite delivers the sun. Savannah is there too, and Ingrid with her fishmonger boyfriend. Cordelia is turning her face to the sky, propped on one elbow, on a red wool rug with the wine glasses and sandwiches and Peter has put the bottles of wine and cherry pop into the river to keep cool. Anna, Briony and Lou are all in just their knickers and dart down the bank holding hands, stopping just at the edge and daring each other to go in. Their pale wispy hair is in ponytails and bunches and as they wave their arms their little shoulder blades stick out from their pink backs, tender as chicken wings. Briony dips her foot into the water.

'The pike, the pike, he's coming,' screams Anna and they all three leap back up the bank and throw themselves onto Cordelia's blanket, kicking their legs and squealing.

'Is no one going to swim today?' says Cordelia, flapping her hands against the bongoes of their three white cotton bottoms. 'What about you big girls, Lizzie? Savannah?'

Lizzie and Savannah are sitting further down the bank, ankle deep in the slick mud. 'Remember how you used to paint yourselves in that, like a pair of little brown savages?' says Peter. 'Go on, what's got into you, have a swim.'

'Age before beauty,' says Savannah, flicking the mud up with her toes, throwing her head back to see him standing above them, her hair coiling behind her on the grass, her body arched like a bridge between the water and the river bank.

'Go on, children first,' says Peter. 'Fifty pee for the first one in.'

The river looks greenish beneath the muffled sky, there are lily pads with tightly closed flowers the size of eggs and a dusting of midges that flit at the water, spotting it here and there with tiny rings.

'Fifty pee?' says Lizzie, crouching with both feet in the water, then retracting them and wiping mud onto the bank. 'But I haven't got my swimsuit.'

'Undies will do,' suggests Cordelia, nudging Ingrid. 'Shy, aren't they? Funny to think that only a couple of years ago they were still running around naked.' And she and Ingrid sigh.

Savannah stands up then, pulls her hair back, twists it into a rubber band from her wrist. She peels her T-shirt over her head, which makes the curve of her backbone stick out like a row of buttons, and unzips her jeans. She stands for a moment with her back to them, a long marble figure in baby pink elastane bra and knickers. Only the fishmonger averts his eyes.

'Okay,' she says to Peter over her shoulder, 'fifty pee,' and she leaps off the bank, just as the sun blazes out from behind the cloud and she hits the water, which breaks around her like a million diamonds and it seems then that everyone gasps.

'Three cheers for my little mermaid,' shrieks Ingrid and Peter says, 'Race you to the other side,' and dives into the water, still in his trousers. The little girls clap their hands together and Anna yells, 'Pike, pike, Daddy, it's coming to eat you all up.'

Lizzie left them all at the river and wandered by herself back through the fields to the house. She picked handfuls of ribwort, twisting the bendy stems into loops that she used to fire the heads at imaginary targets, just as she always did. Muttley appeared through a gap in the hedge, bringing a well-chewed ball in his mouth and dancing around her, dared her to chase him and wrestle the slimy rubber from his mouth. 'Go away, Muttley,' she said, kicking at the brown dust on the path with her bare heel. Her nose felt almost gritty with pollen and she could smell a distant field of rape, pungent as old piss and not at all like beeswax candles, which is how her mother always described the smell. 'Piss, piss, pissy old trousers,' she said, and Muttley cocked his ears at the sound of the others shrieking and laughing down the field and scooted past her towards the river. 'I hate them all,' said Lizzie, tearing a branch from one of the saplings that Peter planted in the autumn and using it to behead buttercups with vicious swipes. A single crow landed on the old oak tree by the post and rails and cackled at her, a low guttural hack, like someone vomiting.

Ingrid found her later, lying on her stomach under the bench in the summerhouse, picking tar from the knots in the old pine floor, and ignoring Cordelia shouting her name for supper. The summerhouse was Victorian, used most recently as a sandwich stall, and re-erected board by board by Peter as a surprise anniversary present for Cordelia soon after Anna was born. Lizzie often hid in there, in the far corner of the garden, with the warm acorn smell of the wood, looking back up at the house through the dimly smeared glass of leaded diamond panes.

'There you are, what's eating you?' Ingrid was squatting on the floor to get a better look at Lizzie under the bench. Lizzie's hair had fallen over her face and Ingrid reached in to smooth it back.

'Leave me alone,' Lizzie flicked her head back as though Ingrid's fingers were electric cattle prods. 'I don't want to talk.'

Ingrid rocked back on her heels. She was wearing a faded Wombles T-shirt that had once been Savannah's though Savannah had recently pointed out that the little-girl illusion fooled no one closer than a hundred yards.

'You worry your mother sick with all your little moods, you know,' Ingrid said and her voice was pure Savannah – post-laughter raspy in a way that made Lizzie think of things French, Left Bank cafés and lace corsets for example.

'Yeah, well, she just wants everyone to think she loves me,' said Lizzie resting her chin on her folded hands, her eyes lit black in the criss-crossing shadows from the cane trelliswork above her. 'Anyway, it's not her, I'm just sick of the lot of them,' she said, more savagely than she intended because she was still unsure why she was feeling so black.

'Have you started your periods yet?' said Ingrid and the careful soft modesty of her voice made Lizzie want to throw up on the spot.

'You're as bad as she is. Why do you always want to go on about such horrible things?'

Ingrid almost slapped her then, but she couldn't reach her under the bench. 'Come out, right now, Lizzie my girl,' she said and Lizzie rolled out and slumped over her knees on the floor, next to Ingrid.

'Now you listen here. I've been wanting to have this out with you for some time. Am I supposed to just stand back and watch you being so mean to your mum? What's she ever done to you?

She's worked herself to the bone to give you everything you need,' said Ingrid. 'Are you such a brat, Lizzie?'

'I don't know what you're going on about,' mumbled Lizzie. 'And anyway you're not here all the time. You don't know what it's really like being me. I bet Mum hasn't even noticed I'm not there.'

'I'm going to tell you something,' said Ingrid, placing her hand on Lizzie's wrist, squeezing between her fingers and thumb as though searching for a pulse. 'Take a deep breath because I'm going to be straight with you.' (What's she on about? Lizzie thought, fighting the claustrophobia of Ingrid clasping her wrist like a cuff. She's always *too* bloody straight. The confiding look on Ingrid's face was the same as it was when she tainted their first school disco with the words, 'Remember that all fourteen-year-old boys have very itchy penises.' Savannah had a fit. 'What does she think we're going to do? *Scratch them?*')

'God help me but you need to hear this,' Ingrid continued. 'Your mum gave up everything for you after that Jack walked out. She had nothing. No place to stay. Nothing.'

'We could've stayed in Cornwall, he'd have been back but she decided to get out of there before he could,' muttered Lizzie still into her knees, quietly though her blood was up and noisy in her ears.

'No. No. No. That's where you're wrong.' Ingrid relinquished her grip on Lizzie's arm. 'She had to get out. Jack gave up the lease on the cottage. You should've seen her then. She was like a skeleton and shaking all the time. She had to take a job sewing. Horrible dresses with tiny beads for women too rich to know better. She gave up all hope of her painting. You were all that mattered. And she got no money from him. Not a penny. And no support either. Just imagine it, Lizzie.

'And you used to ask for him every morning, so she started

every day lost for words. And at night she used to weep over your cot because she thought she'd failed you. And you say she doesn't love you.'

Lizzie wrapped her arms around her legs, pushing her throbbing eye sockets against her knees. She knew that Ingrid was trying to blame her for Cordelia giving up painting but that wasn't what interested her. The truth about Jack was what she wanted. 'He loved her once though,' she said, grasping the opportunity. 'Didn't he?'

'Who knows? What does it matter now?' Ingrid was not prepared to be drawn, her lips were sealed between her front teeth as though they'd been stapled. She held up a hand for Lizzie to pull her to her feet. 'Now, get your act together,' she said, sharply, 'and come in for supper and try to be a bit more pleasant to everyone. Especially your mum.'

When she got to the kitchen, they were all eating ice cream with hot chocolate sauce and Cordelia told her that she'd saved her some macaroni cheese, kept it warm in the oven. Savannah was showing the little girls how to hang a spoon from the end of their noses by breathing on it first and Peter took a fifty-pence piece from his pocket and screwed his eye around it like a monocle. 'Ah, Lizzie, ve haf vays of making you talk,' he said, patting the chair next to him and Lizzie felt her mood lifting, the heavy green fug dissolving, like vapours through the top of her head.

Cordelia and Jack. Ingrid was the only person Lizzie knew who had seen them together. Cordelia and Jack. The sole witness, other than herself of course, and there's little she can remember. Did he love her mother? Had he loved her? She should have pushed for more while she had Ingrid's attention. And now, as she sits, dabbing silver highlights to the ripples in the water in Tony's picture, she wonders if these are things she will ever know.

Chapter Ten

Lizzie doesn't like to take taxis, she can't really afford to for one thing, and she hates the feeling of being trapped inside with a strange man. She thinks of those little red lights that flick on inside the doors as devils' eyes and knows that she can't escape until the driver decides to release them. But she's already late because Katrina made her finish a filing job at the office. She had to go home to change because the filing room is filthy and she didn't want to appear at Tony's house in a bedraggled state. She raided the meter jar of all its fifty-pence pieces before she left, and walked straight past the busking magician with the cheeky smile because she had spotted the yellow light of a cab at the traffic lights. 'Campden Hill Square, please,' she said importantly, and it sounded so good that she hopped in without fearing a thing.

'Stranger danger,' the voice in her head started the moment the driver pulled off the handbrake, activating the devils' eyes in the doors. Stranger danger. That's what Cordelia used to drum into her, and yet here she is riding in a stranger's car, with him asking nosy questions like how long she's been in London and mocking her West Country accent. 'Ooh aah,' he says, 'you'm come from the place where them cider apples grow.' The little picture stuck to his dashboard of crew-cut twin boys with toy guns does little to reassure her.

Once, when she was really late for work, she recklessly hailed a cab on the way, and realised too late how little money she had in her purse. She sat in the back, trying not to breathe in the ancient ashtray air, chewing her lip as the clock whirred incessantly around. By the time she got to Holborn, it had clicked up to her limit and she had to tell the driver to stop and then he waited while she fished around in the bottom of her bag for a tip, coming up with a few coppers that she added to the two pound notes in his cupped hand. As she walked to the tube, she felt something hard hit her on the back of her head, and the coppers clattered around her feet. 'What d'you do love, empty your fucking piggy bank?' And she felt ashamed as the taxi pulled away from the lights. Later she remembered his eyes. They were white between the lid and iris, like knife-point rapists' often are in police photofits. Stranger danger, of course.

She grips the metal edge of the open window, despite the fact that it's frosty on her fingertips and she knows that it's ludicrous to have these panic attacks every time she gets into a cab.

'So Campden Hill Square it is,' says the driver.

'Yeah,' says Lizzie, 'Stranger danger, stranger danger,' Cordelia's voice an urgent whisper in her head.

'D'you live up there then?'

'Not yet,' she says. 'My boyfriend does. I'm moving in soon, though.'

'Pretty young thing like you,' says the driver, whistling through his teeth, 'he must be a happy bloke.'

Lizzie keeps her face close to the open window and the wet,

cool air. The cab rattles on up the Bayswater Road, past the wine shop, the butcher's and the late-night delicatessens with their striped awnings and the purposeful women emerging in smart coats. That'll be me, one day, she thinks.

'Here we are then,' says the driver, drawing up alongside Tony's black Mercedes and his pulling of the handbrake extinguishes the devils' eyes on the doors and Lizzie knows that she is free to go.

'You tell him from me that he's a lucky man,' he says when she pays, tipping him handsomely, in fifty-pence pieces. 'And make sure he takes good care of you.'

Lizzie has been to Tony's house before. Not inside, of course, but she sneaked past, just once, to see what sort of place it was. Before they'd even kissed. She stopped at his front gate, late one night, and peered up the garden path at his black front door, with the lion's-head door knocker and the clipped box balls growing from terracotta pots on either side. She stood in the dark and saw a glimmer of gold through a gap in the curtains on the tall front window and smelled the sweet honeysuckle and orange blossom beyond the wall of his front garden.

The garden is bare now, just black skeletons of trees and shrubs that shake their fingers, admonishing her and whispering as she waits. She hears the slap of his shoes along the hall, the clanking of the latch. Her heart performs a little drum roll as he opens the door. 'Ah, Lizzie, come in,' he says, without so much as a welcome. 'This way.' Lizzie is left closing the door behind herself as he turns with only a hunch of his shoulder to suggest she follow him.

Lizzie has his Christmas present in a Selfridges carrier bag. She has wrapped the jumper in spangled silver paper with a broad red ribbon but, in the end, left the painting out and just shoved it under the bed with the others. It got too personal; the river, the children; it had nothing to do with Christmas. She should have painted the Three Kings or people skating on a lake. Still, the jumper might suit him. Wordlessly she grips the plastic bag as she follows him down the grey flagged hall, past a wide stone staircase, to a door on the left. He throws open the door, and holds it wide. He flinches from her hand on his arm. 'Just step into the library,' he says, in his dull businessman's voice, devoid of high notes. 'We need to talk.' His eyes will not meet hers. He doesn't answer when she asks him if something's wrong.

The house is threateningly silent. Just the click of the library door as he shuts it behind her. Lizzie feels herself shrink, physically, like a cake from the oven. Her stomach sinks, as though her skeleton is crumbling under the weight of vital organs.

The library is long and thin and green, with dark wood bookshelves on either side that reach up to the ornate plaster ceiling. Before her, at the far end, is a vast leather-topped mahogany desk and the blurred folds of heavy velvet curtains that are drawn to the street. Lizzie sees that the only light is a pool from a green glass lamp on the desk and now she can hear the ticking of a clock that she can't see. Tony strides past her to the desk and sits down behind it, leaning forward into the pool from the lamp. She follows him to his desk, a wretched pupil on heavy legs, dreading that she has been summoned to the office to be expelled. 'What is it?'

'This has got to stop,' he says, pushing his fingers over the desk's leather top. Lizzie's hands feel clammy around the twisting handles of the Selfridges bag and she drops it to the floor. As soon as the words have left his mouth she realises that this is what she has been expecting all along, though it had been diverting to imagine him declaring undying love. She can feel his eyes on her, but she can only stare at her feet. She is frozen, suddenly unable to bear the thought of being deserted by him again. Coldness is striking from the inside out, she needs warm arms to wrap around her, to fall into. At this instant anyone's would do. For a moment she pictures herself sinking to her knees, begging him to hold her, but she gets herself under control by breathing in deep, shuddery breaths through her nose.

'What? Tony, what is it?' She already knows what it is. A fairground organ drones discordantly around her head.

'We can't carry on with this. I don't want this to go on. I felt so ashamed when Sophie saw us, kissing like that on that stupid merry-go-round.' He sounds rehearsed, still heartless. 'I'm forty-six, for Christ's sake.'

'I don't mind how old you are.' She can taste the faint vinegar tang of blood on her bottom lip as she speaks.

'That's hardly the point.' The sickly light is making his eyes look hollow between his hands in his hair. 'I mind, that's the thing.'

'You're going away tomorrow,' she says weakly, still standing before him. 'You'll feel better.'

He gets up from behind the desk, so suddenly that she can't help hunching her head aside, for a moment thinking he's going to strike her. The telephone rings but he ignores it. He picks up a brown bottle from the side table and pours them each an inch of drink. 'Brandy,' he says.

And while she takes her glass he tells her that he wants her to find herself another job. That he'll keep paying her for six months, whatever. He just wants her somewhere else, where he doesn't have to see her.

She should feel flattered, he almost seems to say. She stares at his hand on his glass, swilling the brandy.

'What are you going on about?' she says.

'You and me, it's got to stop.'

'Why?' She can't believe he really wants to end it, not since the last time when he said that he couldn't live without her. 'You said you love me,' she almost wails, despising herself.

'I don't know what that means. *Love*,' he spits out the word. But as he does, she notices a faint glimmer, something close to a smile, a small crack in his armour. He's trying to be nasty to me, she thinks. He's enjoying himself. Don't let him upset you. Lizzie, of all people, recognises the signs and his eyes are scanning her all over, settling anywhere but on her eyes. He huffs out his cheeks and blows the air out defeatedly, then plonks himself down on the end of his desk. 'Sophie's in a state,' he says. 'My ex-wife is taking her to a counsellor.'

'What's that to do with me?' Lizzie is pushing up the sleeves of her jumper. She sees him watching her arms.

'It doesn't help,' he says.

'Well, she isn't here, she doesn't need to know.'

A shaky silence falls between them. Somewhere outside a dog is barking. Lizzie can see the rumpled bag with his present at her feet. Cordelia's face floats into her mind. Her puffy wet face, the one that Lizzie closed the door on. She waits in the silence for Tony to speak.

'Will you stop doing that?' he says, finally, his voice more animated now that he has downed the brandy.

'What am I doing?' Lizzie is genuinely confused, she has nothing but her glass in her hands.

'That.'

'What?'

'Looking at my flies like that.'

'Oh,' says Lizzie, looking at the front of his trousers for the first time that she's been aware of. 'Oh, I see,' she adds, moving her eyes up to meet his, trying to keep all signs of triumph at bay.

But failing as she holds his gaze and then becoming dizzy with relief as with heavy arms he hauls her towards him.

Minutes later she can feel the Oriental rug, its knots rough against her bare back, and she knows she will have grazes, carpet burns, along her spine by the morning. But it's not that making her cry as Tony shoves her back and forth against the rug, his whole face screwed shut, and drops of sweat from his chest stinging her skin. She is clinging to him and crying with relief, then pain, as he opens his eyes and screams out, and the dog starts barking again outside. 'Sophie, my Sophie,' he cries again, and then she knows that he wasn't lying just now, that he really doesn't love her at all. She has never seen him this anguished. He sits upright beside her, banging his fists against the floor then slapping the top of his head. 'Sophie, I'm sorry,' he moans.

'Tony, she's your daughter,' Lizzie is gathering herself together, trying to unclench his fists from his face. 'What's this got to do with her?'

'Oh Christ,' he gasps, bolting from the floor. 'Everything's such a mess. You must go, let me call you a taxi.'

'That's how it's always been, always someone more important than me.' Lizzie is talking to a photograph on the floor in her room. She thinks she's going mad but there's an empty bottle of Harveys Bristol Cream by her side. All the girls got a bottle, and a fifty-pound Christmas bonus too, from Tony. 'With thanks,' read the merry Christmas tree-shaped label, 'for all your hard work this year. Happy Christmas!' Katrina doled them out like bloody Santa Claus on Christmas Eve. Santa Claus in a push-up bra, Lizzie thought. She and the others drank glasses of champagne beneath the coloured paper chains in the office, with Paula complaining about her cold sore and Siobhan, the part-timer, swearing that by next Christmas she'd have a boyfriend to spend it with, though with her newly shaved head as shiny as a hard-boiled egg Lizzie doubted that she'd succeed. Lizzie lied; she told them she was spending Christmas with a family in Wales. Katrina popped the cork on another bottle. It was just the four of them and three or four of the photographers who could be bothered to turn up, what with the boss not even being there himself. 'St Lucia,' they said. 'Very nice too.' And Katrina sat swinging her legs on her desk and announced that she would be going to the Caribbean herself, on Boxing Day, after she'd done the family stuff.

'The family stuff, la-di-da,' says Lizzie to the photograph in her hands. The photograph has a caption on the back, SEY-MOUR, Jack, it says. Lizzie stole it from the office and keeps it in her knife drawer, just gets it out to shout at occasionally. And sometimes, because Jack's mouth is contorted open like that, it feels as though he shouts back.

But it's Christmas Eve and despite all the sherry he just looks vacantly back at her, from the dog-eared print. 'Never anything for me. Lovey, lovey Mum and Peter, fucking Savannah too. Anna darling, Briony dear, oh sweet little baby Lou. Sophie this, Sophie that. Sophie doesn't like it. Well stuff Sophie. Stuff the lot of them. And you too,' she says. 'I'm going to find you,' and she stabs her finger at the photograph. 'Just you watch me.' If it wasn't so dark she'd go out and buy herself another bottle of something to drink. As it is she can feel her temples throbbing and her nose has started to run. She should get an early night. There are things to be planned. She drains her glass. She says, 'Happy Christmas.'

Chapter Eleven

Every New Year's Eve, since Lizzie can remember, Peter and Cordelia put on a fancy-dress party in the big barn. There was always a live band, made up of architects from Peter's firm, netted balloons that fell from the roof at midnight and a bring-a-bottle punch that ensured that everyone there started the new year with a head full of snakes.

The fancy dresses got pretty serious, some years. The whole family spent from Boxing Day onwards planning their costumes and Cordelia sewed them all herself. Lizzie's favourite was when she was ten and Cordelia made her a floppy top hat in red and white stripes and a black velvet catsuit with a tail. She was the Cat in the Hat, complete with rolled umbrella and carved carrot goldfish in a bowl, and Anna and Briony continued the homage to Dr Seuss with fuzzy turquoise wigs and little Thing One and Thing Two T-shirts. Savannah came as Pippi Longstocking, or perhaps that was the year before.

Last year, because they were eighteen, Lizzie and Savannah made their own outfits in the attic while Cordelia worked downstairs with papier mâché and an old fur rug to make a wolf outfit for Peter, three fluffy cotton wool sheep suits for the younger girls and some gingham and stiff petticoats for her own Bo Peep. Much to Savannah's delight, Ingrid had announced that she would be coming as Snow White. 'Please, please, let this mean that Donald will finally find his vocation as one of the dwarfs,' she said while she and Lizzie took turns at the sewing machine. 'Is there one called Stupid?' enquired Lizzie. 'Nah,' giggled Savannah, 'but there is Dopey . . .'

Lizzie and Savannah were still sewing sequins when the party started. Cars were crunching to a halt on the gravel and they could hear the buzz of the amplifiers and Nick and Charles from Peter's office tuning their guitars. Lizzie pulled open the curtains and looked across to the drive, at the bare trees that Anna and Briony had strung with a hundred candles in jam jars glowing like fireflies to the road. The barn was festooned with fairy lights and the leaded windows of Cordelia's summerhouse were rosy from the red lightbulb that Lizzie had bought. The younger generation would be huddled in there later, playing spin the bottle or the truth game, no doubt. She saw her mother standing with her shepherdess crook at the barn door welcoming an ageing Marilyn Monroe and a pair of Charlie Chaplins inside. 'I don't know if I can go through with it,' Lizzie was reluctantly strapping a borrowed sandal around her ankle. 'I feel like a prostitute.'

'Bah,' Savannah batted her false eyelashes at her. 'You look great. Here, stuff a bit more cotton wool down your bra.'

The bunny girl outfits had been Savannah's idea and she'd come up with the fishnet tights and two pairs of Ingrid's old stilettos. Lizzie was going along with it only because Sam bet Savannah that she wouldn't when she asked him to lend them a couple of his father's bow ties.

'Jesus,' said Cordelia when she caught them prancing in their sequinned swimsuits. 'You'll give Peter's friends heart attacks dressed like that.' Savannah giggled and waggled her tail, Lizzie said that she might need a couple of drinks before she made it to the barn.

'Please don't get so drunk you throw up again,' said Cordelia. 'Come on, you'd better get your grand entrance over and done with before all the food runs out.'

'Dutch courage,' said Savannah, passing her friend a bottle of beer from the crate they had stowed in Lizzie's room.

'Cheers.'

'Chin-chin.'

'I can't walk in these shoes.'

That was just last year, but now as Lizzie sits alone in her flat, surrounded by crumpled balls of used paper hankies, her nose and upper lip stinging raw, she shivers and thinks how it seems like a lifetime ago. Someone else's life. That sparkly girl getting tipsy in the barn is a stranger; remote to her now as the star of a silent movie. It's New Year's Eve and she has nowhere to go. She has been alone since the night before Christmas. Christmas lunch was a pork chop, mash and frozen peas finished off with Sainsbury's mince pies and half a bottle of Benylin to bring on sleep. She has been sleeping twelve hours a day and wandering around in a daze for the rest, through deserted streets and empty parks under dense sulphur skies.

She had to go out to buy Lemsip one day. Yesterday? The day before? And as she stood in the chemist a woman touched her lightly on the arm.

'Are you all right, dear?' Lizzie looked into the woman's lined face, not a face she recognised. 'Yes, I'm fine,' she said. 'Why?' It was only when she left the shop that she felt the wet-ness on her cheeks and realised she was crying.

Would Peter and Cordelia have their party as usual? Lizzie tries not to think about it. She's given up worrying about Tony, it's thoughts of her mother that plague her through the uncomforted nights. She tries not to dwell on that last day at the office, and what Anna said on the phone while Katrina mouthed at her about office policy and personal calls.

'Mum's not well. She's got pills.'

'Oh, sorry.'

'It's all your fault. Why don't you love us?'

'Not now, Anna. I'm at work.'

'You're not coming, are you?'

'No.'

'But it's Christmas.'

'I'll see you one day. Not now though.'

'I've got a boyfriend.'

'Good. I've got to get on now, Anna.'

'Please Lizzie . . .'

After that Siobhan staggered back late from lunch with a tinsel halo around her bald head and Katrina took her into Tony's deserted office to give her hell. And Paula asked Lizzie if she and her man would like to come round to her place for New Year's Eve. 'Nothing special,' she said. 'Just two other couples from Ian's work and a leg of lamb.' Paula emphasised the word 'couples', and Lizzie could see how awkward it would be when the clock struck midnight and she was left in a sea of champagne bubbles while these pairs welcomed the New Year with their lovers' kisses.

'Thanks,' she told Paula. 'Thanks a lot but I think we'll be spending the evening just the two of us.'

'Ah yes,' said Paula. 'New love.'

If only. Right now she can't imagine ever having anything to celebrate again. She couldn't seem to pass a building site these days without someone yelling, 'Cheer up, love, it might never happen.' Which wasn't very cheering.

Elena Mankowitz stands at her front door, which is open the full width the security chain allows. Even with such a thin slice of red jumper and yellow paisley shawl to go on, Lizzie recognises in the skin of white silk, now unironed, the woman from the painting in the Tate. She is here on impulse, in the rain, clutching a supermarket bouquet of disappointing freesias, knowing she should have called first.

'Yes?' says Elena, peering out through the crack in the door, then shutting it in Lizzie's face to release the chain. She swings the door wide open then, and stands erect with bare balletic feet, heels together, beneath yards of maroon knitted skirt. Elena is as long and graceful as the house in which Lizzie finds her. Her pale-blue eyes scan Lizzie's wet face and in it she sees something that makes her throw her hands to her lips, fingertips pressed together as though forming a steeple. Elena's hair hangs loose about her shoulders; it is no longer the dangerous auburn of Jack Seymour's painting but a lustrous white against her brightly patterned shawl. She looks more like a picture in the flesh than she does in the Tate. Unreal. Ethereal. A swan. Lizzie knows that were she an artist she would ask to paint her.

'My name's Lizzie Weller, but I'm Lizzie Seymour really,' she blurts, pushing her wet hair from her face, feeling her ears blaze. 'I hope you don't mind me coming here like this but I wanted to meet you.'

'Yes,' says Elena, weakly.

'I think you know my father,' continues Lizzie, regretting her decision, less confident already.

'Seymour. Oh Lord, I must sit down. Please come in.' Elena is stepping back to steady herself against a solid dark table in the hallway. Lizzie holds out the flowers and with barely a nod of thanks Elena lays them on the table, then stands with her hands still gripping it behind her, very straight, staring at Lizzie's face until Lizzie feels she will boil with embarrassment.

'Hello,' she says again. 'I'm Lizzie.'

'Yes. I know who you are,' whispers Elena. And as she leads the way to a pale sitting room, Lizzie hears her again, even softer this time, five short words on a breath: 'I can't hate you now.'

'What?'

'What indeed,' she says. 'Ignore me. Please sit down. I can see you've come here to talk.'

Lizzie, still in her wet coat, sinks into a cream fireside chair, its cushions muffling like an eiderdown, drawing her down. The air is heavy with the scent of lilies and a parchment-coloured cat stretches in a fluid S before the fire, lazily observing Lizzie through unblinking citronella eyes. Elena sits for a moment on a formal high-backed chair, still studying her, while she tries to explain what she wants. She stiffens when Lizzie says the word father, but promises nothing before springing to her feet. 'I shall make some tea. Please take off your wet things.'

As Elena closes the door behind her, Lizzie wishes she had not come. She can discern something salty in her throat, like blood, her swollen glands, the taste of panic. She doesn't know why Elena has frightened her, but she has. She half expects her to hiss at her, an evil spell or a prophesy that she will not be able to shake off. The Devil Child, she might spit in her sibilant voice, faintly tinged by Eastern Europe, her long finger pointing straight ahead, accusing as a knife. Or she could poison her tea.

Lizzie shivers before the fire, keeps her damp coat pulled around her. She doesn't like this room with its susurrating logs that seem to give off little warmth and the heavy ebony tables between chairs and sofas the colour of bones. She heard the woman say something about hating her. What is she doing here? Elena could be insane. Or perhaps the sickness of the last few lonely days has turned her own mind, making her see and hear things that are not there. The smallest things have been turning her rigid with fright lately. I'm the one that's unwell, she thinks, pulling a soggy handkerchief from her pocket.

Even with her cold, Lizzie finds the smell of lilies overpowering. They are in a tall glass vase, each bloom full and saffron-throated. Ranged around the flowers on the sidetable are silver photograph frames in front of which two miniature silver candelabra glint with triumvirates of candles, weeping wax and flickering orange onto the picture glass. It's like a shrine, and as Lizzie is too nervous to just sit while she waits, she tiptoes across the bleached floor to scrutinise the pictures.

In each of the frames she finds black and white prints. Several portraits of Elena, and one misty nude of her holding a baby to her breast. The other three photographs are too much. Lizzie's legs buckle, she realises that she shouldn't have come out with a temperature. She is on her knees, eyes involuntarily closing in her head, which feels too heavy for her neck. When she looks again, the portraits are still there, as before: three stark images amongst the candles. They are of herself. One as a baby, another as a toddler on Elena's lap and the third – how could it be? – a double profile, like the trick pictures that appear to be people one moment and a candlestick the next. A double profile of her four-year-old self nose to nose with Jack Seymour.

Elena has still not returned with the tea and the house is silent. Lizzie stumbles back across the floor to the chair, tries to steady her breathing. The cat snakes onto her lap, soft as warm clay, and starts to purr and, at last, she hears the rattling of porcelain and Elena glides back into the room bearing a tray.

'Excellent,' she says setting the tray down. 'I see you have made friends with Ying. Ying is a good judge of character, aren't you Ying?'

'Ying?'

'Yes, handsome, isn't he? A lavender Burmese. I have others. Tell me, little one, do you like cats?'

'Yes . . . Elena, do I already know you?' Lizzie's voice is quavering but Elena appears not to hear her as she lifts the lid on the teapot.

'Lord. Now I've forgotten the milk. Help yourself to a biscuit. I'm afraid they're not chocolate. You like chocolate, don't you? I'm sure you do.' Elena is on her feet again and Lizzie stands too, puts her shaking fingers to Elena's wrist.

'The photographs . . .' she says. 'I don't understand.'

'Perhaps I'll fetch us a proper drink,' says Elena, covering Lizzie's bitten fingers with her own cloudy hand. 'After all, it's New Year's Eve. Do you like champagne? Oh dear, perhaps I shouldn't though. Do little girls drink alcohol?'

'I'm nineteen.'

'Yes, of course you are. Nineteen. I suppose you would be by now. But you're such a little thing, you must excuse me. Time does strange things when you get to my age. Please sit.'

Elena's pale eyes shimmer. 'Nineteen,' she whispers, again, and she presses her fingers to Lizzie's face, feeling her cheeks and temples as though searching for the skeleton beneath the flesh. Like a blind woman. 'Beautiful,' she sighs. 'But tragic. I wish I'd found you before now. You're not happy, are you?'

Lizzie bites her lip, tries to stop herself shaking as Elena's icicle fingers trace her jaw. 'What am I to you?' she says, terrified of the answer. 'Why am I in those photographs over there?'

Elena takes her hands from Lizzie's face. Her eyes blaze. 'You don't know, do you?' Lizzie shakes her head. She has a flashing image of herself standing by a plate-glass window, unable to move although she knows at any moment there will be an explosion, the noise of a thousand firecrackers and razor shards will fly into her, the innocent bystander. Recently she's been unable to walk past shopfronts without considering the possibility. And stranger danger has been shadowing her for days, lurking in the supermarket queue, in the dark outlines of men walking towards the night bus. Cars might veer out of control and mount the pavement where she walks, psychopaths on the loose, hammers falling from building sites.

'I always wondered if he even told Cordelia about me,' continues Elena. 'About poor Laura. It would be so typical of him to keep it all to himself. Your father is a moral coward. Do you really know nothing of this? Oh dear, you don't look well. Let me get you a blanket, you're shaking.'

Later, much later, long after Elena has finished her confession, Lizzie sits again in her empty flat, safely wrapped in her quilt while below she can hear the party revellers starting the new year with bottles smashing in the street, their shouts ringing out as they stumble in twos and rowdy groups to Paddington. They'll bed down amongst starbursts of vomit and the hopelessly homeless on cold station seats, waiting for their early trains. Never again, they'll say. Off with the old and on with the new. Did you see that copper's face? Happy New Year! Hey, I'm dying for a fag already. If she wasn't so scared of them all, Lizzie would be down there too: on her way to the phone box to call her mother and demand to know why she never told her of what Elena revealed tonight.

All Cordelia ever managed were whimsical tales of bluebells and apple trees but never anything to explain why Jack Seymour walked out like that. Her only words on the subject rang hollow as carillons and she always changed the subject to what

a marvellous dad Peter was, how lucky she was to have him.
How much *he* loves you Lizzie. And then she would hug her
close, too close, as though trying to silence her against her
bosom.

'Of course your *biological father* loved you too. He just couldn't
carry on living with us. Emotional ties make him ill. One day
you'll understand . . .' And Lizzie, who couldn't make sense of
a word her mother spoke, presumed it was somehow her fault
that her father lived but never to see her.

She has a better explanation now. And his address too. At
least what Elena believes to be his address. She said she hasn't
seen him since the funeral and, after what she told Lizzie earlier,
Lizzie cannot blame her. If she was angry with Jack Seymour
before, that is as nothing now that she carries Elena's burden too.
The fury burns inside her: boiling poison acid in her stomach.
It's as though Elena has slipped a cloak of hatred from her own
shoulders and wrapped it around Lizzie. Lizzie goes to the knife
drawer and takes out Jack Seymour's picture. She quarters it
with the sharpest knife and holds each piece over the gas flame,
until only curled ashes remain on the lino at her feet. Her own
life has already caused a death. Alone now in her flat she feels
almost ready for another.

Elena made her promise not to make trouble. 'It's over,' she
said. 'For me and for you. Leave well alone.' But that was after
she told her about Jack and the terrible things that happened
soon after Lizzie's birth. He planted an orchard of trees, she
thinks. For me. And the thought of Jack Seymour digging
holes in the winter earth makes her shiver. Elena never did get
the champagne: there was little to celebrate and she talked in
barely a whisper while Lizzie huddled in the chair and the fire
died to embers as her story unfolded.

She said she no longer held Jack responsible for the tragedy but Lizzie didn't believe her. 'For a long time I did blame him, I was eaten up with wanting to damage him. Every night I used to dream of going after him with a knife. I would wake up sweating, my hand still clenched around the handle, disappointed that it was only a dream. But not now. It was my fault Laura died. Years it's taken me to accept that. She was lovely, you know. She had these eyes that seemed brighter than anyone else's, an almost faceted brilliance, like a diamond. She stopped people in their tracks, it was as though there was light shining around her. And that flesh, it was so sweet I wanted to eat her, I had to stop myself from sinking my teeth into her bottom.

'Jack was good with her – not like a conventional father, but he understood her, had all the amazing conversations: whispered stories of a magical land in the mountains where children ate rainbow sandwiches. It wasn't as though Jack lived here, though. This has always been my house, it was my mother's before she died and this is where I shall die too. But Jack, he never lived anywhere. He was here when he was here and not when he was not. Laura loved it when he was with us but learned not to ask when he would be again. It was an easy way of life for him: a conscience-free option, you might say. Rather like his vegetarianism: 'I eat meat when meat meets me,' was how he put it. I think meat met Jack as often as any other carnivore – he never cooked for himself. There was always someone who wanted to break the bread with him. Rich people and other artists and some writers. He was welcome to stay in lots of places besides here. I think that's how he defends himself: says that he never actually lived with me and our daughter, and I suppose he never really did. That's how he deals with it: Laura's death, I mean.

'She was only four when he told me about your mother. About Cordelia. He hadn't been around much for a while, I supposed he was buried in his painting. That's how he worked;

he'd spend years alone, feverish with ideas in someone's attic, or alone at his cottage. He never invited me there, Laura never saw it. I respected his need for privacy, I suppose. You see, I knew him as an artist first. I sat for him for years before anything happened between us. I just got used to trusting him, to doing what he said. Bend this way. Eyes down. Hold it. I was trained to accept his point of view, well before Laura was born.

'Laura ran to him when he finally showed up, and he held her, breathing her in. I remember him burying his head in her hair. But he put her down to tell me about Cordelia. My soulmate, he called her. The woman I love. His words were unrelenting, like a rain of bullets. Laura started to cry because I was crying but he stuck to what he said, emotionless as one of those messenger boys. Just repeating what he had come to tell me. He had already left in his mind, it was obvious. He was already in Cornwall with your mother. How I hated that woman. I never met her but I found out what I could. She was so young and she painted! She painted quite well: I made a point of seeing some of her stuff at a gallery off the Portobello Road. I despised those little canvases, I would quite happily have slashed them to ribbons.

'Worse was to come. She got pregnant. Jack rang me in an agitated state. I told him to tell her to have an abortion. He said that you couldn't kill someone for bad timing, that he and Cordelia had been bound to have a child from the first time their eyes met. He didn't spare my feelings. Instead he stayed there in Cornwall playing Daddy Bear with Mummy Bear and Baby Bear while Laura danced at ballet school and was the only child there not to have a father applauding in the audience. Just an inadequate mother. All I did was cry and have temper tantrums about Jack and Cordelia and how their baby daughter was stealing all the love and attention that Laura was due. She hugged me all the time because she knew that I was sad.

'The day she died, Jack came here for the last time to show me some photographs of his new daughter. So like Laura, he said. A considerable resemblance. He thought I should see them; he was determined not to be cowardly. He liked to face the music but was the first to turn heel when the orchestra got too loud. Ask Cordelia: she knows how that feels now. I've often thought of contacting her: we should start a Jack Seymour survivors' group. Ha. I would like to ask her forgiveness for having wished her such ill. Sometimes I feel that it was me that forced him to walk out on her. And you. I made sure it was painful for him, after the way Laura died. I said some bad things.

'Anyway, even before then I wanted to exert as much damage as I could. I willed his daughter to be ugly. I glared at these photographs, but Jack's new daughter looked so like Laura when she was just born that my heart melted for a moment. There you were, a chubby babushka with bright black eyes. I had to smile. He has strong genes, I suppose. Then he told me that he wouldn't be coming for Christmas. It wouldn't be fair on Cordelia, he said. He couldn't desert her with a tiny baby in Cornwall over Christmas. And no parents to go to. We were arguing about it in the kitchen when it happened, me shouting, him with his head in his hands.

'They said she had been dead for over an hour when we found her. Out there in the garden, face down in the pond. It's not there now. I had it filled in and planted with snowberry bushes because those were her favourites. She liked the way the berries popped under her feet. We always had to stop if we came across a snowberry bush so that she could scatter some around to stamp on. They make that squish, and she would laugh and jump up in the air. So there it is. I hadn't been paying attention, I'd been too busy trying to get my own way.'

It's New Year's Eve and Lizzie doesn't have a place to go.

There is no party, no family to share it with: to dance in the new year and jeer at each others' drunken resolutions. But she is not alone, after all. At midnight she stands at the tiny grave of the sister she has never met, watching her own breath leave her body as clouds in the cold night air. She stands with a photograph in her hands of little Laura who loved cats and wanted to be a ballet dancer when she grew up and then died before Lizzie's first Christmas. Laura, the sister who like herself was not enough for Jack, not loved enough to keep him near. The sister who is like her. Elena lays the lilies beneath the marble headstone while Lizzie runs her finger around the frosting carved inscription: Laura Seymour, beloved daughter of Elena Mankovitz and Jack Seymour. 1956–1961.

Chapter Twelve

Katrina wears her suntan like ceremonial battledress; her sun-bleached hair, a laurel wreath. She perches at her desk by the window, dabbing moisturiser at her peeling nose, wrinkling it in the little silver mirror that she takes from her crocodile briefcase. Although Tony isn't in, she hasn't yet retreated to his office. Instead she turns her triumphantly sautéed face to the others, asks if everyone had a good break.

Paula holds up her left hand, wriggles her fingers and her new emerald flares obediently in the light from her desk lamp. The others have already admired it. About time too, they said. They already have the date of the wedding in their diaries. Katrina snaps the mirror shut, slips it back between the jaws of her bag.

'Is that an engagement ring?' she manages.

'Certainly is. It was Ian's grandma's, an antique.' Paula lays her ring finger along the palm of her other hand, smiles down at the emerald. It's the sort of smile normally reserved for the newborn.

'I was there,' says Siobhan. 'When Ian popped the question. He was down on his knees as the clock struck midnight. He got the ring out of his pocket. You should've seen Paula's face.'

'Best start to the year I've ever had,' says Paula, still admiring her ring.

Lizzie has heard all this several times already this morning. She has other things on her mind.

'Well, I suppose I should congratulate you!' says Katrina smartly, before too swiftly turning her attention to Lizzie.

'And you Lizzie, did you have a good Christmas break? What did you find to do with yourself?'

'I spent most of it in bed,' says Lizzie, though she dreads an onslaught of sympathy from the others.

'That flu again, I suppose,' says Katrina dismissively, and Lizzie feels a wave of hatred so strong that it sparks something of her old self. It's almost as though Savannah sits at her shoulder, egging her on as she replies.

'No, not flu,' she can't help smiling, 'fucking.' She is holding Katrina's gaze, staring her out. 'Non-stop fucking.'

It's almost lunchtime before Lizzie finds herself alone in the office for long enough to make the call that she's been waiting to make. Since leaving Elena at Laura's grave that night, she has cursed herself for not having a phone. She tried to call first when she woke at lunchtime on New Year's Day but got no reply and was too terrorised by the dark streets to risk the phone box later and there has been no reply all weekend. She came in early to use the office phone this morning but Paula was already here, a blushing bride to be, impatient to broadcast her news. Lizzie has been going through the motions since eight thirty: sharing Paula's excitement, hearing about Siobhan's mother's arthritis, wiping the smile off Katrina's face. In between she's been keeping one eye on the door, jumping each time she hears the rattle and ting of the lift, thinking it's Tony arriving. To sack her? To apologise? To tell her where she stands.

She knows he's back in the country because she went to his house yesterday, and stood at the gate and saw the broad outline of his back at his desk in the golden window. She hovered there a while just watching, until he got up and drew the curtains and she ran down the hill then, breathless and guilty as a child playing knock down ginger.

But she forgets about Tony as Paula and Siobhan disappear into the filing room with a copy of *Brides* magazine secreted beneath Paula's jumper and Katrina hastens into Tony's office soon after what she terms Lizzie's 'crude outburst'.

Lizzie's fingers are crossed as she holds the receiver between her chin and her ear. Please God, let Peter be at work, but her prayers are ignored as he picks up the phone. Lizzie slams it down when she hears him; waits a moment, then dials again. Three times she puts the receiver down, three times she hears the once reassuring voice that now turns her stomach, before finally her mother is on the line.

'Yes, who is this?' Cordelia sounds angry.

'Mum, it's me.'

'Lizzie. Was that you just now?'

'Yes, listen Mum, I haven't got long. I'm not supposed to use the phone here.'

'What is it?' Cordelia does nothing to disguise her mistrust. Lizzie can feel her own heart beating somewhere near her throat as she forces herself to speak.

'Why did you never tell me about Laura?' she says, finding her voice but not her breath.

'What? Laura who?' And that is all Lizzie needs to hear for now.

'Nothing,' she mumbles while Cordelia protests. And

Cordelia's words tumble into one another as she demands to know what she thinks she's doing putting the phone down on Peter like that and does she realise the pain she's causing everyone.

Shaking with grief, Lizzie cuts the line and sits wiping her eyes on her sleeves while all around the shrill telephones go unanswered.

What am I? she thinks. Like Jack? So cruel? And she wonders what sort of emotional blankness got him through those winter months after Laura's death. The same months he spent with her mother, celebrating their new baby daughter, without once revealing the tragedy he had left behind in London. How did he hide the pain?

And she thinks about her poor mother being kept in ignorant bliss while this emotionally crippled man bent over the earth, digging holes, planting trees. She imagines Cordelia singing songs and filling the cottage with pine cones and cinnamon sticks and holly and kissing Jack Seymour beneath the poisonous mistletoe berries.

Cordelia always put so much artistry into decorating the house at Christmas; she said it had something to do with her not being able to paint any more. She made swags of yew branches that she hung above the fire and studded with burnished crab apples, red velvet bows and walnuts and pine cones that she sprayed gold. She framed pictures and mirrors with holly and turned all the windows to stained glass by hanging them with paper-thin slices of citrus fruits, dried flat so they looked like crystallised stars. She made Christmas puddings from her grandmother's recipe and Lizzie was always the first to stir the ingredients and make her wish.

Lizzie was five when they spent their last Christmas alone. Before Peter turned them into a family and other stockings got nailed up beside hers beneath the chimney each year.

They were house-sitting for some friends of Cordelia's at a small farmhouse in the Cotswolds. They roasted chestnuts in the open fire, which exploded like gunfire, making them both jump. The house smelled of toast and pine resin from the burning logs and upstairs there was a huge iron bed that they shared to keep warm. In the mornings it creaked and pinged as Lizzie trampolined her mother awake.

Outside on Christmas Day, the house sparkled like frosted gingerbread and Cordelia read her mind and said that the grass that scrunched beneath their boots was really peppermint brittle and all the trees were carved from chocolate.

There were animals to be fed, too. Cows and horses. They struggled through the mud to the paddocks each morning and evening, Cordelia pushing a barrow of hay, Lizzie by her side dragging plastic buckets of cattle cubes and pony nuts and sometimes turnips. They would lean on the gate, blowing on their frozen fingers, and watch the horses pulling at the hay, turning on each other with squeals and bared teeth and steaming breath, and the cows more peaceful, almost courteous, a ruminative community at the trough.

There was a pony in the nearest paddock. A small dun mare called Sukie. Cordelia's friends said that Lizzie was welcome to have a ride on her if she felt like it. Cordelia and Lizzie found Sukie's tack in the barn, veiled by cobwebs and stiff with mildew. Cordelia remembered enough from her own childhood to show Lizzie how to treat the saddle and bridle with the neat's-foot oil that they found in a rusting tin in the feed store. It took them a while to get the tack on the pony because Sukie refused to open her teeth for the bit and then blew her stomach up and held her breath so that it took all of Cordelia's strength to fasten the girth. But then sitting high up on the pony's back was the most thrilling thing about that Christmas Day.

For the next couple of days, Cordelia led Sukie around the fields while Lizzie clung to handfuls of mud-encrusted mane, her mother's steadying hand on her leg. After a while she grew braver, and even tried to trot, with her mother running beside her, and she bumped up and down until she feared that her insides would jump out of her mouth. On about the fifth day she was brave enough to attempt a solo circuit of the field while Cordelia stood anxiously by the gate. The pony walked off willingly enough with Lizzie remembering all the things Cordelia had been telling her: heels down, grip with your knees, look straight ahead.

She was moving across the field, admiring the tips of Sukie's ears, which were the exact brown on cream of singed paper, and confident enough to try a trot when the pony saw a plastic bag caught in a tree, flapping there in the wind like a ruined bird. All at once she took off, at a jarring run and then pounding the ground at canter. Lizzie could hear her mother's scream over by the gate and the next moment she was flying through the air, with the wind like the sea in her ears. Somehow, impossibly, Cordelia made it across the field and threw herself between Lizzie and the hard ground and Lizzie heard a crack, like a branch snapping, as she landed on top of her, the pony still careering madly ahead, splattering them both with mud.

For years they talked about it every Christmas, about how when the pony bucked it was as though in that split second Cordelia was able to fly. They wondered how else she could have got across the field in time to cushion Lizzie's fall. And about how she didn't realise her collarbone was broken until they were back home.

Lizzie sits at her desk and thinks about her mother. Her wonderful mother who was always there to save her and never complained about the pains that still shoot down her arm before it rains, a legacy from that Christmas. Cordelia always seemed to sizzle with something compelling, like a magnetic force. She was the sort of mother that Lizzie's friends talked to: she wasn't an embarrassment. When they got in, late from the rugby club disco or the pub, she made them toast and let them help themselves to leftovers from the fridge. 'Bugger,' she'd say when she pulled the plug on the toaster, 'that thing always gives me a shock.' In fact Cordelia was forever getting electrocuted. She seemed to attract static energy: her long hair crackled when she brushed it and she'd throw the brush down. And car-door handles, too, she needed someone else to open them for her. But it seemed natural when you were around her. All that electric energy. Elemental.

Lizzie is glad the others are still out of the room. She wraps her arms around her own shoulders, hugging herself. Missing her mother makes her despise Peter all the more for what he did. Why should she protect him? Sometimes she doesn't know how she puts herself through all this loneliness and misery just to save their marriage when all that means is depriving herself of her mother's love. What a saint I must be, she thinks bitterly. But then she pictures Cordelia and Peter and the three little girls. She imagines them at home like they've always been. She sees Cordelia looking at Peter, adoring him. Her eyes follow him around the room as a puppy watches its master and then Lizzie thinks that after everything that's happened her mum deserves something better than the truth.

She doesn't hear the lift when Tony arrives. 'Sweet thing,' he says, 'you're still here.' His eyes look brighter with his face so tanned. 'I'm glad.'

Lizzie never talks about her parents to anyone, but Paula has this way of probing. They are sitting in the Three Bells after work, waiting for Ian and a couple of his friends from the city. Paula has recommended the mulled wine and the barman pours it scalding from a saucepan into their glasses. It's too sweet and Lizzie can see powdered cinnamon dusting the surface and the oily ghost of someone else's lips on the rim of the glass.

'So how come you never see them?' asks Paula, shovelling Golden Wonders into her mouth as they sit on high stools at the bar, then holding up a spectacularly large crisp with a bubble in it for Lizzie. Lizzie always thinks Paula smells faintly of spermicide but she tries to put that from her mind as she takes it.

'Aw, it's just my dad. He's a bastard.' she says. 'I had to get away from him. My mum's okay though, it's just impossible to see her without telling her about him, so I don't.'

'What, does he hit you or something?' Paula's eyes are wide with possibilities. She and Ian spend every Sunday with her parents in Orpington, eating roast chicken and playing gin rummy. It's growing up in Orpington that makes her vowels so cosy, her words so inviting of confidences. Lizzie is a harder nut to crack than most and she can tell that something pretty dreadful must've happened because Lizzie's eyes are glistening.

'I think he only ever hit me once,' says Lizzie. 'When I was about ten.' It's not something she's thought about much since, but she tells Paula about it because she can sense that Paula won't leave her alone until she does.

'All I was doing,' she says, 'was playing with the broom. It was Halloween. I was a witch, still in my Brownies outfit from earlier, and I told the broomstick to giddy up around the kitchen. My dad was reading the evening paper at the table. Anna and Briony were being a pain about the pumpkin lanterns that beamed down from the dresser. You can't touch them at all, he said, they're hot. So they were both already crying and getting on his nerves when I knocked into him with the broom. I didn't mean to but he snatched the stick and walloped me across the legs with it.'

'What, hard?'

It had been actually, it had left a bruise. But she's losing heart already and longing to change the subject. 'No, not really. I was just shocked because he never hit us.'

Paula looks so disappointed that Lizzie regrets not making something up about him breaking her leg. But the thought of keeping track with yet more lies is too much: Andrew, the fictitious Camberwell boyfriend, is already causing enough trouble, especially since Paula told everyone else all about him. Now she has to ask advice about handling his five young sons and Siobhan said she needed a good dentist and could she have his number? 'No,' Lizzie had said, thinking fast. 'No, you can't. He might fancy you!'

Paula has finished her wine and it's Lizzie's turn to buy another, although she'd much rather leave. They move to a table because Ian is due at any moment. Lizzie brings a steaming glass in each hand and another bag of crisps tucked under her chin. Paula swipes the crisps and opens them with a pop.

'What did he do to you, Lizzie?' Paula is not going to let the subject drop and Lizzie considers telling her the truth. She swallows half the glass of wine, her stomach is grateful and warm. The winebar is dark with a vaulted ceiling and sawdust on the floor. Paula smiles encouragingly. Lizzie drinks from her glass again, starts to peel the corner of a beer mat. She is struggling to find the right words, uneasy because it's not something she's ever told. Paula strokes the back of her hand. Lizzie feels the words swirling, still unspoken. A cold blast of air from the door to the street breaks the spell, bringing with it Ian and his friends.

For the first time ever, Paula seems almost disgruntled as Ian throws his arms towards her but she gets over it. 'Ah, there's my

beautiful fiancée,' he says, and plants a kiss on his dead grandmother's emerald ring.

The three accountants give off the chill of the street as they
unwrap their navy-blue wool coats. 'It's sleeting outside now,'
says Ian and introduces the others to Lizzie before offering to get
everyone a drink. Lizzie starts to decline, nervously pulling at
her coat. She must get going, she says. She has her father's
address in her pocket, at least she hopes he still lives there – it's
the address that Elena gave her. She has been planning a visit;
the mulled wine was simply for courage.

'Good heavens,' says Ian, 'you're not leaving us the moment
we arrive, are you Lizzie?'

'You'll upset the boys,' says Paula wickedly. 'Anyway, I
thought you said you'd broken up with your man.' Lizzie has
spared Paula the news that it's all back on again. Tony's behaviour is beginning to sound eccentric. Especially for a dentist.

'It's bloody cold out there,' says Ian, rubbing his hands vigor-
ously together then clicking his fingers for effect. 'I forbid you
to leave without another drink to warm you.'

'Did you say your name was Liza?' says the older of Ian's colleagues, whom Ian introduced as Christopher. He has an old
man's leeriness in a young man's face, or perhaps a young man's
eagerness in an old face; Lizzie can't decide which. He's obviously well fed though, and the shoulders of his pin-striped jacket
are salted with dandruff. He laughs louder than anyone else and
tells them a disgusting joke, something about anchovies and
female genitalia. He whispers the word 'fanny' straight at Lizzie
as she recoils from his spicy breath and the white beads of spit
that have collected in the corners of his mouth. He finishes his
drink long before his colleagues, although he's doing most of the
talking.

James, the other one, is nice enough though. He flashes a

toothpaste smile when he is introduced and holds Lizzie's hand for longer than he would a man's. She notices his skin: loose, like a puppy. And that his hair is cut in a teen-idol hairstyle: longer at the front so that his forelock flops over one eye every now and then, especially when he laughs.

Lizzie is certain that under his suit James would be wearing designer pants, probably with a festive motif, and that he'd have checked them out in the mirror before he put his trousers on. If Savannah were there, they'd lay a bet, then beg him to reveal. Together they were safe to muse aloud about the underwear of young men they'd only just met. It's a habit that Lizzie wishes she could break. On his right hand she notices a silver ring, engraved with a Greek key pattern, that might once have been worn by a girlfriend. As an identity tag, Lizzie supposes, 'James' girl'. Not James' girl now though, because there isn't one. Paula made a point of putting Lizzie straight about that in the ladies'. He might as well have 'Situation Vacant' emblazoned across his chest, Lizzie thought, as Paula pushed the hairbrush towards her.

When they leave, James insists on giving Lizzie a lift home and she sits in the passenger seat while Ian and Paula climb into the back. Christopher's car is parked in front and they watch him fumble for his keys, bloody from wine and swearing. A drunk lumbers past and stops to sway awhile and raise his beer can in the air as though waiting for God to rain a refill. Christopher yells something at him, Lizzie doesn't hear what, but the man staggers back as though he's had sand thrown in his eyes. Lizzie meets the man's watery, pall-bearer's gaze. Minutely she points to Christopher and grimaces: a silent 'Yeuch' and a thumbs down that only he sees. The man's face creases in half, his black mouth gappy as a jack-o'-lantern's. As they drive off he is still standing there, pointing after Lizzie, his thumb raised in approval.

James asks her questions about herself all the way home and

she can feel Paula's happiness radiating through the back of her seat. She thinks of her all fluffed up back there and keeps expecting her to cluck little chirrups of satisfaction each time James speaks.

'Do you like shellfish?' he asks as they pull up outside her door, and Lizzie knows what's coming next when she tells him that she does. She thinks how little Tony has bothered with her since he got back from the Caribbean. And not even a proper apology for the way he treated her before he went.

'Dinner on Saturday?' Paula has time for an impatient cough between James asking and Lizzie's reply.

'Why not?' she agrees, while in the back Paula smiles over them, a slightly sozzled Cupid in a Marks and Spencer skirt.

Lizzie rests her elbows on the windowsill by her bed; she is blind to the streetlamps and the cars and the people passing below, deaf to the sirens and shouts. She is thinking about Jack Seymour, about going to Marylebone. 'It's part of the Portman Estate, just off Manchester Square,' Elena told her. 'He's had it for years, got it through one of his rich connections from school.' It's too late to go there now. It's not the rudeness of the hour that bothers her, just the darkness of the streets.

She will see him one day soon, possibly even tomorrow, though she wouldn't be introducing herself: that would be risky, after all, look at what happened to Savannah. Lizzie can remember Savannah returning from Halifax last summer. It's something she tries not to think about given the circumstances: Savannah's face pale as washed-out linen, her trembling sorrow turning to banshee rage in Lizzie's arms. Between sobs her telling Lizzie what happened.

The taxi from the train station, her father at the door staring at her as though she was trying to sell him something, a woman demanding to know who was there, a baby crying somewhere inside. 'I had an overwhelming urge not to speak, just to throw myself into his arms,' Savannah said. She did speak though: 'Hello Dad, it's me, Savannah, and I'm nineteen today.' Wordlessly her father had shut the door in her face.

Savannah said that after that she kept her finger on the bell for almost an hour, but he didn't come back. Lizzie thought she was a fool to go there. It's not a mistake she intends to make with Jack Seymour: a closed door would not be the most advantageous situation for revenge.

Someone is whistling further down the street, a tune that breaks through Lizzie's preoccupation. It makes her smile. Hi ho, hi ho, it's off to work we go. It's what she and Savannah used to hum whenever Donald was just out of earshot. It's hard to whistle when you're laughing.

She cranes her neck to see where the whistling is coming from, then draws herself back inside and switches off the bedside lamp. It's the busking magician from the tube. She's sure it's him by the way he walks: long legs almost dancing along as he whistles and swings a holdall from arm to arm. It's definitely him, she can see his face now, impish in the glare from a passing car, and when he's almost directly outside she notices the three silver juggling clubs poking through the zipper of the bag. He seems to slow down then, and he glances up at her window, to where she sits in the dark, looking out like a sentinel.

She is still at the window as his whistling fades to nothing and he turns the corner. The street is empty now; it's long past closing time. Thinking of Savannah and the day she went on her pilgrimage to Halifax sets Lizzie's mind on a track from which there is no return. She tries to wipe the tape, as she has so many times, but the pictures flash by in her mind, indelible as blood. That other time, looking out of her bedroom window at home, a sleepless night, long after Savannah had gone to bed in the

spare room, dosed up with double brandies from Peter and dec-
larations of love and sympathy from Lizzie.

'Will she be okay?' Lizzie asked Peter who was damping
down the fire but he just shrugged. 'I love you,' she said, kissing
the back of his neck before she went up to her own room. And
she meant it. What had happened to Savannah that day had
recemented her love for Peter after some pretty rocky teenage
moments. She would never think it again, but at that moment
he was the best thing that had ever happened to her: her
mother's saviour, her own dear father.

She lay in bed and worried about her friend, railing against
the man who made Savannah and along with him the man who
made her. She was missing her mother, wishing she hadn't gone
to India with Ingrid when they were needed at home to give
comfort and reassurance. Her own words had been so useless in
the face of Savannah's misery. She could almost hear her
thoughts: at least you have Peter. It was written all over her face.
'At least you've got Peter,' she said, aloud at last, as Lizzie stroked
her arm, just like she used to.

That night. Was it a dream? How many times has she tried
to convince herself it was. Looking out of that other window,
but not so long ago. Though it feels like a lifetime. Her bed a
tangle of ravaged sheets and blankets behind her. Feverish from
lack of sleep, the cool air beckoning her to the window, then
standing leaning out over the garden, at the monotones of the
hushed trees and conspiratorial bushes, their branches blurring
silver from the full moon. A shroud of mist hanging over the
grass, Lou's forgotten tricycle, and Cordelia's summerhouse
looming out beyond, distant stark black.

Lizzie screws her fists into her eye sockets to try and rid herself of the vision but it's always there, like bright lights imprinted
on her retina. The full picture: Savannah, a pale Rapunzel with

her hair hanging out of the summerhouse window, metallic almost against the black. Savannah rocking to and fro, back and forth, in and out of the window, getting faster and faster. And behind her, moving with her, another face. A face as familiar as the moon.

Chapter Thirteen

Lizzie feels conspicuous as she hovers in the entrance of the underground car park opposite Jack Seymour's house. She is in a narrow mews, just off the main drag, the only place that affords a clear view. His door remains black and closed within the peeling, grubby white stucco walls; plain dark curtains block the only window to the street. There is no name beneath the bell, just a yellowing piece of paper and, strangely, his is the only door without a letterbox. But she knows that she's in the right place because on the second evening of her vigil she saw an old woman locking up the house next door and after agonising in the street, watching her corn-plastered amble towards the bus stop, she ran after her. 'Please, am I in the right place for Jack Seymour?' and to her relief the woman nodded, yes, and then asked Lizzie if she would kindly help her up into the bus.

Lizzie has been here every evening after work. Although she's over her initial paranoia and need for subterfuge, she still hates the way men look at her as they drive in and out of the car park. She's careful to wear neither lipstick nor any skirt above her ankles. But now she no longer hides behind the pages of the *Evening Standard* nor stands ostentatiously looking at her watch and then up the street as though waiting for someone who is late. Now she feels she's almost invisible and the excitement has ebbed away.

Today is the first time that she's been here in daylight hours. It's Saturday, and for once the weather is being kind to her, taking a break from showering her with icy needles and sand-blasting her face with grit. There's no warmth but there is sunshine and Lizzie stands with her back against the garage wall, squinting through the glare at the closed door and the shrouded window. Come on, she thinks, you have to emerge sometime.

A man walks towards her swinging a yellow carrier bag. Fair hair, she notices, and as he gets closer it's greying at the temples. But he's too fat. Fat cat banker. Name? Possibly Henry. Around here, she scrutinises people more than she's ever done before. All her life she's seen Jack's face in strangers, often moved closer or followed some unsuspecting old man just to make sure. She's often wondered if she's sat next to him on the tube or queued behind him in the supermarket but now, in Marylebone, no man goes by without suspicion.

She left home so early this morning that she met the postman on the way out. He handed her the mail for the flats, bundles of letters that she slipped out of the rubber band, assuming none would be for her. She flicked through them, just to be nosy really: jolly postcards for the Australian girls with wallabies on the stamps; the usual letters from banks in the Channel Islands for the unpleasant middle-aged man with the Filipina girlfriend on the first floor; some bills for the old couple; flyers for a pizza parlour; and amongst it all a cream envelope addressed to herself in an old-fashioned script.

She opened it at the bus stop. Inside was a bevel-edged card, just two sentences, innocuous at first reading but inexplicably more chilling each time she looked again. *Dearest L*, it said, and Lizzie noted that unfortunate initial, rather than her name. *I have been thinking about you. I would love you to visit me more often.* And it was signed, *Elena*. Later, outside Jack Seymour's house, she read it again and by then the warmth of her pocket had released from it the faint smell of lilies.

Lizzie watches two women turn the corner from the main street into the mews. Sybil and Adelaide, she says to herself, rich widows. To help with the aching boredom of her surveillance she has started to give everyone names and occupations. Sybil and Adelaide clip along, arm in arm, purposeful as a pair of clothes pegs. They stop at the first house in the mews and ring the bell. Lizzie sees an Asian man come to the door, shake his head and look down the street. She sees Sybil and Adelaide move on to the next house, and ring that bell too. She can't hear what they say to the blank-faced woman who answers but now her blood is drumming in her ears. Sybil and Adelaide are doing door-to-door something or other and they are just two away from Jack's.

No one is in at the next house, nor is the old lady whom Lizzie helped onto the bus the other day. And now Sybil and Adelaide are ringing Jack's bell and Lizzie pulls her coat around her face, pushing her hair, with trembling fingers, inside the collar. She hardly dares look as Jack's door opens wide to the street, and there, at last, he is. His head and scrawny neck emerge from a heavy green jumper, poking left and right, like a suspicious turtle. Lizzie cowers as she sees the man with the bonfire hair, grey now, so old and frail-looking that she almost forgets to dislike him. She hears the women ask about a lost cat, sees Jack's bony hands clench together, his black eyes at that moment seem to find her as he shakes his head and disappears again, wordlessly, behind the black door. Lizzie's heart is beating so fast that she has to crouch down on the pavement to catch her breath.

It's almost eighteen years since she last saw him. Her only real memory is of the day he left, just that fleeting glimpse of his face through the steam and the bluebells in the bathroom. Now there is this other secret face, old and ravaged, lurking behind the dark door that she's been haunting. Secret, yet not a stranger, even now.

You bastard, she thinks, but softly. I've found you, why have you never tried to find me?

The few times she asked her mother straight why her real father was never there, Cordelia's only response was to tell her how protective he used to be, as though this very fact excused his subsequent disappearance and proved that she was loved by him, despite all evidence to the contrary. As Lizzie walks away from his house, she remembers something of what she used to say, and one story in particular that gave her something to cling to whenever the feelings of worthlessness threatened to submerge her, like the time that Peter's mother hissed at her, in a moment of senile cruelty: 'You're not really his daughter, you know, you're not a proper grandchild.'

'He carried you everywhere when you were a baby,' Cordelia told her then. 'And as soon as you could walk, he watched you like a hawk. I remember one time, I took you to explore down the field, beyond the well. It was a beautiful day, and the first time you'd worn shoes. Little red lace-up boots, they were. We kept them as an ornament when you outgrew them, dangling by their laces from the reading lamp. So sweet . . . no, I don't know where they are now.

'Anyway, you tottered by my side, singing away in your funny little tuneless voice. At the bottom of the field was an iron five-bar gate and beyond that the river that used to flood its banks and freeze in the winter, where schoolkids used to skate. But it was a lovely day and I took you down there to see if we could find some frogspawn. You had a little fishing net on a long bamboo pole and I was carrying a jam jar. I was sitting on the riverbank and you were picking water buttercups when there was a shout and I looked up past the gate to see him haring down the field, waving his arms.

"Stop, stop," he was screaming at me. "Get her away from the river." He was shaking when he reached us and scooped you up, buttercups falling from your hands, making you cry. He was in a white-hot rage. I'll never forget how he looked at me: an accusing stare that said "unfit mother". "What do you think you're doing leading her down here?" I didn't know what to say, and he was in such a panic. He said he thought there would be no stopping you, now you knew the way to the water. It was as though he was scared the river would call out to you while we were asleep . . .'

What a bloody fraud, Lizzie thinks now, as she trudges between the blank red towers of Chilton Street, disillusioned as a child who's just been told there's no such thing as Santa Claus. Of course Jack would have panicked about water. If only she could see her mother so that she could share all she knows. But what would she say? My father left because – guess what? – He had another little daughter that you never even knew existed because he never once mentioned her. She drowned shortly after I was born and he didn't tell you about that either. Oh, and by the way, another thing you don't know. Last summer I watched your husband fucking your best friend's daughter in the summerhouse. Hey Mum, you sure can pick them!

Cordelia would have approved of James if she met him. Any mother would have. He is close-shaven, with clean hair and bright teeth and under his smart jacket he is wearing a pale-green aertex shirt with a little green crocodile embroidered on the breast. He arrived on time and stood waiting for Lizzie on the pavement. In the drizzle. He walked around his gleaming company car to hold open the passenger door, his black umbrella angled above her head. His car smelled vaguely of citrus fruit, subtle and clean as his aftershave.

Lizzie stifles a yawn as he starts to tell her about his plans to get a job at the Stock Exchange. Many of his friends already have, he explains, they're making good money. He's bought his own flat, he tells her. His father is big in medical equipment, his brother too. Sade is his favourite singer and he eats BLTs from a sandwich bar most lunchtimes. It's relaxing as a warm bath sitting in the restaurant, listening to James. This isn't the sort of place Tony takes her to either: there are posters of Toulouse Lautrec café society on the red-brick walls and at the far end, next to the bar, a kohl-eyed woman perches on a high stool strumming a guitar and singing in a little-girl voice like Françoise Hardy. They eat with their fingers: hot buttery lobster and moules marinières, steaming garlic, heaped in glazed earthenware bowls in bright blues and greens.

The woman sings and James translates for Lizzie: '*Je suis d'accord pour tous que tu voudras, mais ne compte pas sur moi pour aller chez toi.* I agree to everything that you want, but don't expect me to go home with you.'

Lizzie laughs, says that she doesn't.

'*Pas pour un seul café?*' And he acts shocked when she tells him that she doesn't speak a word of French because her French teacher was blind enough not to notice her absence from class.

'You never went on an exchange then?'

She shakes her head. She never did stuff like that, because to be honest she's never really enjoyed long spells away from her mother. When other girls were breaking free, she still thought of Cordelia as her best friend, although with so many sisters and Peter competing, a friend whose company she had to snatch in cherished moments between the others' demands.

'I never really wanted to,' she says. 'I couldn't bear the thought of being stuck with a family I didn't know.'

'Best thing I ever did,' says James. 'I went from bottom of the class to top after that summer. They were really poor, Bernard's folks, and didn't speak a word of English. Every morning they gave Bernard and me a loaf of French bread and we weren't allowed back in until suppertime. We spent the whole summer on the beach and I learned to dive. We lived on raw sea urchins from the bottom of the sea, we used to scoop out their insides with the bread.'

'Ugh,' says Lizzie.

'Delicious,' says James, and at that moment Lizzie likes him.

It's strange as time travel for Lizzie: this finding herself with someone her own age, talking about school and careers and pop concerts. It's a shame her mind keeps wandering off. She's trying to fix the image of Jack Seymour in her head. Not the usual impression of his face through the steam, but the one she saw earlier: the querulous eyes and the papery pale skin, the bony neck, the chaotic grey hair. She is striving to think of that face as her father. Sometimes she can sense James waiting for a response and she has to jolt herself back to the present.

'What about *Hunky Dory*?' he says suddenly.

'Sorry?'

'You know, David Bowie, the one with "Changes" on it?' He enunciates his words as though talking to a small disobedient child.

'Yes. What about it?'

'Never mind. It's what we were just talking about, that's all.'

James starts to laugh, flicks a piece of bread at her across the table. Dizzy Lizzie he calls her, and she wonders if he is regretting this dinner already. When the bill comes he doesn't argue about her paying half. 'You're not with it tonight, are you?' he says as they stand up to leave, and the word tonight makes her wonder why he imagines she's any more with it any other night of the week.

It's obvious when they get to her front door that James *does* expect to be asked inside and, as she finds her key, Lizzie thinks why the hell not? The door doesn't shut properly behind him, the lock has been dodgy ever since one of the Australians slammed it too hard. Lizzie is about to go back down the first flight of steps to jiggle it into place but changes her mind: James won't be staying long, she can ask him to do it on his way out.

When they reach the top of the seventy-seven stairs, she leaves her own door open too. It's not that she's scared of James exactly, but you never can tell. She tries not to think of the open door as an escape route but it's always struck her as odd, the whole dating convention. One dinner or a night at the pictures, it seems, and you're expected to let a relative stranger into your private space, which in Lizzie's case is nothing more than a bed-room with a kitchen and bathroom tacked on. It wasn't something she thought about much when she lived at home. In any case Cordelia was always there to dole out the cups of tea and ask if they had a good time.

'Hey, nice mirror,' says James as he circles the room. 'Big.'

'I hope you don't take sugar,' she says, hating the mirror and the heat that's spreading up from her neck as she rinses a couple of mugs at the sink.

They drink their coffee sitting on stools at the kitchen work-top, the mirror and the bed behind them, the silences between them longer now, more awkward than in the restaurant.

'Got any music?' James asks and Lizzie hates to admit that she only has classical, some opera and a bit of J.J. Cale, but she doesn't tell him why.

'I thought you said you liked Steely Dan,' he says but she can't possibly explain to him that she's put her own musical taste on hold because of Tony.

James squats on his heels with Lizzie beside him going through her second-hand record collection on the floor. He has found some Prokofiev he likes, *Lieutenant Kije*, and is putting it on the turntable when they hear the creak of the stairs followed by footsteps on the landing. Lizzie rises to her feet as Tony appears in the doorway, breathing hard from the stairs.

'Andrew, hello!' she bellows. 'What a surprise.'

Tony's smile fades. 'What?' he says. 'Who?'

James is also on his feet, his hair flopping over one eye, left hand extended towards Tony.

'Hello Andrew,' she says again, with more emphasis on the Andrew this time.

'Andrew, this is James, he's a friend of Paula's, you know, one of the girls from work.'

Tony is still looking at her as he takes James' outstretched hand. He's shaking his head as he pumps it up and down once. Lizzie almost giggles; it's as though she and James are naughty children who've just been caught with their fingers in the trifle.

'You know,' she says again, enjoying her own panic, 'Paula, I've told you about her. Would you like a coffee? There's still some hot.'

'Andrew,' says James courteously, 'tell me, is it still raining outside?'

Later when Lizzie is alone again she waits in the dark at her window for the magician to walk past. He often does at this time of night, usually alone, always whistling. It's almost as though he wishes her goodnight as he strains his neck to look up at her window. Sometimes she wonders if he knows she's there watching him as he wends his way down the street.

She's trying to sleep, attempting to hold on to that glimpse of Jack Seymour, to persuade her subconscious to allow her real father into her dreams. But the word father just brings Peter to her mind. She tries to conjure up the good things about him: all those years they had as father and daughter before she saw him with Savannah in the summerhouse that night. But it's like scrambled egg after someone's made it for you with shell in, or a restaurant that has served you something raw, like sinewy pink chicken. It tarnishes your memories. You no longer salivate when you look at the menu; you only remember the crunchy shell stuck at the back of your throat making you want to vomit.

She saw him, that night, hands kneading Savannah's bare flesh, her moonlit breasts, him behind pushing against her faster and faster, in and out of the summerhouse window. Since then Lizzie has only been able to remember the bad things about him. Like that time he hit her with the broomstick, and the day he swabbed her mouth with the soapy dishcloth when she swore at her mother, or when he banned her from seeing Sam because it became obvious they were sleeping together.

But it's mainly pictures of him with Savannah that disturb her, not just in the summerhouse, but earlier ones too: Savannah, aged about seven, riding on his shoulders when she twisted her ankle in the woods; Peter bringing Savannah the same wooden doll from Prague that he brought Lizzie; Peter teaching them both to jive, Savannah's red skirt flying up as he swung her between his legs; Peter and Savannah swimming in the river while Cordelia clapped her hands at the water's edge.

And so the images go on, flaring and subsiding, until on Sunday morning Lizzie wakes with a Benylin hangover. I've got to get a grip on this habit she thinks as she chucks the empty syrup-encrusted bottle into the bin where it clanks against its twin, consumed on some other insomniac night less than a week before. She's always considered herself vehemently anti-drugs. Savannah too. At parties they stood together, not gasping at rainbow auras or elephants emerging from the wallpaper, nor sucking on the soggy stumps of joints. They always agreed that there's no warning quite so salutary as seeing one's parents inanely grinning in a cannabis haze, pink-eyed and talking rubbish all night, waking late and bleary.

Of course, like everyone else they flirted with glue when they were fifteen or so. When punk was cool and they wanted to be Siouxsie Sioux. They hung out at the children's swings in the park near their school, taking turns with the Bostik poured into a crisp packet, inhaling deeply, driving the oxygen from their brains, then greeting the swirling clouds as they all piled high, girl, boy, girl, boy, toppling like layers of dominoes from a park bench. Or staggered through the botanical gardens, dressed in ripped bin-liners, yelling the lyrics from 'Anarchy in the UK' to frighten the old people. 'She was a girl from Birming-ham, she'd just had an abor-shun.' But that was only once or twice, before the headaches brought her to her senses and someone alerted Peter that they thought they'd seen her there 'with some unpleasant types.'

'So what, you smoke dope,' she cried. 'What's the difference?' Cordelia said there was a very big difference, because Lizzie had her whole life ahead of her, and her exams. 'And marijuana is organic. It helps me unwind after a day with you kids.'

'Any more of this type of thing,' said Peter interrupting her mother before she incriminated herself further, 'and you'll be kept in every evening after school. Understand?'

'And you'll get spots,' added Cordelia, looking at her sternly down the raised barrel of her index finger.

It's almost lunchtime, later than she intended to get up, but that's because of the Benylin. She sits on the lavatory, shivering and holding the plastic showerhead dribbling lukewarm water from her neck over her stomach. The gas water heater seems amplified to an almost industrial roar in the small space. What to do today, she thinks. She has a choice: either to take up James' offer of lunch in a pub on the river near his flat in Hammersmith or to wander over to Stanley Mews and find out what Jack gets up to on a Sunday. There's no choice really: she knows what she'll do.

Her new hat collection is piled high on the dressing table. Sixteen hats. Some straw with wide floppy brims, a battered brown felt trilby, two berets (one red, one black), a yellow cro-cheted cap, a black pillbox with a widow's veil and several others of the types worn by old ladies to weddings, with netting and flowers and shiny red cherries around the brims. Sixteen hats, all picked up from the charity shops in Westbourne Grove. Sixteen disguises, that's how she likes to think of them.

Lizzie wraps herself up in the least unpleasant of the five new coats that she bought from the same shops as the hats for the same purpose. It's a man's overcoat of rough lovat tweed that smells like Marmite and both pockets are worn through. She adds the brown felt trilby, sees herself in the mirror, a latter-day Mata Hari, with just a small triangle of nose and eyes between the brim of the hat and the pulled-up collar of the coat. She nods to her reflection, satisfied that even a father would fail to recognise his own daughter shrouded like this.

The sun is still trying to put on a show, emerging every now and then, dazzling as magic from the sulky sky, as Lizzie walks through Manchester Square. She turns the corner before the mews and stops at the newsagents to buy a Sunday newspaper. She'll do the crossword. The cryptic one. Since she's been spending so much time standing around, she's become quite good at them.

Two small boys that she's seen there before are playing football, using two metal dustbins in the entrance to the mews as a goal. She passes a man further down the street, legs emerging from his open garage, fixing his car, his head in the maw between engine and bonnet like Jonah being swallowed by the whale. She stops to watch the smaller boy score a goal, walks on and only then clocks the grey-haired man coming straight towards her. In that instant, as her blood freezes, she understands what Savannah meant about the sudden urge to throw herself into her father's arms.

Jack Seymour is just a few steps away, reading a folded newspaper as he shuffles along, a cigarette hanging from his lips. She takes in the long striped scarf looped around his neck, his floor-length grey coat with bulging pockets, then reluctantly forces her eyes to his feet: tractor-soled walking boots, one two, left right, left right. She staggers past on legs of string, close enough to smell his tobacco smoke, close enough, she fears, for him to hear the thudding in her ribcage.

Lizzie is back at Paddington, but at the train station. She's absorbed now, safe to watch Jack from the cloak of anonymity offered by the crowds. Everyone in big coats, nobody staring at anyone else, not even at the teenage prostitutes in their ankle boots and fishnets, nor the man who is bellowing about the end of the world.

She stands behind Jack as he waits at the inquiry desk. She is close enough to see his watch when he rolls up his sleeve, it has a golden moon on the blue face, and his calcimine arm is smooth as pasta. For the first time in eighteen years she hears his voice: the unsurprising gravel and tar, even after he has cleared his throat.

'Is the ten fifty-two to Harlington running today?' She could reach out and touch him from where she stands. She stuffs her hands in the shredded pockets of her coat.

'No, there's one at ten forty though, you might still catch it. Platform four.'

He scoots past her to the platform, surprisingly sprightly in his heavy boots. Lizzie daren't run after him. She watches him board the carriage just as the guard is slamming doors and the train pulls out of the station.

Chapter Fourteen

'That's okay, love, we'll bring them up, you'll never manage this lot.' Lizzie stands at the top of the stairs in her man-sized dressing gown, flapping with excitement. Flowers, too many for her to carry! She hears heavy feet on the lino round-ing the final landing: two men breathing noisily, between them a galvanised tub, almost the size of an old-fashioned hip-bath. But she smells the flowers, sweet and deep, an unseasonal breath of hothouse summer, before she sees them. Iridescent spires of purple delphiniums, deep carnelian roses and sprays of silver eucalyptus spill from the tub above clusters of nervous blue scabi-ous on trembling stems.

'Somebody loves you!' says one of the men, the one awk-wardly manoeuvring backwards past her and through the door.

'Where do you want them? Over here by the bed?'

Lizzie nods and they set the tub on the floor and straighten themselves up. One of them wishes her a happy Valentine's day, the other asks how she manages with all those stairs, and they wipe their foreheads on the sleeves of their jumpers before they leave. Lizzie snatches the card that's stuck in with the flowers, tears open the envelope. 'With love from your dentist' – not Tony's writing, she sees, but a backward-sloping hand, probably of someone from the florist's.

Lizzie can hardly believe it, after the other evening with James. Neither man left immediately, each behaving as though he was staking his own claim. They all three sat gulping at too hot coffee, Lizzie desperately feeding Tony the script, watching James become increasingly aware that he was caught in some sort of game where no one had explained the rules and unsure how to proceed.

'Many teeth to fill today?'

'Oh, I see, it was your day off, well then how did the boys enjoy the zoo?'

Each time she spoke, she could see Tony tense up, his fingers flexing as though he wanted to strangle her. But he had to maintain his cool and stick with the charade, even when James started asking his advice about amalgam fillings. 'No, I'm not one to advocate their removal,' said Tony, foolishly inspecting James' glistening teeth. 'All this stuff about leaking mercury, it's just another scare story.'

James, having initially assumed he was one of her relatives, possibly an uncle, grew increasingly uncertain. He pretended not to notice when Lizzie stood to refill their cups and Tony's hand rested casually on her bottom, patting it in the way that one might a favourite horse: pistols at dawn weren't really James' thing. Tony had been boozing, it was obvious. He was red around his wattles, reminding Lizzie of a strutting cockerel. At one stage, after dentistry but just before cars, he let his animosity get the better of him, addressing James as 'sonny' and asking if it was okay for him to be out so late. It was a terrible end to the evening. Then, to make matters worse, they both stood up to leave at the same moment and couldn't sit down again and had to keep up their ludicrous conversation, down the seventy-seven stairs and out into the street.

Tony didn't return once James was out of the way, though Lizzie expected him to. Since then, she's only seen him once, briefly at the office, when he flipped her over the head with a pile of papers. 'Don't you ever try anything like that again,' was all he said. And from James there's been not a word and, with Paula off sick, no feedback either. Which is quite a relief given the way things worked out.

Everything's going to be all right now though, the flowers prove it. Lizzie has to stop herself from skipping when she gets to the bottom of the escalators at the tube.

'Hey, stop, wait.' Arranging those flowers has made Lizzie late and the doors to the tube train are opening, she's even spotted a seat, but now she won't be able to get on. Another train might be an age in coming and she's more anxious than usual to get to the office. The boy is wearing his top hat, his hand is on her arm as she steps towards the train.

'I've been here since eight,' he pleads. 'I've got something for you.' Reluctantly she stands down as the doors swish together and the two of them are left alone watching the last of the sparks through the tunnel.

'You again,' she says, though she didn't mean it to sound as rude as it came out. He smiles at her, the clown's face, only the corners of his mouth upturned. 'How's tricks?' she says, relenting.

'Just one for you today.'

'Me?' Lizzie is still impatient to be at work. Tony will be there, surely he will, after the flowers. The boy looks too young, his cheeks smooth beneath the ridiculous hat. She would like to ask how he knows where she lives, why he looks up at her window, but as usual decides against it. What if he's a friend of someone else in the building? She'd feel a fool.

The platform rumbles beneath her feet: another train.

'Okay, then, quick,' she says. 'I'm late for work.'

'I know.'

He shows her his hands, flips them from palm to back and back to palm three times. They are empty. He bows to her and sweeps his hat from his head. When he's upright again, he holds out his left hand to her chin and smiles. There, suddenly, before her eyes is a single white rose. It seems to grow from his fist, almost fluorescent white. It's as though it's been there all along; as though they are in darkness and someone has simply switched on a spotlight above it. The arrival of the train blows dust into their eyes but she doesn't see him blink. 'For you,' he says, with a flourish and the tube doors sigh, leaving her pressed inside against rancid gaberdine. She looks back and sees him, just a flash of him, still waving within the arced light, as her train rattles and lurches into the dark.

It's quite a tatty rose, this white one, some of the petals splotched pink from the rain. Lizzie smiles each time she sees it on her desk, wilting now in her coffee mug.

'Who sent you the flower?' asks Tony, making her jump, his hands on her shoulders.

'Wouldn't you like to know?'

'Gawd, these teenagers, just look at them, pissed the lot of them.' Tony *is* looking at them, he's hardly taken his eyes off them all night as they stagger around the houseboat as if it's in motion even though the tide hasn't reached it yet, won't do until about three in the morning in this part of Chelsea.

'I only invited them to help serve the drinks, not to drink the bloody stuff themselves.' Eric is shouting to make himself heard above the music. 'Greedy little tarts!' Well, it's his houseboat and his party, but all the same, Lizzie finds his condemnation of his nieces a little harsh. Besides which Eric's been leering at one of their friends all night himself. Lizzie saw him.

'So, darling,' he said to the young girl as she poured and the champagne overflowed from his glass, 'are you going to be my lucky Valentine?' Lizzie nudged Tony when she spotted him disappearing into the boiler room with the tiny blonde and Tony laughed and said that old Eric had always been that way. 'He's the same as any other photographer who got spoiled rotten with nubile attention in the sixties.' And Lizzie knew that, in part, he was referring to himself when he said that.

'Oi, tarts, over here with the wine!' Eric points to another young girl, shimmying up the stairs in thigh-skimming chocolate satin, a different colour of nail polish on each toe. 'Apart from Jessie,' he says. 'She's not a tart, she's a good girl.' Jessie walks past them, smiles nervously at Eric and then falls against an older woman with close-shorn hair who is leaning against the wall. They wrap their arms around one another and sway together to the music, the older woman's long silver earring brushes the girl's naked shoulder. Tony nudges Eric and points.

'That's her mother! Tony really!' Eric does his best to scold.

'Thank God for that,' says Tony, spluttering into his wine.

'Ah, you dirty bugger.'

Lizzie doesn't know what to think. She was watching the pair of them too, as they danced; remembering the safety of her own mother's arms; not once mistaking them for lovers.

All the same, she's been drinking too much and the room is spinning slightly. Conversations come at her, loud, soft, loud, as though someone is twiddling with the volume control. She doesn't want to talk because she's scared she'll slur her words; besides which, the Electric Light Orchestra is drowning everything out. She is standing outside the cloakroom, inside which, Eric tells anyone who's interested, a couple are bonking each other's brains out. Tony dares him to walk in. A man in brown suede says better not, because it's his turn next, and Lizzie isn't sure that he's joking. Tony's hands keep sliding under her skirt. She's aware of people, Eric and the others, clocking her legs, licentiously observing her with Tony, like some seedy floor show, as his fingers slip inside her knickers.

Paula has been keeping up a sniffy silence with Lizzie since she got back from her sickbed. 'Pah, she hasn't been ill,' says Siobhan, 'she's been shopping for her wedding dress, I'll put money on it.' Lizzie is sick of the job and her colleagues, exhausted by the endless speculation and prying into out-of-hours intrigues that accompany the tedium of office life. She can't get excited at the prospect of cream cakes like they do. She doesn't worry about her weight. She doesn't care who shot J.R. She doesn't want to buy anything by weekly instalments from their Freemans catalogues.

'Look at that,' says Siobhan, shifting from her desk to peer out of Katrina's window. 'It's trying to snow.'

Lizzie shivers beneath her thickest jumper. She still hasn't recovered from St Valentine's night when she drank herself to near oblivion at the party on the boat. Underneath the wool, her arms still bear fading yellow bruises from where Tony held her down on Eric's bed, rough with alcohol and mean-mouthed. It hardly seems possible that the man who that same morning had filled her flat with flowers could have called her those things, and hurt her like that, and then been so dismissive once it was over. She is filled with self-loathing because when he had finished and just before she threw up she swears she saw Eric's leering disembodied face: a pop-eyed gargoyle, pressed up against the round porthole between the bedroom and the deck.

'Are you all right?' says Siobhan coming back from the window. 'You look peaky.'

'Yeah, well, I've had a bit of a rough time.'

'It's that man again, isn't it?' says Siobhan as Paula sweeps back in from the coffee machine.

'Trouble again?' Paula asks, the first words she's spoken to Lizzie all day.

'Yeah.'

'Well, I could throttle you for the way you treated James. I thought I was doing you a favour.' Just so Lizzie realises the graveness of her crime, she has brought a coffee for Siobhan too, but not one for Lizzie.

'I couldn't help it,' mutters Lizzie, looking away to the square of bruised sky and the first flakes of snow that flit like moths past the window. 'I didn't know my boyfriend was going to turn up like that.'

'Bit of a rude one, that dentist of yours, from what James said,' says Paula just as Tony arrives, shaking the snow from his hair.

'Morning everybody, I suppose Katrina's in my office as usual. Bloody cuckoo.' His eyes are viridescent from the cold.

They all smile, except Lizzie who stamps out to fetch herself a coffee.

'Someone been rattling her cage this morning?' says Tony before she's out of earshot.

'Boyfriend troubles,' says Paula gravely.

Lizzie doesn't want to go drinking after work but the Calor gas has run out back home and her flat will be freezing. Tony is cosseted in his office with Katrina, sorting out a muddle-up that someone's made with two rival photographers' sets of transparencies. An easy mistake, Lizzie reckons, their subject matter

is completely interchangeable, and of no interest to her whatso-
ever. Once you've seen one shot of Joan Collins' cleavage
you've seen them all. She can't understand the ceaseless appetite
for Britt Ekland and Björn Borg, Victoria Principal and Simon
Le Bon, and the ubiquitous sequinned women showing their
knickers as they climb out of limousines. The same old people
whose photographs pass over her desk and from her desk to the
files and back again. Like a troupe of pantomime dames, but
bread and butter to Tony.

'I'm going to be stuck doing this for half an hour yet,' he mumbles on his way through; half a wink tells her it's an invitation.
'Get lost,' she wants to say but she's too raw to manage even that,
despite his gaudy gold buttons and the slight sheen on his suit
trousers that quite suddenly she despises. She notices that his hair
has been newly streaked: the colour of piss she thinks, repellent,
though perhaps not repellent enough. The danger is that she
aches to be held. Since she saw Jack in the flesh, she's been like
that. It's as though she's become brittle and needs to be wrapped
up. She could do with time to think about it. She doesn't want
to put herself at risk by being home if Tony calls round later.

What she could really do with is someone to talk to. Not
Siobhan or Paula, obviously. Confession would be handy, if
only she were a Catholic. For the first time she admits to herself how much she misses Savannah: the old Savannah, the one
who hadn't yet revealed her true colours. That Savannah would
tell her what to do right now.

She remembers Savannah on that last evening, when she was
crying and her eyes the colour of forget-me-nots with bright
yellow rings around the pupils and Peter standing helpless at the
door while she stroked her arm.

And before then it was Savannah who always did the comforting: turning up when Lizzie was sad, as though by instinct.

She brought her chocolate and tarot cards in a gold foil box and Lizzie would believe every word she said as she slid pictures of priestesses and jugglers and stars and moons and diamonds to her across the table and told her that everything would work out fine. That Savannah would be able to tell if it's just the cocaine that turns Tony so violent. Lizzie's sure he has it; she's tasted it like bitter lemon in his kisses and seen the folded paper envelope fall out of his wallet.

'Lucy's coming over, she's pregnant!' Paula's voice saws like a bread knife into Lizzie's thoughts. 'Are you going to join us, Lizzie?' Lizzie barely knows Lucy. Since her predecessor left for her new and better job she has called in a couple of times, rather gloating in black designer clothes that draw attention to her improved salary away from Tony's agency. Paula and Siobhan still talk about her though, and at the rate they talk Lizzie knows Lucy as she would her best friend. If she had one. Lizzie's been shown which underwear Lucy selected from Siobhan's catalogue, and knows about her husband's hernia operation. She's been told that Lucy, naughty girl, considers Colonel Gaddafi, Alan Bates and John Conteh sexy.

'So Lizzie, how're you finding the job?' asks Lucy after the four of them have tucked themselves around a table in the Three Bells and they've exclaimed over Lucy's glowing cheeks and tactfully neat bulge. 'Is Tony treating you okay?'

'Tony?' Alarm bells ring, for a moment, before Lizzie calms herself. 'He's not in much.' She manages a yawn. 'I'd rather work for him than Katrina though.'

'Oh, Katrina's not so bad when you get to know her,' says Lucy, moving the ashtray to divert the smoke. Siobhan has left her cigarette burning there. Neither she nor Paula have taken their eyes from Lizzie since Lucy started on her.

'Katrina used to be quite a laugh,' says Paula.

'Well she sure ain't anymore.' Siobhan grinds out the cigarette as she says it. 'Someone should send her to niceness school.'

'Is she being tough on you, Lizzie?' Lucy seems concerned and Lizzie nods her head.

'She's a bitch,' says Siobhan. 'Thinks Lizzie's after her man.'

Lizzie is suddenly queasy, she knows what Siobhan is getting at: where she's leading the others. A paranoid part of her brain wonders if they've planned to challenge her tonight. She flounders around for something with which to change the subject while the other three agree and sigh that Tony's always had a bit of a thing for the young and pretty.

'I remember when I had a waist like Lizzie's.'

'Yeah, in your dreams.'

'Shut up, I used to be a size ten you know.'

'You should see Tony's face when our Lizzie walks across the room.'

'Yeah, and Katrina's!'

'So are you having morning sickness?' Lizzie butts in. 'How far gone are you?'

'Baby's due on Midsummer Day.'

'Lovely. Has your mum been knitting?' asks Paula, and Lizzie feels like kissing her.

They get giggly quite quickly, just a couple of glasses of house white each, apart from Lucy who rubs her tummy, fondly, and says that her husband would never forgive her if she turned their baby into an alcoholic in the womb.

'Any side effects?' Lizzie asks. It's hard enough already to contain herself, she's determined not to let the conversation veer away from pregnancy and babies again.

'I get God-awful indigestion,' Lucy says and Siobhan smothers a happy sigh. 'And my gums keep bleeding.'

'They say you lose a tooth for every baby, you know. They

leach all your calcium. Hard luck.' Sympathy is not Siobhan's forte.

'Lizzie's boyfriend's a dentist,' offers Paula, her hands placed broodily now over her own stomach.

'Is that so?' says Lucy and Lizzie finds her eyes too cognisant and wonders again if Lucy, and perhaps the others too, know the truth. 'Married, is he?'

'About to be divorced,' Siobhan answers for her.

'He won't marry you, you know,' says Lucy with such authority that Lizzie grows hot, certain now that Lucy knows that her dentist is really Tony.

'What do you mean?' asks Paula.

'There are two types of women,' Lucy hasn't taken her eyes from Lizzie. 'The wives and the mistresses. You, my dear, you're a mistress. Paula's a wife.'

'Hey, thanks,' says Lizzie.

'Just be careful you don't get trapped like poor old Katrina. Forty-odd and still a mistress. Bloody Tony robbed her of her thirties.' Lizzie notices that both Siobhan and Paula are looking down at their hands now as Lucy continues. 'Always hanging on, waiting for him to be free. And is he about to marry her now the wife's gone? I don't think so.'

It's past ten when Lizzie gets home. She had to stay on at the wine bar for the second bottle just to show the others that she wasn't rattled by what they said. Inside she was burning, she had to keep her hands wrapped in the sleeves of her jumper so that they wouldn't see them shake. How dare he, she inwardly fumed. How dare he string me along as a stopgap between Katrina and goodness only knows who else. No wonder he always wanted to see me in my dingy flat and in the same old restaurants where we never met anyone we knew.

No wonder his own bedroom remained a mystery to her.

Lizzie shivers in her duvet; it's so cold without the gas. Tony and Katrina. It's a fact then. It's all she needs to shake him off. This, and what he did to her on the boat. She tries to make herself cry in front of the mirror for a while but the tears don't come; she just feels impatient to tell him it's all over.

She is pacing up and down her room. It's even colder now she's opened the window, but she doesn't feel it. Outside the streets are muffled by new snow; she can hear twigs cracking and someone screaming far away. It's dark out there but her adrenaline is up and her usual fears do not assault her as she makes her way out into the snow-strewn street.

Her feet find their own path along the gutters, where the snow gives way to a rusty slush of salt and sand. Stranger danger is the last thing on her mind. She is out of her mind and on auto pilot, marching herself towards Marylebone though she doesn't know what she'll do when she gets there. When she set off, it was for Campden Hill Square, but somehow she has found herself heading for Jack's, and it is his name and not Tony's that she is cursing in time with the crunch of her shoes. She hasn't taken her normal route and when she gets to the Bayswater Road she has no idea how she came to be there, nor how long she has been out in the freezing air. She calms and stops outside the big iron gates to Hyde Park. Stretching ahead she can see the park, clothed in acres of untrodden eiderdown, patterned only with the perse-blue shadows of the trees. She stops and rests her burning forehead against the iced metal of the closed gate.

The boy's voice makes her jump when she hears it, inches from her ear.

'Mad March,' he says.

'How do you know, have you been following me?' She turns around to face him, not sure if she's pleased to see him. The brim of his black hat is filled with snow, a dramatic floor-length cape makes him look like a proper magician.

'Sometimes, yes.' His eyebrows have knitted together, he's obviously puzzled by her asking. His face is at the same time both anxious and comical.

Lizzie doesn't know what to say then. She certainly doesn't want to ask him why he pursues her; she'd like things to stay the way they are.

'So how do you know I'm mad, just by the way I walk?'

'Sorry?' And he starts to laugh and without knowing what the joke is, Lizzie joins in.

'I meant the month. Mad March. Sunshine and snow flurries, crazy weather.'

'Oh I see, sorry,' Lizzie says, wiping her eyes. 'Any tricks for me today then? I could do with cheering up.'

'Not a single one, I'm afraid. I'm all out of magic.' He's already done a show for some Rotarians' wives and a charity ball at the Dorchester. He claims that he's exhausted his supplies of fairy dust for one night. 'Here, I've got this though,' he says and he produces from under his cape two steaming blue mugs of hot chocolate and hands one to Lizzie. He clunks his mug against hers, says, 'Nasdrovje', and tells her that it was the snow in Russia that got Napoleon's Army in the end. 'You should do up your coat,' he says.

'The trees look like they're shivering under all this snow.' Lizzie feels self-conscious as she says it. She's swallowed the last of her drink, and the mug has disappeared again somewhere inside the cape. 'Did you know they were all planted by one man?'

She finds herself wanting to impress him, mimicking Tony's speech from months before. 'He sat with his binoculars while men held poles in the places where he would later plant the trees for future generations. Capability Brown . . .'

'Bullshit,' interrupts the boy.

'I beg your pardon?'

'Bullshit,' he says again. 'Capability Brown had nothing to do with this place. He never planted trees in avenues. You want to check your sources.'

After that, and just to see her smile again, he spun round three times and from under his flaring cape produced some refills of hot chocolate, in yellow mugs this time. Lizzie found herself telling him all about Tony, and not only him but about how her father planted an orchard of trees for her when she was born and everything about Savannah and Peter too. They made snowballs while she talked: Lizzie's were streaked yellowish and grubby in places from the road but in his hands they turned the colour of raspberries, like sorbets. When he rolled them on the snow, they left a comet's tail of pink smiles in their wake. His hands were still so icy when he took hers that she wondered if he was an apparition, Houdini's ghost perhaps.

He saw her shiver as a flurry of snow, fine as pillow feathers, flittered from a branch above, lit by headlamps.

'Cold hands, warm heart,' he said before he walked her back through the meltwater, taking the outside to protect her from the spindrift dished up by the cars that night.

Chapter Fifteen

Lizzie is watching Jack in a café, dunking his toast, the usual four sugars in his tea. She is wearing a curly auburn wig today, one of several that she's collected. Not that she needs to bother with a disguise, Jack never looks up from his newspapers anyway. She just enjoys dressing up, even adopting a new persona with each combination of wig, coat and hat. Cool and severe in the black bob and trilby; sweet hippy in the honey afro and long olive corduroy coat; art student in the baggy tweed. Before she left home she tried her new waist-length blonde, from the bargain bin at Hair We Go Again in Camden Town, teamed with a white vinyl mini-skirt and knee-high boots. She stood with her back to the mirror, seducing herself over her own shoulder and Savannah stared back, fluttering her eyelashes, pouting lewdly, thrusting her pelvis back and forth. 'You know I have always wanted you to fuck me,' lisped Savannah.

'Bitch Savannah!' Lizzie cried tearing the wig from her head. 'Why did you do that?' She kicked the wig across the floor where it lay defying her in a shaft of sunlight from the window, as though it had a life of its own and had decided to take centre stage. That was the thing about Savannah that used to drive Lizzie nuts: that artless way she always had of positioning herself in the spotlight. Lizzie remembers how the light from a window would fall onto her face, turning her cheek a powdery white, smooth as royal icing. She always suspected it was deliberate. Savannah had an almost innate ability to sit anywhere that best illuminated her face: where the shadows fell below her cheekbones or the candle put fire into her eyes. Savannah, ever the star, thought Lizzie savagely as she picked up the wig, distastefully, as though it were a cat she were holding by the scruff of its neck. And the vision of Savannah in the summerhouse that night flashed through her mind: the moon reflecting white from the leaded glass onto Savannah's face, lighting her bare skin china bright. Lizzie shoved the attention-seeking pile of long blonde nylon into the bin and rinsed her hands under the hot tap at the sink. Instead she would be a muse, that's what she decided, as she replaced the call-girl outfit with a belted black mac and pinned up curly hair under a black beret.

Lizzie knows that Jack buys all the newspapers from the corner shop near Manchester Square, even the tabloids. He carries them around with him all day, and sits at café tables, like this one, just as he always does, a hefty magnifying glass in his hand, snuffling over the print, in a way that reminds Lizzie of a truffle pig that she once saw on a documentary.

Although he rarely looks up, his hands are always busy: not only with the magnifying glass but constantly scraping back his hair, flicking ash into his saucer from his Gauloises. Sometimes he tears things from the newspapers; expertly with razor-straight rips. In a way she wishes he would notice her: that he'd look around him for once and demand to know who she is and why she keeps following him. Then she'd ask him what it is he collects from the papers. If he wasn't her father, she'd do just that.

She has plenty of time for haunting him these days: she's taken her leave from the office, cashed Tony's cheque. Six months' pay all in one go. She could almost feel her mother's disapproval as she took it from him. '*Lizzie really! It's more than you deserve. Should you be accepting his money?*' But then she'd think about Tony: the lies, the bullying, the way he kept her dangling like some wretched yo-yo, drawing her back and forth, holding her to him, pushing her away. She'd think about Katrina, about Paula saying, 'Yeah, of course she's still got a key to his place, go on, ask her yourself if you don't believe me.' And then she'd remember him holding her down on a leopard-print bedspread, the mean-ness of his voice in her ear whispering 'little whore' and Eric's red face pressed against the porthole, looking in. The self-disgust, the need, the way he set out to dazzle her. Those were the things she thought about when she cashed that cheque.

Once she'd finally got over the night-time absences, she rel-ished that her days had become her own. Tony thought it was for the best, too, at least that's what he said as he signed over the full amount with the casual air of a man paying for groceries. His wife has been threatening a move with her boyfriend to Canada, taking Sophie with them. There's a major court case looming, he's too exhausted even to begin to discuss Katrina with her. Lizzie congratulates herself on her independence.

She's becoming an expert in the art of cutting free. It must be in her blood she thinks. Like painting.

Lizzie sleeps in late most mornings. There's no point in waking any earlier: during the week Jack rarely leaves his house. Her face has grown plumper from sleep, which suits her, and she's been painting most days. She's even sold a couple of water-colours to a greetings-card company. They haven't been produced yet, they still might not be, but she earned an advance and the woman who runs the firm has asked to see more. She likes Lizzie's colour sense, says that pictures of puppies and kittens always do well, and Lizzie can paint Muttley from memory.

She has a windowbox now and some daffodil bulbs that the magician gave her are already sprouting. Soon the green tips will split open to release the yellow faces like jesters into the sunlight.

Saturdays are spent in cafés like this one, sometimes at galleries around the Portobello Road, and at the market. She's seen Jack buy turnips and sweet potatoes; she's sat behind him in the cinema, *The Deer Hunter* at the Electric and a revival of Fellini's *Eight and A Half* at the National.

She couldn't help but laugh when she trailed him to a retrospective of Theodore Smolski's work. 'Jazz Musicians' was written with the painter's name in the gallery window and that made her laugh out loud because she'd once overheard Cordelia's claims about Jack and Theodore Smolski's daughter, the walnut-faced Joan. The paintings were of trumpeters with bubblegum cheeks and fat, glistening men with veined eyes bulging like marbles, painted in smoky halls. Looking at them you could almost feel the heat of the people around you. In front of a lithograph of a man with a torn shirt stooped sideways over his saxophone, she saw Jack deflecting from the crêpe-paper kisses of a liver-spotted woman whose earlobes were weighted down with heavy drops of gold. 'Joan,' he said, and Lizzie found herself distracted, still connected to the plangent timbre of his voice. 'How lovely to see you after all these years.'

She's been following him long enough, she knows his routine. She's even been to Harlington two Sundays in a row, concealed behind her newspaper in the adjoining carriage on the ten forty from Paddington, then following him from the train, through the village with its chocolate-box thatched cottages and green front doors, past the school and on up the hill. Both times she diverted through a gate, and crept on up through the Forestry Commission land, on a higher track than the road, where she could still observe him climbing the tarmac hill below. She darted between the evergreen crops, negotiating a cat's cradle of fallen twigs, inhaling the damp pine, the soft new needles wetting her face.

She's watched him from the churchyard beyond as he's stood at the studded oak gate to Harlington Court, ringing the brass bell on the door to the lodge, set between the twelve-foot-high stone walls. She's seen him pass through, twice, close enough to hear his boots scrape on the gravel within.

Her sketchbook is crammed with Indian inks of the lodge-house and pencil details from the carved door, and of the crumbling sandstone gargoyle that leers down from the archway. She has waited there among the granite headstones and the yew trees, watching and sketching two hours, three the second time, and seen him re-emerge, sniffing the air like a fox. She didn't dare take the same train back – they would almost certainly have ended up alone together and conspicuous at the station if she had – but instead she had hung around the village, drinking tea from her thermos and sketching the ducks on the pond. She went in to the shop once and spoke to the postmistress but she said she had never heard of Jack Seymour. According to her, Harlington Court was the seat of the seventh Earl of Croxley and his family. Lizzie still has no idea what Jack does inside the gates. Paints the Earl's portrait perhaps? Or visits his mistress? She intends to find out.

Today is unusual. It's a Friday and Lizzie's only with him because she happened to catch him leaving his flat when she swung by there on her way back from buying Paula's wedding present at Selfridges. It's a bonus, an extra, and they are in the

Cherry Tree Café, with Lizzie watching the top of Jack's head as he bends over his papers. He is at his usual seat against the counter with his back to the door: the best position for avoiding anyone attempting to join him or start a conversation. Lizzie is at the other end of the café, by the window, hot in her wig, the almost completed *Telegraph* crossword spread out before her. She wishes Jack would hurry up with that second cup of tea; it's still such a crisp day outside and she wonders where they'll be going – where he will lead her – once he's finished here. She noticed him clock the cinema on the way: a new film with Meryl Streep is showing.

Lizzie shifts in her seat, her cup is long empty. Her watch shows that it's almost half past eleven, experience tells her it won't be long before the early edition of the *Evening Standard* arrives on the news-stands. Jack is still busy with his papers and there's a newsagent's five doors away, just past the deli. She knows it's stupid, but she can't wait another moment. As she makes her way across the floor she has to force herself to look straight ahead and not to turn around and peer back through the glass at him as the café door pings shut behind her. It sounds louder than usual.

The girl chewing gum in the newsagent's is still cutting the bindings from the first delivery of *Standard*s. There's a man in front of Lizzie who is paying for a box of Roses chocolates but changes his mind and opts for Quality Street instead. 'Because the lady loves the green triangles!' he explains apologetically after the girl has already rung up for the Roses, which leads to lengthy correction procedures involving the till and much sighing all round. Jack waits alone and unwatched in the café while Lizzie throws down her coins and snatches a paper from the top of the pile, ignores the girl's mutterings, and has the page open at 58 before she has even left the shop. Patric Walker smiles benignly out at her from his byline like a fond uncle. 'Scorpio,' she reads Jack's first, as she hastens back to the café. 'A good day for discovering new friends. But with Venus in the ascendant be sure to make time for your family.'

Savannah used to say that you know you're in love when you catch yourself reading someone else's horoscope, but what has Savannah ever known about anything? Jack is already gone, his ashtray and the two cups have been cleared away, the table wiped smeary clean. Perhaps she'll just go to the Meryl Streep movie anyway, by herself. She misses him already.

Chapter Sixteen

'Anna, what are you doing here?' Lizzie has been shocked from her sleep by the persistent buzzing of the doorbell. Anna has to speak her name into the intercom several times before Lizzie is awake enough to realise that her sister is waiting at the front door.

Anna is not how she remembers her. It's only been seven months but when Lizzie fled Anna was still playing with dolls. She now looks something like a Barbie herself. The sight of her makes Lizzie feel that she left home a long time ago. She is wearing lipstick, bright red too, but she might just as well have grown wings, so complete is her metamorphosis. Lizzie gawps at her.

'Mum said it was a squalid flat,' says Anna when they reach the top of the stairs. 'I think it's nice.'

'Used to have cockroaches,' Lizzie mumbles.

Anna lays her handbag (a handbag!) on the chair, stands in her zip-up boots towering over Lizzie. 'Good God, Anna, look at you!'

'I can't stay long,' Anna says. 'I'm supposed to be at the British Museum. We're doing Xanthos this term.'

'How are the others, Briony and Lou?' Lizzie asks. Anna pulls a face, pushes her nose up into a snout. 'Annoying,' she squeaks, adding a few piggy grunts that make them both laugh. 'But seriously Lizzie,' she says after they've hugged, 'you must come home. Mum's been in hospital.'

'God, what's wrong?'

'She's okay now.'

'But?' Suddenly Lizzie doesn't want to hear what Anna's come to tell her, she knows before she speaks what she'll say.

'I'm not supposed to know this, but she took loads of pills. Dad's told everyone it was appendicitis. She did it while I was out at Sam's twenty-first. I thought you'd be there.'

Lizzie is confused, aware that she should be expressing an emotion but which one? For a split second she can't decipher which is the more shocking: her mother's suicide attempt or the fact that one of her little sisters is now hanging out with her old friends. She feels like saying, 'Sam, what *my Sam*,' but gets herself under control. 'You don't think she'll try it again, do you?'

'I dunno,' says Anna. 'But you should come home.'

Lizzie can see herself reflected in the window of the train. A double image of a fuzzy white ghost person with her own sharply focused face within. She settles in the seat and slowly turns her head a few degrees, watching the angles change, thinking of Savannah. She smiles at herself, satisfied with the way she looks reflected like this. As the train pulls out she opens her book and folds her coat as a pillow against the black window, tucks her feet onto the empty seat beside her. It's better than the train to Harlington, this Intercity 125; it's sleek as an aircraft, with a table to every four seats. Hygienic, orange velour and grey plastic. The train to Harlington rattles and creaks and smells of dirty laundry.

'Sorry, love, these seats are reserved. Here, look, I've got the tickets.'

An elderly man in a sheepskin coat waves a piece of paper between her eyes and the book. His companion is huffing up the aisle behind him, carrying a yellow cake tin in her hands. 'Those our seats there, Ivan?'

'Yeah. Reserved, I'm afraid, love.'

The couple stand apologetically waiting while Lizzie gathers her coat and stuffs her book back into her bag. She sways between taken seats up and down the train. Every one is reserved. Regular commuters are better prepared than her for the end-of-week crush. Thirty pounds her ticket cost her. For goodness' sake.

She stands steadying herself against the window in the buffet car, where men in unflattering suits and students with Walkmans growing from their ears balance piles of sandwiches, cans of lager and miniature green bottles of gin between their hands and their chins as they lurch back to their seats.

She only has a twenty-pound note and the man behind the counter says he can't change it. She tries to resume reading but people keep falling against her as they weave to and from the buffet car. She needs somewhere to sit and think. She really ought to compose herself before she gets home. She still hasn't worked out what she'll say, nor how she'll deal with Peter.

There is a luggage compartment further up the train. It is almost dark in there, but it's better than the buffet car. Lizzie pulls open the rattling cage gates and settles herself amongst the lumpy grey mail bags, squinting down at her book by the jumping lights from the track and the dim bulbs of the corridor. The stations rush by, this train doesn't have time to pause anywhere insignificant. More's the pity.

Bristol Temple Meads will be the next station stop. She might get off there, that's her plan, if she can't face a scene at home after all. But then she gets absorbed in her biography of Picasso and Françoise Gilot's problems seem more immediate than her own and before she knows it almost everyone else has departed at Bristol and she is still there, pitching ever closer to Exeter St Davids. At least there are plenty of seats to choose from now, and she resumes her position next to the window, tucked up with her coat and her book. Someone further down the carriage is peeling an orange. The smell is intoxicating. Imagine if you were told that you'd never again get the chance to eat an orange. Now that would be bad, she thinks. The first thing she'll do when she gets there is ask for an orange.

It's a short bus ride from the station to Stonleigh. Lizzie walks from the bus stop, through the town centre. The smell of the chip shop is achingly familiar but she doesn't stop there. Opposite there's the park where an old man once flashed at her, and the sweet shop where she and Savannah had a brief fling with shoplifting sherbet fountains and Curly Wurlies: long thin things that they could slide up their sleeves. There's the café that has three of her mum's paintings on the wall and the toy shop where she used to spend her pocket money, collecting Britain's model animals. Any minute now, she'll pass someone she knows; an old teacher or parent of one of her friends, or worse, someone who knows her mother. They'll call to tell her they saw her and there will be no going back, which is what Lizzie has decided to do, now that she is close enough to taste the metallic dread, indelible as a mouthful of ink. There's no way she can face Peter, there isn't a thing she can say to her mother.

The Golden Globe is across the road from her now. Her pub.

Everyone's pub. The G-G where they used to go, to play pool in mock rococo splendour and get served at the bar without anyone ever being questioned about their age. It's Friday night and through the open door she can see the golden lights and the peacock-feather wallpaper of the saloon. It's not like London; it feels an age since she's been able to walk alone into a pub. She would like things to be the way they were, if only until she's got her mind in order.

It's early still for the Globe, but out of habit she walks straight into the pool room. Benji and Moby are there, just as they always have been, though she hadn't noticed their bikes outside. The brightly lit room smells of their rolling tobacco, of patchouli oil and leather, and Moby gets her a Bacardi and Coke without a question about where she's been for the last few months. Benji has a new tattoo of a red rose on his arm, still risen and scabbed, and she looks at the familiar one around his neck, the dotted line of permanent blue ink and the words 'cut here' and realises how scared of these men she'd be if they weren't part of her teenage landscape.

'Shit hot,' says Moby when he pockets the black, although he pronounces it 'shi-ot' and anyone else might think he'd said 'Shot', but Lizzie's been around them long enough. 'You play-ing or what?' Lizzie's finished her drink and their pint glasses are empty. She knocks on the hatch to the bar, lines up the refills on the edge of the pool table.

'Got a match?' says Moby, dangling half a sodden roll-up between his lips. 'Your face, my arse,' says Benji, just like she knew he would. 'Your round again if you lose,' says Moby as Lizzie jiggles the balls in the wooden triangle and she says, 'I won't,' which makes them both throw their heads back and strum imaginary guitars, howling like the wolves off Roxy Music.

She gets a better reaction from Sam, three games and two Bacardis later. Sam arrives with Harris, his brother, both of them in matching Harley Davidson leathers and a girl that Lizzie's never met before with hair that's flipped in a perfect peroxide coil around her face like a fallen halo.

'Frig-a-pig, Lizzie, where've you been?' says Sam. 'You missed a good party, you know.'

Lizzie laughs. The months that she has been away are getting shorter all the time. Tony, Jack, Paddington, her job; all that seems suddenly improbable; insignificant as a daydream. 'London,' she says.

'Horrible,' says Sam. 'By the way, this is Carol. She's from London.'

'Herne Hill,' says Carol.

'Where's everyone else?' Lizzie asks. 'It's a bit quiet for a Friday night, isn't it?'

'All broke, I expect, student grants.' Sam gulps dolefully from his pint. 'Haven't seen anyone much since my party. No one bothers to come home anymore, bloody dump this place out of season.'

Lizzie loses count of the drinks long before closing time. Sam's leather leg is pressing against her own. They are playing spoof around the corner table, shaking their fists with varying numbers of coins in their hands, betting on the total. Getting the rounds in before it's too late. The new girl, Carol, seems unhappy with her presence and scowls each time Lizzie guesses right. Sitting on the other side of Sam, she keeps referring to things they've done together, a party at the beach, and the day Sam trapped three wild mink at the river.

Sam and Harris are huddled over the jukebox, while Lizzie sits with Carol in whoozy silence. Lizzie flips beer mats but Carol is watching Sam as the jut of his chin gives away the urgency of his instructions to his younger brother. The jukebox whirrs and clicks. Carly Simon. 'Nobody Does It Better'. Quite meaningful in the days of Sam and Lizzie. Lizzie tries not to look pleased. 'Baby, you're the best,' yodels Sam across the room.

'For fuck's sake, why don't you just screw her here on the floor,' screams Carol as Carly Simon fades and Sam tells her to go on the back of Harris's bike with Benji and Moby to Mr Matt's in Torquay and he'll join her later once he's caught up with Lizzie's news. 'Cool it, Carol,' drawls Harris in the movie-star Americanese that he must have acquired at about the same time as his bike. He's leaning over Lizzie, attempting to help Carol from her seat. But Carol's up in a flash and snatches Moby's half-finished pint from his hands and empties it over Sam's head before she runs from the room with Moby and Benji's laughter pursuing her through the door.

Sam shakes lager from his hair. 'You'd better go with them,' Lizzie says.

'Not a chance,' he says and they are still sitting at the beer-drenched table when they hear the motorbikes roar up the street.

Despite all the drink, Lizzie feels dull and lonely, too cowardly after all to see her mother, and she does want to be held.

'Do you mind if we don't make love?' she says later in the gentle darkness of Sam's bed. But Sam does quite mind and the sex isn't great. But then it's over and he holds her as though she were the most precious thing in the world and, well, that didn't happen to her very often. In the morning she leaves him, still asleep, child-like without his leathers, a thin arm thrown across the pillow, his beard in infancy. She tiptoes down the stairs and through the kitchen, stopping only to steal an orange from the fruit bowl, terrified she might wake his mother. What if she knew that the Devil Child had stayed the night?

It's a ten-minute walk through the village. The houses get bigger the further she gets from Sam's house and the closer to her own. The roads are wider here, the houses spaced further apart with increasingly longer drives and higher front gates. The Grange is at the top of the hill, she can already see the monkey-puzzle tree poking like a diseased dinosaur above the dense forestation that stretches from the front gates to the house. They'll have left by now; Cordelia with her earthenware dishes wrapped in silver foil piled into a basket; the little girls sulking because, like Lizzie, they hate having to visit Peter's widowed mother every Saturday for brunch.

Lizzie finds the spare key where it always has been, under the loose paving stone. There is no sign of Muttley when she steps through the door, he should be barking by now, but everything else is the same as it ever was. She gulps at the air, the scent of her family flows around her in the warm house, comforting as milk. Firewood and baking, roast potatoes, roses and damp wool. The pendulum clock is a familiar heartbeat, Cordelia's African violets are in flower on the hall table, muddy wellington boots line the skirting boards from the door to the bottom of the stairs.

There is still no sign of Muttley though. They must have taken him with them, though Peter's mother hates him, says he has fleas. Well, she mustn't stay long. She heads straight for the attic to see if it still is her room, or if they have already moved Anna or Briony up there.

It is the same as the day she left: as much hers as her signature. Moderately untidy, though her bed is made with smooth unslept-in sheets. Maybelline and Miners crowd the dressing table, her dressing gown is hanging over a chair, there are piles of her LPs on the floor, the Blondie album she knows by heart is on the turntable. She can smell Youth Dew, which catches in her throat, a souvenir from her own less troubled past. They have left it all as though they are just waiting for her to return, from a holiday perhaps. Or a tantrum.

Cordelia has never been particularly surprised by her daughters' unanimous lack of enthusiasm for their grandmother but she's trained them to keep it to themselves. Peter is the only person allowed to criticise his mother, though Cordelia wishes he'd speak up when the crazed old bat says she has three lovely grand-daughters, not four. Thankfully, these days, she's too infirm to cook them a meal and Cordelia takes the Saturday brunch in a basket, a more sanitary arrangement in her opinion as Peter's mother has the sort of kitchen where the butter has been licked by the cat and there are rancid crumbs suspended in the honey like flies in amber. The whole house reeks of untended hamster cages, though she's never kept a hamster.

Anna, Briony and Lou slouch up the path behind their parents, hands deep in coat pockets as though searching for excuses to be elsewhere. Peter swings the food basket from one arm and pulls Cordelia closer to him with the other while they wait at the front door. He feels Cordelia flinch as he kisses her neck and he knows that she can't help it.

'The bread rolls,' says Cordelia flatly, as his arm falls back to his side. 'I left them by the cooker.'

'Right,' says Peter, 'I'll go back for them.' His mother opens the door and scowls at them as though they are Jehovah's Witnesses who have deliberately interrupted *The Archers* and not her family at all.

Lizzie lies down on her old bed and looks across her room to the window. The curtains are drawn, a relief, because she never wants to look out of there across the garden to the summerhouse

again. She would like to sleep though, she'd like to close her eyes
and wake from this long, tormenting dream that her life has
become. Reluctantly she leaves the familiar cool smoothness of
her blue and white checked eiderdown, finds an empty school
bag and starts loading a few things into it. Muttley's framed photograph from the chest of drawers, a chunk of lucky rose quartz,
the cabled cream sweater that Cordelia knitted for her fifteenth
birthday, her Parker 51 ink pen and some Steely Dan and David
Bowie albums.

She has started leafing through some old sketchbooks when
she hears it. The unmistakable scrape of a chair downstairs and
the creak of a door. She freezes, the Daler pad insubstantial in
her hands. She can hear heavy footfalls on the main stairs.
There is no other way out and the footsteps are mounting the
bottom of the attic stairs now, scraping on the wood. She
curls up with her head on her knees in the cubby hole under
the dressing table, appalled, like when she was in trouble as a
child.

'Gotcha!'

'Dad, it's me.' She knows his footfalls before she hears his
voice. She looks out to see Peter standing in the stairwell with
his head in the attic, an iron poker shaking in his fist, ready to
club her to death.

'Oh Lizzie, it's you. You frightened the life out of me. What
are you doing under there?' Peter still has the poker in his hands
as he climbs onto the attic landing; he stands staring at her as she
crawls out from her hiding place. His hair is stragglier than she
remembers, not as clean; he needs a haircut. He tries to smile
but he looks more terrified than if she really were a burglar.

'Getting some things, I thought you'd be out.' She gestures at
her bag on the floor, at the LPs spilling out of it.

'The others are,' he says, still gaping at her, as though she has come back from the dead, not overjoyed about it either. 'I'm glad you've come home.' He's lying, she thinks, and she stares at his brown boots as he continues: 'We've got things to talk about, though I don't know what to say.'

'No,' she says. 'Don't bother.'

He takes another step towards her. 'You have every reason to hate me,' he says.

Lizzie cannot look at him. She turns her face to the wall. 'Go away,' she cries. It's even worse seeing him than she'd imagined. 'Let me go, don't try to explain.' He is moving in on her; she shudders as she feels his breath against the back of her neck, like a moth.

'I know what you saw,' he says.

'Well, fuck off then, leave me alone,' she twists herself away, savagely, as he stands his ground, too close.

'Lizzie, you don't understand,' he says. 'If I had one wish in the world, it would be that the thing with Savannah never happened. She made herself irresistible, so young . . .' Lizzie puts her hands to her ears. 'So pretty.' She is banging her forehead against the wall to drown him out, crying, 'Why?' though it feels like someone else's voice screaming from far away.

'I was horribly drunk, and she was crying because her dad . . . you remember, of course it shouldn't have happened.'

'Why?'

'I found her crying in the summerhouse.' Lizzie is still banging her head, harder now, he tries to turn her around, to still her, but again she wrenches herself free of his touch. 'Why?'

'She was like a broken bird in my arms. I got her another brandy. She was wearing a dressing gown, Anna's, I think. It was too short for her. Her hair smelled of apples . . .'

'So when did it start?' Lizzie pushes past him. She wants to end his reminiscence. No more details, she wants to scream, and slap; but not him. Just someone. Alberto Green Apple VO5, her mum's shampoo. They all used it then.

'What do you mean start?'

'She was pregnant the summer before, was that you too?'

'Jesus Christ, Lizzie, what do you think I am?'

'Do you really want me to answer that?'

'No.' Suddenly they are both in danger of laughing, not that anything's funny. Years ago they discovered that they suffered from the same crossed wires, those terrible spontaneous bursts of laughter in response to tragedy. It was at his uncle's funeral, and surrounded by solemnity they both giggled at the cemetery. Cordelia was exasperated. 'Hysterical,' she said but that had only set them both off again. 'Not quite *that* funny,' Peter had spluttered while he and Lizzie clung to each other by the grave. 'She must have inherited it from me,' he said then, bringing a note of real discomfort to the proceedings.

'Are you telling me it was just that once?' Lizzie is determined to keep up the pain level. Serve him right.

'Yes, for Christ's sake.' He's shame-faced but she's lived with him most of her life, long enough to notice him falter, to know for certain that he is lying to her.

'It wasn't just once, was it?' she insists nastily.

Peter sighs, so weary and broken that for a moment she almost forgives him. His hands are shaking, despite the fact that he is still gripping the poker, his eyes downcast. 'The next day, before we knew you'd disappeared. Yes, in the morning. She came into my bedroom.'

'Yes?'

The poker clangs as he drops it to the floor, she would like to pick it up and batter him with it.

'Yes?' she repeats. 'The next day?'

'What?' He knows he has no authority, that she will make

him answer the question. She is tiny and fierce in a way that her mother will never manage.

'You know what,' he says wearily. 'Lizzie, please, it was a stupid mistake. What can I do about it now? Think of your poor mother, you've got to stop this. She needs you.'

'I can't . . .' she starts to shout, though she can't think what to call him. 'Don't you realise, I can't see her because I don't know what to say about you.'

'I'm going to tell her, I've got to, haven't I? There's no other way. I'll have to tell her right now.' He's half threatening, half begging Lizzie to forbid him saying a word. 'It's the only thing I can do, isn't it? She'll leave me. Jesus Christ, what am I going to do?'

'You should have thought about that before.'

'She'll leave me, they'll all leave me. Is that what you want?'

Lizzie finds this brutal. She can't stand to see Peter's defeat. She doesn't answer. This, she realises, was what she had wanted. She's not so sure that it's what she wants now. Peter was her rock. Now it's as though he's been broken down, his big shoulders heaving like an earthquake. He is crumbling in front of her, blocking the exit with his big body reduced to a pile of shale and sand and dust that would slip through her fingers even if she could bare to touch him. She pushes past, half runs, half falls down the stairs and out of the front door. She is scattering gravel as she bolts up the drive and down the street towards the town and the bus stop, swallowing hard to stem the bile and the lumps of vomit that sour her throat.

Chapter Seventeen

Lizzie walks blindly from the bus to the train station. She craves sugar as though her life depends on it. She tries to get chocolate crisp from the machine but it swallows her money and its parted metal lips refuse to deliver the goods. She sits in the station café, at the tea-stained Formica table, drinking Coke from the tin and pulling at a second apricot Danish, waiting for the train. Cordelia finds her there, cramming pastry into her mouth.

'Thank God you're still here, I came straight away.' Cordelia's breath comes in gasps as though she's been running. She's paler and thinner, her once thick hair scraped back and scrunched into a knot with a plain elastic band. Lizzie pulls her eyes away from her mother's bloodless face and takes another bite of the pastry, more pain is the last thing she needs. Cordelia is doing that scanning thing with her eyes. Looking for clues in her daughter's face. Lizzie tries to stop her hands shaking as she builds little walls from sugar cubes on the table. She realises that it's her turn to say something and tears at what's left of the

Danish and swallows it only half chewed. 'I only came to see Muttley,' sticks in her throat.

Cordelia sits down, reaches across the table, and, almost by reflex, unfolds the paper napkin and dabs it at the icing on Lizzie's mouth. Almost by reflex, Lizzie flicks her head away. 'About Muttley,' says her mother quietly, reaching for her hand. 'Lizzie, I'm sorry, he had to be put down.'

'You had my dog killed?' Lizzie stiffens, her voice rises in a wobbly crescendo. She almost seizes the opportunity to be angry, the dog is already insignificant. Her clenched fists hit the table, sending a saucer scuttering.

'He had a lump in his groin, it was cancer.'

'You let them kill him.' Cordelia stands to comfort her, like she should, to stroke her hair as she slumps over her arms on the table. 'He was in pain,' she pats Lizzie's back. 'You're allowed to cry.' Cordelia holds her tight, lets her bury her head against her coat. 'Come home, Lizzie.'

'I wish I wasn't here now,' Lizzie moans, allowing herself to breathe into her mother for the briefest moment.

'Lizzie, what has happened to you?'

But before she has to answer, the rattling of the café's windows signals the imminent arrival of the train. Lizzie jumps up. 'Must go,' she says. Her mother's lips feel cool on her own hot cheek, and she has to brush her off quite literally, and run out to the platform. She pulls open the door of the 125 and climbs into the compartment, but Cordelia is behind her, getting on too, and the tweed-coated man in front of her is complaining. 'You don't have to shove, you know.'

'What are you doing, Mum?' Lizzie has thrown herself into the first available seat travelling forwards.

'I'm coming with you,' says Cordelia, settling herself opposite her daughter, surprising herself. The guard slams the doors, people rush by to stake out their territory of, if possible, at least two seats each. The man in the tweed coat looks irritable and, sighing defeatedly, refolds his paper and squeezes past from his window seat beside Lizzie to somewhere further down the carriage. Two football fans rush by, with green and white striped scarves and parkas, their white with green Plymouth Argyle sportsbags rattling beer bottles and banging against their legs as the train pulls out.

Cordelia and Lizzie have been left alone, thank goodness. No one has plumped for the two remaining seats at their table.

'I'm sorry about everything I said when we rowed in London. Did you get your Christmas parcel okay?' Cordelia removes her coat and settles back in her seat, trying to act normal: the worried mother attempting to tame the tearaway.

'Yeah.' Lizzie would be happy to play the game if it wasn't for all the important stuff: all the things she knows about Jack; about his dead child; about Peter and Savannah.

'It's just we didn't hear, I wondered about the post.'

'Well I didn't get round to any thank you letters this year. You're not coming to London are you?'

Cordelia rummages in her old leather handbag, finds a scruffy packet of Murray Mints, offers one to Lizzie. 'I'm coming as far as it takes to get some answers from you.'

'Peter will tell you everything you need to know,' says Lizzie, concentrating hard on her fingers, fumbling as she unpicks the cellophane. 'If you care about me at all, don't ask me another thing about it.'

'Something did happen between the two of you then.' Cordelia isn't whispering but she is leaning across to Lizzie, half standing over the table.

'Mum, it's not what you think.' Lizzie forces herself to resist the instinct of evasion, she sits perfectly still despite the closeness of her mother's face.

'What do I think?' Cordelia holds up her hand, as though halting an invisible force between them. Her hand signs in the air, no need to answer that. She takes a deep breath, though she's so relieved, anything else will be manageable now her greatest fear has been assuaged. Her next question sounds almost girlish when she asks it, high strung, like a teenager suspecting a boyfriend has slow-danced another. 'He's been unfaithful, hasn't he?'

Lizzie doesn't answer, her silence tells Cordelia everything she needs to know. She can't bear to see her mother then, quietly, rocking back and forth with the motion of the train, turned in on herself, weighing the possibilities, desperate to ask Lizzie for a name, but at the same time not wanting to know, nor ask her daughter to speak it. Lizzie cannot face her, so she changes seats to travel backwards with her head buried against her mother's lambswool shoulder and the sweet smell of almonds and Dreft.

'My poor darling,' whispers Cordelia, holding her so that her own tears fall silently onto Lizzie's hair. And for a while neither mother nor daughter notice the names of the stations rushing past, each of them deaf to the crackle of the announcements and blind to the reflection of the sun gilding the waves that practically beat against the edge of the track on the other side of the train.

It is only when they reach the Tamar that Lizzie looks out and gasps at the stretch of mirrored green below, dotted with boats, as the train races streams of traffic on Brunel's iron bridge. 'Shit, I'm on the wrong train,' she says. 'That was Plymouth back there.'

'I know,' says Cordelia smiling. 'We're in Cornwall.'

It was Lizzie's idea that they should go to the cottage. Cordelia was reluctant at first, but as they stepped from the station at Truro a gust of wind stirred some cherry blossom, swirling pink confetti at their feet as if in exultation. 'The orchard,' said Lizzie, her eyes shining. 'Come on, at least let's see all the blossom.'

'We can't,' said Cordelia but Lizzie was already pulling at her arm.

'You always told me they were my trees, I'd like to see them.'

Cordelia had muttered something about getting back, but then she thought about the recriminations that awaited her there, about Peter and his hangdog shame. There was something celebratory about being in another county, with Lizzie at her side. Time out from her problems and Lizzie back with her, a child again, holding her hand and tugging her towards the taxi rank, chattering about adventure and pilgrimage.

The cottage was not how it appeared in the photographs in the red vinyl album, nor how it lived on in her mother's memory. The plain granite walls had been pebble-dashed and painted pale yellow, like scrambled egg. A two-storey extension jutted out, turning the whole thing L-shaped. The extended part was almost as big as the original, though more uniform in shape, and boxily covered most of the front garden (where the hollyhocks and cabbages used to grow side by side, said Cordelia wistfully). A sign hung above the gate, 'Painter's Pocket'. Cordelia was reeling.

'It was always just "The Cottage",' she said. 'It must be a reference to Jack. Come on Lizzie, let's go.'

'Just the one room?' said Mrs Osman, whose magpie eyes contradicted the impression that she wouldn't let just anyone share a room at the Trevanna guest house further up the hill from Painter's Pocket.

'Overlooking the river?' asked Lizzie.

'No twins left on that side of the house.'

Lizzie was disappointed. She had reckoned on a view to Painter's Pocket and the river.

'You don't mind sleeping in the same bed as your mother?' Mrs Osman's black eyes glittered as she named the price of the room and Lizzie confirmed that a double bed would be just fine.

They were led from the front hall, up the narrow staircase and along a deeply carpeted corridor, Cordelia muttering under her breath about how the whole village had been ruined and Lizzie saying 'Shush' and pointing to the huffy floral nylon back leading the way.

'Good God,' said Cordelia when they were left alone in a room that smelled strongly of synthetic lemon. She sank onto the bed with its custard-coloured candlewick. 'What are we doing here Lizzie? I'll have to call home, the others will be frantic by now.'

Lizzie looked out of the window, towards the river and the cottage but the view was blocked by a high hedge of conifers. There were bluebells though, just a few dotted here and there.

'There are bluebells in the garden,' she said.

'Yes, they come earlier here than the rest of the country,' replied Cordelia from the bed.

Lizzie turned back into the room. 'They were flowering when he left us,' she said. Her words hung between them, heavy with intent yet unintended, as though her speech had flowed from an unexpected place, a more primitive part of her brain like the scream that follows a cut. A shadow settled onto Cordelia's face.

'You were only little,' she said softly, 'you can't remember.'

'You were singing,' said Lizzie. 'There were candles.' She was defensive now. 'He came to the door, said it was more than he deserved.'

'Did he? How can you possibly know?' Cordelia was trying to remember whether she had ever described that day to Lizzie. She could remember the bluebells, because she and Jack had picked them that morning. And they had sent some in a parcel to his mother, for her seventieth birthday, wrapped in wet cotton wool and a flannel and protected within a cut-down Fairy Liquid bottle. And the bath she had been sharing with Lizzie that night was candlelit because she knew he'd be home from painting that old tree soon, and she wanted to make a welcoming picture for him.

'Let's go outside before it gets dark,' she said to Lizzie, shivering slightly in the draughty corridor. 'We'd better walk down the hill and take a look at that orchard before it gets too late.'

There was no one in at Painter's Pocket and Cordelia and Lizzie scrambled uninvited over a low broken wall of mud and crumbling granite to the back of the cottage. Before they turned the corner they could see further down the hill, and the grass etched with the long shadows of old trees, to where the hedge was blurring in the rising mist. Cordelia pointed out the well, its pumphouse with a green-painted door, and beyond that they could make out the iron gate to the river that had so alarmed Jack, though she wasn't sure if she'd ever told Lizzie about that. They walked arm in arm around the corner and through two granite gate posts, with sturdy iron hinges weeping thin triangles of rust onto the lumpy grey stone.

'About that time at the river . . .' Lizzie suddenly felt the moment was right to tell her mother all she knew about Jack and Elena and poor little Laura but Cordelia was gasping by then, her hands fluttering to her face.

'Not a tree, Lizzie,' she said with the gateway behind them. 'This is where it was, this is where he planted your orchard.' Between where they stood and the tall black hedge that separated the cottage from the woods was nothing but a rough hillocky paddock where three white nanny goats grazed among the clumps of nettles and crimson mottled docks. A light breeze carried the smell from the septic tank towards where they stood; either that, or it was the goats. At the edges of the field a few frothy-cream-capped giant hogweeds lorded it over silvery spires of thistles, but there wasn't a fruit tree to be seen, not even a stump.

The goats came running, their bells tinkering and Cordelia reached for Lizzie's hand, giving it an apologetic squeeze. Later, in the dining room at Trevanna Cottage, Mrs Osman told them it was the honey fungus that got the trees, a veil of poison that spread out beneath the earth, picking them off, one by one, before they had ever borne fruit.

The goats followed them, nudging at their pockets, to an old stone shed in the corner of the field, its once painted timber door hanging from buckled iron hinges.

'Some of our stuff used to be in here,' said Cordelia, rubbing the rough, bumpy head of the most insistent goat. 'I wonder . . .'

The corrugated tin roof had corroded in places, allowing shafts of late sunlight to fall on Cordelia's old bicycle, rusted up, its basket gone mossy and home to rodents of some sort. There were four tea chests in the far corner with a few old carrier bags heaped on top. The smell of mice and damp was overpowering and although Cordelia was shaking a fraying old towelling dressing gown out of one rotting box, Lizzie didn't want to delve her hands into any, fearing what she might pull out of the grisly lucky dip. Cordelia kicked over one of the wooden tea chests and a broken teapot and some battered aluminium milkpans clattered out onto the stone floor. She started cursing Jack while she pulled at mildewing clothes and blankets, emptying dead bluebottles that fell from their folds like currants. She rummaged among the ruins of her first marriage and retrieved a carrier bag, tied by the handles and sticky with generations of cobwebs.

'Jack dumped all this stuff here, I'm afraid,' she said.

Lizzie was sad to see her first pair of shoes were there too, the red ones that Cordelia said used to hang over the reading lamp as an ornament. The leather had hardened thick and was streaked like malachite from frosts and mould. Cordelia considered the tiny boots, turning them over and over in her hands.

'So that's where these ended up,' she said sorrowfully. 'They'll clean up okay, though.' She shoved them and the plastic carrier bag under her jumper. 'Come on Lizzie,' she said, panicking more than was strictly necessary. 'We can't stay in here, if the owners come back they'll think we're a pair of thieves.'

Back in their room the floodgates opened. The baby clothes and toys that Cordelia had brought back in the bag were rotten and damp. But there was a rusting ring of keys and she regretted her sentimentality as she handed them to Lizzie.

'You loved these,' she said. 'They were Jack's. He gave them to you when you were teething and you refused to give them back. You were such a little madam, you even used to sleep with them in case he tried to retrieve them after you'd gone to bed. Quite often in the morning, your cheek was indented with a perfect impression of one of the keys but you wouldn't be without them.'

Lizzie turned them over in her hands. Old brass keys, on a plain metal ring, thick with greeny-black gunk. She wished she could remember treasuring them before, but the memory is too deeply buried for her to reach it.

Cordelia told Lizzie about the times that Jack would disappear. How once when he was gone, she lay down in the woods – she pointed at them through the window, looming black in the hollow – and waited to die. She told Lizzie how sorry he was whenever he returned. She told her that when he left for the last time, she stayed on in the cottage, shivering, unable to eat, certain that he would still come back to her. Ingrid had found them there, two weeks later, Lizzie daubing the walls with finger paints, Cordelia talking to a mouse that lived in the cupboard under the stairs, insistent that it was the reincarnation of her dead mother.

They lay together on the bed. Lizzie thought how strange it was to end up with her mother all to herself for the night. She couldn't remember the last time. She longed to loosen Cordelia's hair from the elastic band, to see it as lustrous brown curtains on either side of her face, and to stroke away the damage from around her eyes.

She sensed her mother's need to talk. It was Cordelia's way of escaping the questions that were crowding her brain, quite apart from which they had missed each other more than they each thought possible. They propped themselves up against the pillows, looking out at the sky as it flooded from pink, to purple, to black. Occasionally through the evening, Cordelia shuddered, said things like, 'I suppose all men do it, mid-life crisis. Don't they?' But then immediately asked Lizzie something else about herself, sparing them both the need for her to answer.

All the pain that Jack had caused her was just a distant memory, and she described those times with an uncharacteristic detachment, as though she were reviewing a film. Peter was the real thing, a good man, a bit of real life that had let her down. Lizzie said that she hated him.

'He saved me, you know. You can't understand how bad things got.' Cordelia sighed, her face on the pillow was a sad dark oval in the fading light.

'I know about sewing dresses, and no money,' said Lizzie gently, 'Ingrid told me once.'

'Something else though,' said Cordelia.

'Ingrid told me how bad it was,' said Lizzie, impervious to the promise of discretion she had made to Ingrid that time after Savannah showed off at the river.

Cordelia turned her head until it was almost buried in the pillow, she held Lizzie's hand and told her that she had almost given her up for adoption in the aftermath of Jack's disappearance. 'I lost my head for a while,' she whispered.

'Oh Mum, I'm sorry.' Lizzie had still wanted to tell her about Elena and Laura, but now decided against it. It wouldn't have helped, even if it might provide an answer to the question that her mother must have asked herself over and over: namely, why did Jack leave?

'There was something else. I've only ever told Ingrid about this, not even Peter knows. Not long after Ingrid had taken us in, I was driving with you in the back of the car, I was coming back here to try to make sense of what had happened. That's when I discovered that Jack had already given up the lease. It was empty. He'd chucked all our stuff in the outhouse. I remember driving back to Ingrid's, and a Cadbury's lorry in front of me on the A38. I put my foot down hard on the accelerator, I'd forgotten you were in the back. I was speeding towards the back of the lorry, I could see the purple tailgate getting closer even with my eyes shut. Then you screamed and I hit the brake.'

Cordelia was breathless from confession. Outside a vixen cried so humanly that the hairs stood up on the back of Lizzie's neck and she burrowed like her younger self into the warm confectionery scents of her mother's skin. They tried to talk about the normal things then. Lizzie told her about Tony, 'a bad mistake,' she said.

'I'd like to wring his neck,' agreed Cordelia. And then Lizzie told her about the magician and the greetings-card company that had bought two of her Muttley pictures and Cordelia brightened and said that she was glad that Lizzie wasn't wasting her talents.

'Will you go to art college in September?' she asked. 'Lots of people take a year out.' And Lizzie nodded her head. It's what she'd been planning. 'If they'll still have me.' It was comforting to think that she could simply step back into her real life, like Alice walking out of the Looking Glass, that she could just think of this time as nothing more significant than a year out. Cordelia drew the curtains after that and they got into the bed and Lizzie leant over and clicked out the bedside light.

They whispered together in the dark for a while. Cordelia didn't confess her recent attempt with the pills but Lizzie said that after what she'd told her about the lorry she had to promise she would never do anything so desperate again, however bad things got with Peter. Cordelia clasped her hand beneath the covers and told her not to get worked up, their marriage was strong, though she'd make his life hell for a while. And then, before the tears started again, she changed the subject. 'I suppose you've heard about Savannah,' she said. 'Have you seen her?'

Lizzie could feel her blood jump, not just her heart, but her veins pulsed too, and her mother was still holding her hand beneath the sheet. 'I bumped into her the other day . . .' she started to lie, then thought better of it. 'No,' she said. 'What is she up to now?' Lizzie hoped that Cordelia hadn't noticed the quavers in her voice.

'She dropped out of college. She's on a kibbutz now. Of course Ingrid's in a right old state, sees it as some sort of break-down, made Savannah see a shrink before she left.'

'Oh God.' Suddenly, Lizzie felt bad about turning her back on Savannah.

Cordelia squeezed her hand. 'What happened between you two? You used to be inseparable.'

Lizzie didn't answer, how could she? For the second time that day, her silence told Cordelia all she needed to know.

Chapter Eighteen

The keys cleaned up well. The grime and verdigris came off on blackened wads of Duraglit and Lizzie jangles them in her pocket, where they are warm and comforting as worry beads. Her fingers always smell of their brass and occasionally she puts the keys to her mouth, where they taste bitter and familiar against her tongue. Today is the day that she will put them to the test, but first she must go to Paddington and see Jack safely onto his train.

The key-ring was in her pocket when she took tea with Elena last week. It was impossible to ignore her invitations any longer and Elena said it was her birthday. Lizzie painted her a card of a Burmese cat and bought a strawberry meringue cake from Patisserie Sagnes. The card didn't take her long, just a sliver of a cat in mushroom and silver. It wasn't so good that Elena would read too much into it.

'You darling girl,' she said when she opened it, her long fingers shaking. 'Is it Ying?'

It was a fine day and Elena insisted they take the cake and the tea into the conservatory. They sat in creaky bamboo chairs at the mosaic table, while half a dozen Oriental cats wound themselves around their shins. Elena was swaddled in a cashmere blanket the colour of blackberries, from the folds of which her pale hands and face emerged, more frail than Lizzie remembered. Lizzie sat with her back to the garden, knowing that Elena looked beyond her to the place where the pond used to be, where the snowberry bushes were now.

'Sshh,' said Elena, holding up her hand, 'we will not talk about Jack.' But there were things Lizzie needed to know. About Stanley Mews mainly. How long had he lived there? Before she was born? Before Cornwall? She pressed Elena despite her protestations. She felt for the keys in her pocket and said, 'How long?'

'Forever,' said Elena, wearily, 'I don't know, since art school. He only had it for painting.'

'But it's where he lives?'

'He lives where he paints. I only ever went there to sit for him, that thing in the Tate was painted there.' And then she changed the subject, told Lizzie about her mother who escaped from Budapest with her jewels sewn into the hems of her dresses, and about her father, the poet, who never got out. But mostly she talked about Laura and she wanted to know if Lizzie had ever wanted to dance.

There was something too cloying about it all, and it wasn't just the scent of the lilies that were giving her a headache. Elena didn't want her to leave, she said that she would like Lizzie to stay forever and she enclosed her in her arms, binding them together in the cashmere blanket as they stood in the hall. 'If you need somewhere to live, my dear, this house is big.' And as if that wasn't enough, before that she had tried to give her some sapphires.

'Please,' she said as Lizzie shook her head and folded the sparkling blue necklace and bracelet back into Elena's hands.

'Then choose.' Elena had pushed her jewel case across the table with the air of someone offering a box of chocolates to a favourite child. 'Anything you like.' Inside the smooth walnut and brass box intricate brooches of ivory and gold, glittering rings, ruby chokers and ropes of black pearls lay tangled on a bed of green velvet. It might just as well have been the Crown Jewels. A small gold elephant on a chain caught Lizzie's eye, just for a moment, but she ignored it and pushed the box back.

'No Elena,' she said, 'I can't accept any of your treasures. I've only just met you.'

'All right,' Elena sighed, closing the lid, regretfully. 'But you will take this.' She slipped a black pendant from over her head and looped it over Lizzie's while it was still warm from her skin. It was a snowflake obsidian, a single white splotch in the centre of the polished jet on a long silver chain with links so close that it felt like snakeskin. 'It's the only thing Jack ever gave me,' she said.

'Sweetheart, stop!' Tony slams his car door as Lizzie rushes past him, and he tries to grab her arm. He is wearing the navy jumper with the fuzzy pale blue hoops. It feels so long ago that she knitted it and now she doesn't care at all if it suits him or not. It doesn't. She thinks about wolves in sheep's clothing and almost giggles.

'I'm in a hurry,' she says, but still he overtakes her to bar her path, his arms reaching out to her as again she tries to push past. He looks ridiculous in jeans, they are too short, and his shoes are his usual shiny slip-ons with miniature gilt snaffles. She shudders when she looks at his shoes. She shudders whenever she thinks about them.

'I've missed you.' His voice is no longer familiar, his mohair arm itchy where it brushes her face.

'Sorry, Tony, not now.' It's already past ten thirty and Lizzie needs to be at Paddington before the train to Harlington departs.

'Where are you going?'

'I've got someone to see onto a train.'

Lizzie has never done anything this wicked before. She stands at Jack Seymour's door, waiting until she is quite sure the mews is empty. She turns to check again, over her left shoulder and the right to confirm that no face watches her from any of the windows. She is alert to the twitching of curtains. Her breathing is shaky, as though her lungs want no part in this treachery. She daren't look at her hands. Her mouth tastes bitter from the brass keys that she is now jiggling, one after the other, in the single lock in Jack's plain front door.

Even while she had stood on the station platform watching his face through the window, thinking ruefully that as his daughter she should wave, even then when the train pulled out she was still unsure if she would be able to go through with this. The third key clicks into place, she feels the mortice start to fold back with the sudden jerk as the key turns in the lock, startling as electricity. Her disbelieving fingers pull open the door, just enough to slide herself through before, with an echoing clunk, she shuts out the daylight behind her.

She is standing in a tiny hall, in the dim light, with another door to her right that must lead to the garage, and there's a flight of stairs running up straight ahead. She can smell varnish and turpentine and as she flicks on the light she sees that the switch is caked in layers of painty fingerprints and the bare wooden steps are patinated with splotches, as though someone has spent years deliberately splattering them with oils or finger painting on the way up.

'Hello,' she calls in a nervous tremelo that was supposed to sound casual. She still has one hand on the door, if there's anyone there she'll run for it. 'Ridiculous,' she mutters to herself, 'that's what you are. Just go. There's nothing here for you.' But already her feet are finding the stairs and her left hand is running up the banister before her, and the greasy warmth of the blackened wood makes her think of his hand gripping it just half an hour before on his way out to the train.

She stands at the top of the stairs looking straight into Jack's room. The air feels thick, as though it has oxygenated other lungs before hers. She remembers Cordelia once telling her that for every breath we take we inhale six million atoms of oxygen that Leonardo da Vinci once breathed. Light and dust motes shaft from the curtainless window ahead. The one to the street, she can now see, is blinded with old wooden shutters. Her eyes water in the fug of stale Gauloises and dust, and she can hear rumbling, which could be from her stomach or from the ancient plumbing or a distant tube train. There is furniture and probably a carpet too, but every available space and surface is buried under overflowing piles of books and yellowing newspapers and supermarket cardboard boxes that spill yet more newspaper clippings over the floor. The walls are nicotined, pasted in places in an overlapping collage of newsprint and old posters: Picasso's Dove of Peace, Che Guevara, Ban the Bomb. She can see three closed doors leading off to the right but her eye is drawn to a single dark painting over by the window.

Her breath comes deep and noisy as a dolphin surfacing for air when she lurches forward, into her father's room, towards the picture. She passes the cream damask day bed that she recognises from his painting of Elena, although it too is heaped with old magazines, *New Scientist* and *The Lancet* and *New Statesman*. There are used coffee cups, everywhere, some with curdled insides of floating green discs, like mini-moonscapes. Others have squashed dog-ends in the bottom, and crowd a small table tucked up against a threadbare and greasy maroon plush fireside chair. On the floor next to that Jack's magnifying glass weighs down folded sheets of yet more newspaper. She is careful not to disturb the clutter as she weaves towards the window and the square of single dark canvas on the wall.

The painting is as she thought from the door: a child, about two years old, with face upturned. The light from the window falls onto a smooth disk of ivory with deep, round black eyes, appealing from the prison bars of a cot. She knows the child in the picture to be herself because she has seen the photograph from which it is painted in Cordelia's red album. There is no confusing her and Laura this time and a warmth of recognition that feels like triumph fuses with the sadness and disappointment that she has found amongst the shambles inside Jack's house. The background to the picture is deep browns and reds, the paint thickly daubed but becoming smooth, transparent almost, melted into a ghostly luminosity around the face.

A bluebottle is beating itself to death against the window. Her hands leave misty starfish on the glass when she pushes up the juddering panes to free the fly and gulp at the thin April air. She wants to see into the other rooms before she leaves, and on her way over to the first door she glances down at Jack's dull brass magnifying glass and lifts it from the pile of folded bits of torn newspaper. She sifts quickly through the newsprint, they are all obituaries of the recently deceased: Sir Cecil Beaton, Oskar Kokoschka, Henry Miller, Peter Sellers, Graham Sutherland, Edward Ardizzone. She doesn't stop to read any but carefully replaces them with the glass on top and opens the first of the doors, her hand slippery on the cool porcelain of the doorknob.

The window is shuttered but in the gloom she takes in the

mattress on the floor with its puddle of old eiderdowns and blankets and the heaps of clothes that pile the chair and chest of drawers. A sheet of brittle newspaper is taped over a full-length mirror; she can see a corner of the reflective glass glinting where the paper has fallen away. From the thin band of blue light projected through a crack in the shutter she squints at the date printed in the top right-hand corner of the newspaper: 28 April 1963. Significant, she realises almost immediately, because that was when he deserted her. Late spring 1963. When the bluebells were flowering. After that, he could no longer look himself in the face; she says it out loud, and can't deny that this idea pleases her. But the air is thick and sulphurous, fetid as a rabbit hutch, and her heart can't take much more.

The other doors lead to his kitchen and bathroom. The kitchen has black and white tiles on the floor that crunch under her feet and dark cupboards and a humming fridge that she daren't open. The bathroom is windowless with a white Victorian bath on lion's feet and a basin that's peppered from his shaving. His shaving soap is in a round plastic dish without a lid and smells of Parma violets. But now it really is getting too much for her heart and without looking back she closes the bathroom door and clatters back down the stairs and cautiously out into the street.

Cordelia sits, untriumphantly, with the larger portion of splintered bone between her fingers.

'You got it, Mum,' says Anna, old enough now to disguise her disappointment. 'Make a wish.'

Lizzie watches Cordelia. The broken wishbone is still trapped in the crook of her little finger and she wonders what she will wish for. If Lizzie had one right now, it would be that she could find a way to confess to her mother about Jack

Seymour and her visit to his house. She has been unable to
relax ever since because of what she found there. In particular,
the part of herself that she discovered amongst the squalor. She
remembers standing there, breathing him in, and being assaulted
with an unedifying urge to tidy up; to throw open the windows, make his bed, to scrub the kitchen floor, cook him
something wholesome for supper. The single painting touched
her deeply. Now she would like to do something for him, to let
him know that she cares for him – not Peter – and to give him
permission to love her back. She watches as Cordelia shuts her
eyes in her tired grey face and realises, beyond any doubt, that
she is on her own. She must not further burden her mother
with talk about Jack.

Cordelia always plans to wish for world peace, she knows she
should, but instead she finds herself asking that she could turn
back the clock. She hasn't made retrospective wishes since she
was a very young girl when she would obsessively watch the
night sky, pinning her hopes on shooting stars to bring her
mother back to life. Later on wishes were always for something
vaguely attainable, or reasonable. Things in the future like a
doll's house or great beauty and later still that one of her paintings would be picked by the Royal Academy, or that she'd find
a thousand pounds in used notes in a phone box, or that Jack
Seymour would notice her.

World peace, that's what everyone should wish for, instead of
something selfish. That's what she's thought since the children
were small, although in those days whenever the chance for a
spell came her way she summoned the gods and the goblins to
provide her family with everlasting health and happiness. That
was then, and now here she sits, with a marrow-greasy needle of
bone, wasting a wish on the impossible. I wish, says the voice in
her head, I wish that the thing between Peter and Savannah had

never happened. And world peace? That, she thinks sadly, isn't possible either.

'What did you wish for?' asks Briony and Cordelia opens her eyes, forces a smile. 'Secret,' she says.

'Anyway,' says Lou, 'if you tell it doesn't come true.'

It's Anna's birthday and Lizzie stands by the door, ready at the light switch while her mother is in the pantry fixing thirteen pink and blue candles into the chocolate fudge icing of the cake.

They all sing 'Happy Birthday', and everything is almost as it ever was, except that without Peter it doesn't sound the same, and he isn't there to turn out the lights and Lou, who has always been the most calm and peachy-skinned of the little girls, has taken to picking at her face and they keep having to tell her to stop. She has a long scab that extends from her left nostril to the corner of her mouth. Briony says it looks like a pork scratching.

Anna wants Lizzie to herself after a while and it's her birthday so what Anna wants Anna gets. It's a family rule. Within reason.

'Let's get away from the kids,' she says, widening her mascara-clogged eyes while Lizzie and Cordelia daren't look at each other across the table for fear of laughing. Anna says she wants to show her the stereo she got for her birthday and play her the new Duran Duran record but really it's the bare-chested photograph of her boyfriend that she keeps secreted between the pages of her lockable diary that she wants to share with her newly prized big sister. 'He's seventeen next birthday,' boasts Anna, 'but don't tell Mum.'

Lizzie sits on the end of Anna's bed in her room that smells sweet and oily, of make-up and pencil sharpenings and bubble gum and synthetic musk. She leafs through one of Anna's true romances comics where photographs of wistful-looking teenagers without spots have thought bubbles coming out of their heads that say things like 'He'll chuck me if he finds out I snogged his friend' and 'Simon never notices me when his mates are around'.

Anna plonks herself down next to Lizzie and asks her if she can keep a secret. 'I think so,' says Lizzie.

'No, promise first,' says Anna and Lizzie makes the expected slicing motion at her throat though she fears that Anna's about to tell her some sort of embarrassing sexual secret.

'Dad's had an affair,' says Anna, gravely. 'That's why he's not here. I expect Mum's told you all that stuff about him having to be away for work, but it's not true.'

Later Lizzie finds Cordelia hunched in her big rose-printed chair. There should be a Scrabble board on the table between her chair and Peter's at this time of the evening and a couple of glasses of red wine, perhaps the bonfire smell of a hurriedly extinguished joint. Instead Cordelia sits alone with the over-loud ticking of the clock and the unread newspaper folded in her hands. Lizzie hovers, wanting to hug her; she hasn't got long before Sam's due to take her to the station on the back of his motorbike.

'I'm sorry it's so gloomy here,' says Cordelia. 'The girls miss Peter.' A silence hangs between them, and a distance. Cordelia bends and unbends her wrists, her laced fingers hinge back and forth. Lizzie draws the curtains to shut out the dark garden, clicks on the reading lamp, wonders what she should say.

'It's all a bit of a mess, isn't it?' Cordelia breaks the silence, her tone is imploring, child-like, as though she expects her daughter to come up with a solution.

Lizzie sits on the arm of the chair and fiddles with some braiding that's come unstitched from the cushion. Though so much is left unspoken, she has a clear sense that Peter has been evicted from family life to make way for herself. Justice: but only if it were all as simple as the guilty making way for the innocent. Earlier, for example, Cordelia asked her if she had thought about moving back home but with college in London looming – and if she could only be honest, her proximity to Jack – she had to say that she thought she should stay put. Cordelia agreed with her when she said that flats were quite hard to come by in such central locations, and she didn't look as crestfallen as Lizzie had expected. She just peered expectantly out of the window when she heard the crunch of tyres on gravel but it was only Anna's boyfriend arriving with his gang in a battered Mini Clubman, bringing Anna armfuls of daffodils that she said smelled of honey.

Some of the daffodils are in a vase on the table in the middle of the room. Anna said she had enough to share, her generosity bounteous as she waved her way out of the door. To the pub, they both knew, though neither of them actually stated it.

'Anna doesn't believe he's just gone for work, you know,' says Lizzie, absently peeling the braiding from the cushion, and Cordelia twists her wedding ring, says that it's impossible to keep secrets in such a small town. 'Perhaps we should move from here,' she adds, without conviction. And then with a heaving sigh she lays her head against Lizzie's arm: 'I miss him,' she says.

Lizzie can taste the sadness in her own throat and swallowing hurts her ears. She finds some matches on the table and starts striking them, attempting to solder them together by holding the head of one against the flame of another. The matches flare and the brimstone catches in her eyes, making them water. 'As long as he never mentions it to me again . . .' she concedes and Cordelia takes the double curls of charcoal from her hands and crumbles them into the ashtray. 'We'll see,' she says.

Chapter Nineteen

Lizzie hasn't noticed Jack's cough before, nor the wheezing in his chest.

She is sitting as close to him as she dares on the Harlington train, her head clothed in scratchy nylon blonde under a black fedora, and he is ratcheting himself in half with the effort from his lungs, rasping into the dark-green wool of his coat sleeves. She can see the shine from a broken button at his cuff. She could almost reach out and pat his back from where she sits behind her newspaper. She would like to tell him about rubbing garlic cloves onto the soles of the feet at bedtime. That always worked for her and her sisters whenever they had a cough, though no one could ever explain why. Peter was the best person to rub the garlic, because he managed to do it without tickling.

She thinks about Peter again, after the train, as she creeps through the roadside forest, watching Jack's laboured stride on the tarmac below. Peter used to take them all mushrooming in coniferous woods, not unlike these. It must be the pine that's reminding her. He had a special knife with a soft brush at one end for cleaning the dirt from the mushrooms. The blade was sharp stainless steel and he said that Lizzie was the only one allowed to use it. Though it wasn't autumn here now, the woods had smelled dank like this, of fermenting bread and damp earth and Christmas trees. Lizzie knew more than the others about mushrooms: she was able to tell them that the ones with white gills were often poisonous, because Peter had shown her with his illustrated book.

One year he had returned from a walk with several different varieties for her in the pockets of his fishing coat, his old brown walking boots caked with soft mud. She catches herself thinking kindly of those boots. She can see them in her mind's eye, knotty laces and worn leather curled to the shape of his foot, stuffed with newspaper and drying in front of the fire. She had painted shaggy parasols, inky wood blewits, nipple-topped liberty caps and, before Cordelia fried them in butter, plump penny buns with their suede tops and yellow spongy insides. She got top marks for her school project on Food for Free. 'Mycology, the most magical of subjects,' said Mr Vizard, who wore his hair in a long grey ponytail. Inspired by the enthusiastic Mr Vizard, or Bob as he liked to be called, she and Savannah had specialised in food for free for a while.

They cooked tender nettle soups and rosehip jellies that glistened like rubies. Once Savannah found an old recipe for Wild Food Shake and banned everyone else from the kitchen while she filled the liquidiser with her secret ingredients. The drink when she emptied it into tumblers was a thick froth the colour of wet cement. It tasted gritty too, so gritty that Lizzie had to spit hers out in the sink.

'But it did say two *whole* eggs,' protested Savannah later, and Peter had to gently break it to her that whole didn't mean still in the shells.

She can remember the fly agaric too, the mushroom's red dome spotted white, just like in the pictures of elves. Peter was proud of her when she named it, warning the others not to touch it. When he tucked her up in bed that night he told her about how the Eskimos fed fly agaric to their reindeer, then siphoned off the pee to drink. 'Gave them funny dreams,' he said and when she grimaced, 'Well, my love, I'd rather drink reindeer pee than Savannah's Wild Food Shake.'

Jack is blowing hard as he approaches the high stone walls of Harlington Court. Lizzie climbs the bit of broken fence where the Forestry Commission land gives way to the churchyard. She runs on stone paths gone slippery with moss, past the forgotten headstones and around the side of the church. She is just in time to see the back of Jack's coat as he passes through the entrance beside the lodge, and then she is left staring at the heavy wooden door and the gargoyle above it.

She doesn't stay in the churchyard today but walks down the path between the lonely graves and out through the lychgate to the lane. The Harlington walls stretch, impenetrable and grey, as far as the eye can see, winding with the road, and she continues in their shadow, up the hill and around the corner. From the top of the hill she still can't see over the wall, though she glimpses the blue leaded roofs and the tops of chimneys and some black squares of attic windows too.

Further ahead, set into the wall, is a second lodge. This one has wooden shutters with hearts cut out just like her old doll's house, and some early yellow roses climbing in clusters over the porch. She has never walked this far around the outskirts of the estate before. There is another gate at this lodge, of wrought iron twisted into fleur-de-lys though less formal and high than the one next to the church. She reaches out and tries the latch and noiselessly the gate swings open to her touch. She passes through, beyond the drive and the lodge garden and on through a stone arch that opens into a market garden. She can see the cloudy panes of a crenellated greenhouse ahead and rows of narrow beds with regimented progressions of leeks, onions and the feathery tops of carrots and other leafy things that she doesn't stop to identify. There are cane wigwams with twisting vines guarding the corners of the crumbling red herringbone paths.

The garden looks deserted, though she passes a wheelbarrow and a tarpaulin spread with early pink fir apples, still with their leaves and muddy from the earth. The garden is walled all around in soft sandstone, against which espaliered fruit trees submit to training with their crabbed branches, some of which carry blossom.

There is an arched doorway beyond the glasshouse, with a green door set into the inside wall. The door is wedged open, with a garden fork, and she can see the grass of the parkland beyond, and more distantly some grazing deer, about four or five of them. Lizzie's heart skips a beat as she realises that this is the way in to Harlington Court. Can she risk it? She's heard reports of the landed gentry and their Rottweiler responses to interlopers. One of Peter's old Cambridge friends was Lord Marlham and Peter often told stories of him laying trip wires and traps for poachers. More fun than shooting, according to Lord Marlham. Lizzie can picture herself hanging by one leg, dangling from a tree, and Jack hearing her screams and finding her there when he's finished whatever it is he does inside Harlington Court.

Lizzie wavers by the open arch, feeling conspicuous, the blonde nylon wig flaring in the perimeter of her vision, each hair lit like an optic fibre in the early afternoon sun. She sees something move further down the garden, just past the glasshouse, a flash of brown, and as she scoots round to the parkland side of the archway she hears whistling and the scuff of boots on brick drawing closer. She glimpses a gardener straight out of Beatrix Potter with roughened face and canvas smock, closer now and following his shadow up the path to the door. Lizzie flattens herself to the inside of the wall, pressing herself against it like one of the espaliered trees on the other side. She hears the scrape of the garden fork, and then the whistling subsides as the door closes with a clunk, leaving her alone with the park spread out before her and the alert deer sniffing the air and looking in her direction.

She is standing in a copse of nut trees with a mown path leading her further in, towards the smooth green lawns and a single huge oak that dominates the centre of the park. Through the hazel branches she can see Harlington itself, grey and castellated, with watchful Gothic windows and two round towers. She daren't move or break cover but crouches in long wet grass between the nut trees, trying to work out what to do next. She can hear splashing water from a tiered fountain, its marble bowls stacked like a wedding cake in front of the house, and the distant hammering of a woodpecker. Now that she's in, she doesn't have the faintest clue what she's doing there, nor how to go about finding Jack.

Harlington Court stares stony and disapproving. He's in there somewhere, she knows, but she's as far from discovering what he does within the grey walls as she ever was. There are other things that she does know about him now, though. Things she's learned. She's seen the bottles of double malt that he keeps by his bed with a plastic cup. Sometimes he spills a drop before he falls asleep. She knows this because she has smelled it on his blankets. He keeps blocks of bitter Bournville chocolate in his fridge. His fridge is framed with snow inside, like the entrance to an igloo. She would like to defrost it.

Last Sunday, while he was here doing whatever it is he does, she was at his house for almost two hours, instead of chickening out after a few minutes as usual. She went through quite a few of his things, books and letters and newspaper cuttings. She read in his chair, with his dressing gown draped over her shoulders, releasing the warm, brown bread and tobacco scent of her father from its frayed wool folds. And she took his shirt. That smelled of him too. When she slept in it, she dreamt of the harbour. She was drifting flat on top of the sea, with the water rising inch by inch. The clanking from the boats was like a warning as she started going under. She couldn't make a noise when she screamed. The water was almost over her face, and she knew that soon her life would be finished, when he came floating down from the sky and lay on top of her. He was warming her and breathing life back into her. Like warm whisky and toast. Not wheezing in the dream.

She crouches in the long grass and starts to count to a hundred, as though she's playing hide and seek. When she catches herself doing this, she tries to stop but the numbers skip on, unbidden. Ninety-seven Mississippi, ninety-eight Mississippi. An aching chant of childhood. Ninety-nine Mississippi, One-hundred. Okay, coming, ready or not. She looks again at the house. There is no way to get to it without having to cross open ground. In any case, once there she'd never be brave enough to creep about, peering in through all those windows. She'd probably get eaten by dogs. She gets up and darts, swiftly, staying close to the ground, to the next circle of trees. Sneaky as a cat. A bird flies up in front of her, a flurry of feathers and alarmed twitterings. It's a flash of pale green that cavorts above her head and then jumps and skips up, swearing, into the sky and beyond. Her eye follows the bird as far as the huge tree. Then something else stirs at the tree and she sees Jack.

Found you. Jack seems to emerge from the very centre of the

trunk. He is stretching and she hears the bark of his cough, despite the distance between them. He walks around the tree, several times, peering up into the branches, raking his hands through his hair, then back around again, and out of sight. Her tenderised heart betrays her with an ache, she feels only sad about him now.

She knows that he is ill. She has read his name on the bottles of pills and the unfilled prescriptions. She has sifted through the dusty piles of newspaper cuttings, the yellowing ones, about radiotherapy, chemotherapy, vitamin therapy, Chinese herbs, new surgical techniques, even spiritual healing. His clippings on these subjects date from 1974 but dwindled in 1978 until they petered out in late November 1979. That's what Lizzie found as her mania grew. She was tipping out cardboard boxes and ransacking his desk and the piles of newspapers on the day bed, searching in vain for something more recent. But for the last two years, he has thought nothing worth saving on the subject of his cancer. Either he is cured, or he's given up all hope.

She tries to imagine what he might have been like as a young man and wishes she could remember him better. She would like to know how he stood when he painted and whether his hands felt warm or cool when he held hers. She can only imagine them as they are now, and thinks they would be fluttery and papery like that bird just now, and cold as marble. He has been alone for years, and now he's ill. Cordelia once said that he was physically irresponsible, like a child; that she would have to cajole him into eating vegetables, or taking proper exercise. In fact, she said she nagged like a health freak. She said he almost died from exhaustion the first and only time she persuaded him to walk along the cliff tops with Lizzie on his back. And Lizzie wishes she could remember that too as she stares towards the tree.

Elena said that he had a 'vampire tan' and that both she and

Laura were lucky not to have inherited such pallid skin. Neither Elena, nor Cordelia, could explain the fascination. And yet he had broken both their hearts.

Last Sunday, after she had finished with his press cuttings, Lizzie started on his desk drawers. The cuttings had told her plenty of what she needed to know; the contents of his desk would reveal more. Of the clippings, the largest collection was all about tragic deaths. There were two cardboard boxes of these; he had been collecting them since 1963, and a new pile from more recent years was growing by his chair. Mostly the deaths were of children, many of whom drowned, almost always in garden ponds. As she sifted through the papers, the sound of their little voices singing became deafening, a playground cacophony, of Laura's voice, and others. The infant roll call would have filled a school. Her head was awash with their canon as she refolded the last front page, halving the cherubic face of three-year-old Thomas who had dimples and the usual black type: *Tragic Toddler Drowns in Pond*. She thought about the place where the snowberries grew in Elena's garden.

Another box contained brittle yellow articles about cathedrals, another old reviews of his shows. There were random piles of recent obituaries, environmental issues, nuclear politics, genetics, euthanasia, and, of course, the cancer studies.

There were three brass-handled drawers in a row above the desktop. Elena's letters rested on green felt in the one on the left. They were in two thick wads that smelled like the inside of a handbag, held in large, perished, elastic bands. Lizzie's eyes pricked as she read of Elena's hopes for their lives together and their old age, getting sweeter, she said, like two peaches in a bowl.

The earliest letters were on crackly, thin paper, translucent like old skin tattooed with ink that had faded to grey. In them Elena spoke mainly of his genius, and often of his absences. She described her aching heart and said that his eyes pierced her soul. She transcribed Keats for him. In later letters she said that Laura missed him too. And there were one or two with scribble pictures of thick crayon on sugar paper folded inside the envelopes. Apparently Jack had been away for Laura's first word. Elena had written 'Egg' in a speech bubble in a pen and ink caricature of a chubby-legged Laura at the fridge. And then the tone had changed. Elena's letters became enraged from 1960, when Jack was already with Cordelia in Cornwall. Her writing elongated to a jagged scrawl that sometimes pierced the paper.

In these letters she calls him a heel. She says that he doesn't deserve another child. She calls him a murderer. She does this every week for over two years.

Jack doesn't reappear from the tree, though she knows he's still there somewhere. From where she stands she would be able to see him walking away in any direction. Elena's later letters were unrelenting, every single one opened, and, presumably, read. She thought about him reading the word 'murderer' again and again whilst holding her in his arms. Or walking into the bathroom that night, with its bluebells and candle glow, and feeling the guilt twisting inside him like a knife. 'This is more than I deserve.' She could almost forgive him when she read Elena's letters, she almost understood why he couldn't stay. Elena had got her way in the end, she thought bitterly as she crammed them back in the drawer. She had to go then, it was late. She didn't want him to catch her red-handed. She didn't have time to look in the middle drawer. She will be less forgiving when she does.

Her stomach is rumbling, she's been stuck here in the hazel

copse since before lunchtime and the sun is getting quite low. While Jack is communing with nature, or reading a book, or whatever it is he does beneath the new leaves of an enormous oak tree, she grows bored and anxious. How on earth is she going to get out of here herself? She retraces her footsteps, keeping an eye out for Jack behind her, to the archway. Cautiously she tries the iron handle of the door, but it is locked or jammed from the other side. She is going to have to get out somehow, though. She's locked in and she'll have to face up to what she's done. She could either bang on the door here and hope the gardener hears her, or brave the lodgehouse across the park, and confess to having slipped inside. On the spur of the moment, she'll have to say, or, even more improbable, I didn't realise it was private property.

She sits down again in the long grass, and draws her knees up to her chest to hug them. However she does decide to do it, she will have to wait for Jack to leave first. It shouldn't be too long now, his usual train leaves in forty minutes. There are looping purple necklaces of wild honeysuckle twining the trees to her left. The scent reminds her of Campden Hill and Tony's front garden, the first time she stood there, looking in.

She doesn't often think about Tony these days, though she has to admit that she's enjoyed scooting around him the times he has turned up with his miss-you face and shiny shoes. She's been gloating like the wicked fairy over his love-struck bouquets. She even tortured a red rose that he had the nerve to send her. It arrived on the morning after Paula and Ian's cock and hen party. She had almost considered a dance with him at one stage, but that was before Sophie and Katrina got there, pink-cheeked and chattering from shopping. Their arms were hung with bags from Etam and Dolcis and Katrina was telling Tony that she'd found Sophie some pretty things. They left the party not long after, because Sophie was allergic to nylon carpets and looked as though she might have an asthma attack.

Tony kissed Paula on the cheek before he left, making her blush. And he yelled to Ian over at the bar, 'Make sure she's not too shagged out from the honeymoon for work.' He looked around for Lizzie, and his eyes found hers at the same moment as his daughter's did. Not pretty eyes, Lizzie noticed. Plain as a fish. Lizzie stared back. At Sophie, not Tony. Sophie took her father's hand in one hand, and Katrina's in the other, making a W of arms with herself as the centre: W for warning, W for warlock, and wedlock. W for who cares, Lizzie thought with relief. Sophie stared hard at Lizzie. Lizzie thought she looked triumphant.

Who cares? Lizzie is thinking about Cordelia drawn up and sighing in the big rose-print chair at home and Peter's empty chair beside her. She thinks about Lou's neurotic scab and Anna's drinking and the cold emptiness of Cordelia's bedroom when she went in to kiss her goodnight. She thinks about Cordelia's hollow eyes and knows then that love is something much softer and less breakable than anything she's ever known.

Her watch shows that it's past five, and Jack should get going if he's going to make his train. Another three minutes pass before she sees him emerge again from behind the tree, folding paper into his pocket. An anxious three minutes because she doesn't want him to miss that train. The next one is her one and the last. She doesn't think the station platform at Harlington is the right place for their reunion. She has been thinking of somewhere quieter, somewhere soft. She sees his lighter flare and his cigarette before he ambles stiffly towards the main lodge, turning around every few steps, to stop and look again towards the oak. She sees a woman in a blue headscarf come to the door of the lodge when Jack knocks on the door. He shakes her hand, they talk a while, though they are too far away for her to hear their voices, and then the heavy wooden door is opening and he leaves Harlington, stopping just once more to look back across the park.

Lizzie feels reckless now he's gone. If she's going to be caught trespassing anyway, she might just as well blow her cover now. She strides out from her hiding place, ears tuned for a shout, leaving the nut copse and the long grass whispering behind her. Her feet on the springy close-cropped parkland march forward, drawing her ever closer to the oak. It's even bigger than she thought.

It rises above her, a solid medieval creature, at least forty feet around its girth. She's never seen a tree like it. It stands in a pool of shadow, majestic, two main branches reaching low and forwards, bent at their elbows like welcoming arms. She walks around the trunk and finds an entrance between two knobbly wooden arteries, low and dark as the opening to a cave. She can hear the whoo-whooing of a wood pigeon and see the sun striping the green with long shadows from the trees on the ridge. She stoops her head through the entrance and finds herself in the warm, brown heart of the tree.

The tree is completely hollow and she is inside, surrounded by its smooth wooden veined walls, where Jack has been moments before. She lies back on the dry, leafy earth and stares up through the branches. The trunk rises above her like a ruined tower, to the sky that appears as a circle of blue glimpsed through a brocade curtain. The new young leaves are shimmering green and speckled gold by the evening light.

For the rest of her life, she imagines that when she shut her eyes that day she could hear the breathing of the tree, strangely in time with her own and that she felt blessed. Perhaps that's not how she felt at the time, but forever more, if anyone asked her what her happiest memory was, it was that hour inside the oak at Harlington.

Chapter Twenty

The boy produces a seemingly endless stream of red gob-stoppers from his mouth. He blows out his cheeks and pops his eyes and plucks out the red balls with his left hand, his right, and places them lovingly into his top hat. Because the sun is shining, people stop to watch a while as he juggles five cans of baked beans and they applaud as painted ladies fly from his pockets. An old woman in a headscarf looks as though she might cry when he fishes a bouquet of sweet williams from her empty shopping basket and presents them to her with a grin. A little girl steps timidly forward to drop some coins into his hat, then runs back to hide behind her mother. He takes Lizzie's watch from his waistcoat to check the time, though she hasn't felt it leave her wrist.

'Coffee?' he says and Lizzie laughs when he catches her sneaking her fingers into his jacket pocket as they walk down the road. He slaps her hand, tells her she should know better than to rummage around in a magician's pocket. 'Careful,' he growls, 'the rabbit bites.'

He hands her one of the red gobstoppers as they sit in the Cherry Tree café. It weighs nothing and is made of red foam that squashes so small that she can conceal it in the crook of her thumb, then make it spring from her open palm as he demonstrates. Though he can make them pop from anywhere, the waitress's ear for example, and already eleven have emerged from the sugar bowl.

'See,' he says, 'nothing to it.'

She asks him again how he makes a cigarette disappear into thin air and he sighs, calls her a heartless nag. He says that if he shows her, she must promise not to tell a soul or he will be out of a job.

'It's quite simple,' he explains, pinning her with his eyes. 'Now, watch carefully. Not my eyes, don't fall for it, I've told you that before.'

He takes his cigarette from his lips. 'Keep watching my hands,' he says, holding them to her over the table. He stubs out the cigarette in his closed fist, grimacing with pain, then rubs his palms together and it has gone.

'Is it in your pocket?' she says hopefully.

'No. Now watch again. This is the same trick.'

He picks up the glass salt shaker from the table and holds it high above his left hand and pours a stream of salt into his fist before presenting her with his empty hands. Again, Lizzie can only believe in magic.

'You're going to kick yourself,' he says and he pulls a fluorescent green plastic tube from his thumb and empties a little mountain of salt into the ashtray. The thumbtip is moulded perfectly, it even has a thumbnail. 'Mine's painted green because I'm a show-off,' he explains. 'Normally they're flesh-coloured. I wear it over my thumb, transfer it into the other fist, pour the salt inside, sneak it back over my thumb with the salt still inside and, hey presto, it's disappeared.'

'I can't believe I didn't spot it,' she says. But when he's finished his next cigarette, she still can't see the green thumb, even though she knows it's there. Sleight of hand has been his trade since before he could walk. 'But I didn't learn to walk until I was seven,' he says. 'I had polio when I was little.'

'Could you saw me in half?' Lizzie asks.

'Easy,' he says. 'Do you want me to?'

'Can you turn water into wine?'

'Do it all the time.'

'Walk on water?'

He raises his eyebrows at her and turns up the corners of his lips. Lizzie finds herself giggling helplessly, as she so often does when she is with him. Instantly he wipes the clown from his face and points her out to the Cherry Tree's other customers, mouthing 'loony', his deadpan making her laugh uncontrolled as a child being tickled.

'I'll tell you what I *can't* do,' he says, relenting with a smile. 'I've seen the maestro crack an egg into a bowl, whisk it to a froth and then whisk it again, anti-clockwise, and the yolk has reseparated from the white. I've seen him put fried eggs back into their shells. That is magic. I've wasted a lot of eggs. And I can't juggle more than seven objects, or make it rain in Africa, or play "Albatross" on the guitar.' He says that he will teach her to juggle one day.

That night she dreamt of the harbour. When she fell she landed on a sea of red foam balls and floated there, looking up at the moon and back to the jetty where Jack stood silently watching her.

From a pile of magazines in Jack's kitchen, Lizzie finds an old colour supplement with an article inside about Elena Mankowitz. Her photograph takes up more space than the type. She is ravishing in a pale gown and pearls. It talks of her being painted by Hockney and Kitaj and of Jack Seymour's *Elena at Rest* in the Tate. It describes her as a Hungarian aristocrat and philanthropist, and founder of the Mankowitz Foundation in Vienna, which housed hundreds of Hungarian refugees. There is no mention of Laura though it talks of Elena's love for children and dedication to the Hungarian orphans who owe her their lives.

Lizzie grips Elena's snowflake obsidian at her throat and feels guilty for all the ill she has wished Elena since reading her letters to Jack. It felt good for a while to have someone to blame for his desertion.

She knows that this is the last time she'll come here like this. There will be no more sneaking around. The wasted and lonely years of obsession that Elena hinted at the last time they met have brought into sharp focus what she has long been considering: that she must either leave him alone or knock at his door and accept the consequences. Trailing him like this has become a mania, a sickness. She strikes a match and, though she doesn't smoke, relights his Gauloise from the ashtray. Her lips where his have been. The sour smoke makes her cough.

The painting of herself as a baby is skewed on the wall and she goes over to straighten it. It is not a big painting and she lifts it down to hold it against the light from the window, and as she does she sees the writing on the back. *For Elena, Hungarian Orphan, 1963*, is scrawled there in black marker pen.

She lets the painting slip from her hands to the floor. An image of Tony slides into her mind, of him watching her in the mirror. Mercilessly living out his rape fantasies, framed by gilded cherubs and vine leaves. 'Instant porn,' he called it. She tries to avoid thinking about those things, her skin feels tight when she does and she shivers. The painting has no heart, it is a device as much as the mirror, the appeal in her eyes simply a stand-in for something less available: Jack's apology to Elena. Her father has used her image for his own ends too. The two thoughts make her queasy.

She moves to Jack's desk with a heavy sigh. Just a few more drawers to go and then she will be through with him. But her heart isn't really in it any more. She pulls open the middle drawer. The photograph of herself is the first thing she sees, the one of her in the cot that Jack used for the painting. Typical that. Cordelia's handwriting is on the back. *Our little frog*, it says. *HOW CAN YOU TURN YOUR BACK ON HER?* It's so like the sentiments of Elena's early letters when he was away from Laura, she's read it all before. He must have been well practised by then in the art of remaining untouched. A couple of Cordelia's letters are there too, begging letters, begging him to visit his child. Lizzie cries for you at night, she says. And Lizzie turned three today.

There is an official letter from the social services inviting him to state if he has any objections to Peter Weller adopting his daughter. Speak now or forever hold your peace is the tone, but written in cool legalese. The letter has been screwed into a ball then straightened and folded back into the envelope. There is another letter from Cordelia, handwritten on sky-blue paper, stuffed inside. It tells him that, though her husband would like to adopt Lizzie, this in no way precludes his involvement, that he will always be welcome to take part in Lizzie's life. That he will forever be her father. Jack has scrawled over the letter black words that burn like acid. Words that make Lizzie throw herself across his desk, violently, sweeping papers and piles of newspapers onto the floor. She picks up a cardboard box, one of those filled with newspaper clippings about medical breakthroughs, and throws it across the room, knocking coffee cups from the table and scattering newsprint.

I do not want this child. I have never wanted this child. Do not send me photographs. Do not send letters. Allow me to forget that you and your child exist. And the *J* at the bottom has slashed through Cordelia's name.

Lizzie runs from her father's room, kicking through piles of newspapers and books, and clatters back down the stairs. She falls shaking against the door at the bottom, trying to get a grip before stepping out into the mews. She moans aloud, she kicks at the door to his garage, breathing fumes of varnish and oil paint. The door swings open on oily hinges to a bright room. It's a studio, not a garage after all. Jack's studio. Of course. She should have guessed before but she's been too wrapped up in his life upstairs. The back wall is conservatory glass from which bluish light floods the room and two enormous canvases face each other across the paint-spattered floorboards. The Harlington oak. One is eight feet high with a step ladder in front of it, the bark etched like human skin seen under a microscope, the branches reaching out in a five-foot span, not all of them painted in detail yet. Propped against the opposite wall is a vast square showing the view from the heart of the tree, a breathtaking perspective of the ruined tower rising high through the leaves to the circle of blue.

Back upstairs in Jack's kitchen Lizzie finds a long meat knife in one of the drawers. She is not shaking any more. Her head feels light with intent. She seems to be floating as she takes the knife back down into Jack's studio. She dives through the open door, into the room and plunges the blade straight into the heart of the oak. She pulls down with both hands on the knife's bone handle, making a three-foot slash. She rips the trunk apart, and stabs at the tree again, at the lower branches and the trunk and then pulls a ragged square straight away from the frame, which makes a noise like a tearing sheet. The tree has been painted thick in places; impasto and paint fall in clumps, pigment and oil and fabric dust taint the air as she slashes through Jack's picture with the knife growing slippery in her hands.

She takes the knife to the other painting. The inside of the tree seems to rise above her, ancient and magical and daring her on, but she can't bring herself to damage it. Instead, she exhausts her rage. She empties brushes and solvents over the bare wood boards and stamps on tubes of paints until the oils explode around her feet like squiggles of dog shit. She is panting among the destruction, the knife still in her hand. Her father could be back any minute.

She drops the knife into her bag. She can feel the falling of her adrenaline level, physical as sand through a sieve, and she looks sadly back at what is left of the largest painting. Canvas hangs from the frame, weighty with paint, like so many rags on a fence.

The tears come later as she sits on a swing in Hyde Park. She is oblivious to the querulous stares from mothers with toddlers waiting their turn as she scuffs her feet along the ground, back and forth, hanging between the creaking chains. When people see her tears, they give the swings a wide berth and point their children to the sand pit or the slide instead.

The boy fails to waylay her, though he's walking backwards, juggling silver balls in an arc before her face. But there's nothing he can do to delay her now. She rushes past, her coat flaring behind her, swearing under her breath. Her boots and her jeans are spattered with paints. She doesn't even slow her step, and he is left holding three silver juggling balls, wondering what it is that he's done wrong. 'I bought them for you,' he objects. 'Hey stop.'

'I'm going to see my father,' she says and the look on her face forbids him from coming with her.

The knife is still in her bag. She's going to face him this time. She stands pressing her finger on the bell, though she doesn't hear it ring inside. No one answers but she has the key anyway. She has nothing to lose. If he's angry with her now, it'll be because he's got a reason. She has destroyed his life's work. Turning her away will have nothing to do with indifference.

She doesn't care who sees her as she lets herself into his house. The door to the studio has been closed now and she can hear the chugging pipes and running water upstairs. At the top of the stairs, his room is how she left it; the desk swept clean, the broken coffee cups, the kicked and trodden newspaper clippings. The pale-faced orphan picture is where she dropped it on the floor by the window.

The door to the bathroom is wide open and she sees him framed and lying motionless in the bath. It feels like a lapse in time: those few slow seconds before he notices her standing at the door, her arms falling to her sides. An angel with wings of lead is what he sees. His head rests against the back of the bath. Steam rises around his face, blurring his features, so that she has an impression that he is made of something grey and insubstantial, like dust or rain. Without saying a word, she runs at him with the knife and plunges it into his centre where close up like this the skin is fish–belly white. It is a silent knifing after the noise of the canvas. All around him the grey water is clouding red.

Of course this is not what Lizzie does, though the thought flashes through her mind. His eyes are ringed white with terror as she shakes out the frayed, greying towel from the chair and holds it up for him. 'Do you know who I am?' She sounds strident. He grasps her hands through the towel, defenceless, as water falls from his chest. This is more than he deserves is what she thinks as she helps him from the bath.

He is frail and shaking as she wraps the towel around him. 'You think I wouldn't recognise you, Lizzie?' He is looking straight into her eyes and she can't tell if he's crying or if it's just hot bathwater and sweat.

'I'm sorry about the painting.' She's quiet, at a loss, as he sinks to the chair with the towel wrapped around his waist and his sunken chest heaving, tinged blue above the towel, as though someone's spilt ink in his bathwater.

'I would never have finished it, anyway.' And she knows that he is dying and tells him that she wishes she had met him before now. She kneels on the floor next to his chair, and he puts his hand to her head and leaves it there. 'You know I've been following you and coming here, don't you?' she says. 'I was scared you wouldn't want to know me.'

'You only had to knock at the door,' he says. 'For all the good it would have done you. I've only ever made people unhappy. I can't be what they want.'

'But you are my dad.'

He seems to flinch at the word dad, or perhaps she's imagining that. But he looks away from her when he speaks, across the room to where she's dropped her bag on the floor.

'You know, Lizzie, I was never going to be any use as a father. I only live to paint.'

'You could have tried.'

His breathing sounds like the sea but his hand is steady where she can feel its warmth through her hair. 'There was something else. Someone else.' He says.

'I know . . .' Lizzie tries to interrupt but he continues. 'I had another daughter. She died.'

'I know,' she says it again but he hasn't finished what he's decided to tell her. 'It's like being lost when it happens, like being stuck in a maze: you think the same thoughts for years – round and round they go until . . . You're dizzy all the time and all you can do is walk up and down, up and down, and suddenly you're too afraid to even look for the way out because there will be other people out there and you'll have to talk again.' Lizzie wants to say that madness excuses nothing. That's what Peter always said to her mother when she heard them talk about Jack but it's not what she feels and they are both lost for words. There are pools of water collecting around his feet on the cork. His eyes are stricken and black but then he smiles at her, and she finds that she can remember his smile and she's glad she came.

'I can't make you understand,' he says, cautiously, 'but let me show you something.'

She follows him from the room. 'I'm just getting some clothes.' He motions for her to wait where she is while he goes into his bedroom. 'It's downstairs, what I want to show you.'

He is barefoot in a shapeless brown jumper and jeans when he holds out his arms to her. 'I would like to hug you,' he says. 'May I?' and he sounds polite, almost formal.

She is self-conscious and disappointed in his arms and she feels his breath in her hair and his heavy sighs of regret as they are locked together at the top of the stairs.

The light has faded to a bronze haze in the studio and the fumes from paint and spilled solvents make them both cough as he leads her back in. 'It's all right,' he says, making light of the destruction with a wave of his arm.

'The tree was beautiful,' she says. She's never felt so ashamed. 'I am sorry.'

'The real thing is better,' he flaps his hands as dismissively as dishrags at the ravaged picture. He steers her by the arm so that they have their backs to the torn canvas and they face only the painting of the inside of the tree towering above them to the sky.

'It's the guardian oak at Harlington. You should go and see it for yourself. It's over four hundred years old.'

'I've been,' she says, 'I followed you there.'

Jack starts to laugh. 'You followed me?' but his lungs won't stand for it and he has to clutch his chest to cough. 'It's in our blood,' he says. 'Wait until you see this.'

He has asked her to help him shift the tree canvas along the wall. He pulls it, creaking and scraping against the floor, towards the window, with Lizzie shoving against the other end with her shoulder. He ducks down behind it and with both hands slides out a second picture and straightens it to the wall.

'It's you,' he gestures, standing up and taking her hand as they both step back. 'And there are others too if you'll allow me to show them to you.'

She feels Jack watching her as she looks at his picture. It is her all right, about nine years old. And there's Muttley too, with his tail fanning out behind him. He has painted her crouching beside the dog on the paving stones at home with a crown of daisies in her hair. She and Muttley are bent low over the ground. 'Watching ants!' she says.

'That's what I reckoned,' says Jack.

'But how?'

'Binoculars,' he says.

In the background, painted grey and insignificant as shadows, she can see her mother with her gourd-shaped pregnant belly bending over the paddling pool with Anna and Briony. 'You were always apart from the others,' says Jack. 'Whenever I watched you, you were in a world of your own but I always thought you looked happy.'

'*You* used to watch *me*!' Lizzie finds her hands on her father's shoulders, his brown eyes are as they have always been in her mind; she can almost smell the bluebells.

He has pulled out three other small paintings and another large one. The large canvas is of Stonmouth Beach, and herself, about sixteen years old, sitting jack-knifed on the freezer reading a book in Mr Milly's gaudy red and white painted ice-cream van. There is a watercolour of her paddling her feet, caked in mud, on the river bank with Muttley, while in the background other people are playing ball and eating sandwiches. There's a heart-breaking portrait of her aged four, when she wore glasses. Another is of herself younger than that, wearing blue and white striped dungarees, learning to throw an orange ball with her arms outstretched towards Cordelia's hands, which are recognisable in the top left-hand corner of the painting.

'I don't understand,' says Lizzie. They are facing each other and Jack is squeezing her arms. 'I can't be a father,' he says, and she finds that she is looking at him as though through a cloud. 'But I can only paint what I love.'

Chapter Twenty-One

Lizzie's face gives nothing away as she comes walking back down the road and I am waiting for her at the corner. The sun is as low as the trees behind her, flaring the ends of her hair, and her hands swing free of her pockets. As I watch her draw closer, I see that her feet barely touch the pavement. She seems to be floating towards me as I stuff the playing cards and the thumb tips and the coins back into my bag. There'll be no need for trickery now.

She takes my arm. I can feel her energy, like electricity from the ends of her fingertips.

'Come on,' I say, 'it's time I taught you to juggle.' And she feels light against me as we walk back through the park.